WILD CREEK
WHISPERS

WILD CREEK WHISPERS

CINDY KEEN REYNDERS

W🌐RLDWIDE

TORONTO • NEW YORK • LONDON
AMSTERDAM • PARIS • SYDNEY • HAMBURG
STOCKHOLM • ATHENS • TOKYO • MILAN
MADRID • WARSAW • BUDAPEST • AUCKLAND

W✷RLDWIDE™

Recycling programs
for this product may
not exist in your area.

ISBN-13: 978-1-335-00832-9

Wild Creek Whispers

First published in 2022 by Camel Press, an imprint of
Epicenter Press, Inc.
This edition published in 2023 with revised text.

For questions and comments about the quality of this book,
please contact us at CustomerService@Harlequin.com.

Harlequin Enterprises ULC
22 Adelaide St. West, 41st Floor
Toronto, Ontario M5H 4E3, Canada
www.ReaderService.com

Printed in U.S.A.

As always, thank you to my husband and my family
for their patience and understanding
when I go into my office and disappear for hours.
They appreciate my writing addiction
and for that I will be eternally grateful.

Also, a huge thank you to my editor Jennifer McCord,
who believed in this story and my ability to write it.

ACKNOWLEDGMENTS

Thank you to the Greater Power
that has blessed me to have my way with words.
Also, I appreciate that Camel Press has allowed me
to join the ranks of their authors.

ONE

Black, glistening, deadly.

Reese Golden studied the black widow as she stretched out, stomach down, on her office carpet. Morbidly fascinated, she watched the spider as it perched in its frothy web between her desk and a file cabinet. It sat motionless, stalking a fluttering moth trapped in the silken strands. When it marched on jointed legs toward the hapless insect, she shivered with revulsion.

After moving home to Meadowlark Valley, Wyoming, which hadn't changed much since she was a little girl, she'd converted the garage of her 1940s brick bungalow into an office. That didn't matter to the previous occupants, mostly those of the eight-legged variety, who continued to prevail.

The vermin didn't realize she'd made this area into habitable space. They were used to having free rein, and she'd invaded *their* territory. Since old habits die hard, apparently even for spiders, she realized the little butt heads weren't going to give up easily.

She recalled as a child when something—must have been a spider—bit her arm, raising a fat, quarter-shaped welt. The doctor had given her mom a hard time, practically accusing her of burning Reese with a cigarette. But Mom wasn't a smoker, and neither were any of her friends. That put a rest to those suspicions.

Mom.

Reese missed her terribly, just as she missed her little

brother, Jesse. Both were taken away far too soon; their car hit by a drunk driver on a rainy night.

Quit thinking about that awful time, she told herself.

The spider sank its fangs into its hapless prey. The moth's wings eventually stopped flapping, and the widow began the cocooning process, wrapping her food up tightly.

Her entire life, Reese had always rooted for the underdog, and right now she actually felt sad for the dumb moth. The moth couldn't do a thing to save itself—the same predicament she'd found herself in at age 12 when she moved in with her grandparents. Now, almost 32, she vowed to stay strong and protect others.

That's why I became a cop, she thought.

Now another voice surfaced, chiding and harsh. *You ran away from the Denver Police Department. Ran away because you feared you'd lost your edge.*

Unfortunately, it was hard not to remember that incident, especially when a familiar ache rippled through her right shoulder. She had a very good reason for leaving the force.

Closing her eyes, she envisioned the event six months ago that compelled her to make that decision. She'd worked a double shift on the homicide division, and she was tired beyond belief. After making a stupid mistake, both she and her partner had been shot.

The docs removed the bullet in her shoulder, but they couldn't stitch her fractured mind back to normal.

None of that mattered now, and even though an internal investigation had cleared her of any wrongdoing, she couldn't prevent a sense of guilt from niggling her consciousness. She'd declined to meet with the department shrink when superiors had requested she do so. Given an ultimatum of receiving counseling or resigning, she'd filled out the paperwork, packed up her gear, and walked out.

She'd never been a quitter, but at that point in her life, she hadn't felt like dealing with bureaucratic nonsense. To make a clean break, she'd returned to her quiet, peaceful hometown, where she'd started a private investigation agency. Now, she could be her own boss.

These days, she stayed clear of guns. She also steered clear of complicated cases. Instead of tracking down criminals and solving murders, she conducted Federal Background Investigations, a job that entailed researching individuals who required security clearances. The work could be considered mundane—possibly even boring. Nevertheless, she knew it was stable and lucrative.

It also felt good to be living in the house where she'd grown up and residing in the town where she'd attended grade school through high school.

Mr. Bojangles, her black cat, wandered over to sit beside her, his tail curling mischievously. Unlike the superstitious beliefs floating around, Bo wasn't bad luck. He was the one thing that made her laugh these days, something she knew she needed to do more. After all, laughter, people claimed, is good for the soul.

Eyes narrowed to glowing green slits, whiskers twitching, he rumbled loudly, "Meow-w-w!"

"Hello to you too," Reese pushed to her feet. She'd had enough of the trip down bad memory lane. Pointing at the web, she said, "Why don't you take care of that spider for me? You know how much I hate those freaks."

Bo blinked, then began to lick his paws slowly and methodically. What did she expect? Like the cat would actually clean out the spider's nest. *Sheesh.* This was a job for insect spray.

Even though she had a snowstorm of paperwork on

her desk, reports to write, and people to research, she reached for her handy can of Raid.

The jangling of the phone stopped her, and she set aside the spray. The beastie would have to wait. Sliding into her chair, she picked up her cell.

As she glowered at the sticky web in the corner, she answered, "Golden Private Investigations. May I help you?"

"Hello, I'd like to speak with Reese Golden," a woman said.

"You're speaking to her," she said.

"My name is Skylar Ellington and I'd like to hire you to find my daughter."

Reese tensed. All at once, the August heat filling the room seemed unbearable, so she switched on her desk fan. As cool air brushed her face, she relaxed.

Once upon a time, she'd been one of the best at missing person's cases. She had a passion for finding people and reuniting them with their families. At the very least, Reese wanted to find answers for relatives and loved ones so they could have closure.

Cases like those always elicited sharp emotions within Reese. She didn't feel ready to take on anything that intense.

"I'm going to refer you to a really good private investigator I know in Cheyenne," Reese offered. "I'm sure he'll be able to help you."

"It's not Paul Cicarelli, is it?" Skylar asked.

"Yes," Reese said.

"I've already tried him," Skylar said. "No luck. He said he's overloaded with cases right now."

"Hmm, what about—"

"Miss Golden, my daughter was kidnapped back in June, and it's killing me not knowing what happened to her," Skylar said. "The police, the FBI and everyone else haven't come up with anything. And I'd do anything to find her."

"I read about the case in the newspaper," Reese said recalling the article in the Meadowlark Valley Chronicle. "I'm so sorry."

"Daisy's only four," Skylar said, her voice trembling. "She must be confused and upset. She's all I can think about night and day. Pl-please help me. Don't turn me down. Otherwise, I think… I think I'll go insane."

Reese closed her eyes as Skylar's plea plucked at her heart strings. Right now, she didn't feel confident enough to take on a case of this magnitude. Yet, how could she turn away such a desperate plea?

"I'll tell you what," Reese said. "Let's meet somewhere and talk."

"You'll help me?"

Reese's mouth went dry. The ice around her heart melted and began to chink away slowly, like a spring thaw in her soul.

You need to step up and do this, Reese.

No way could she remain in her home office and manage this case properly. She'd have to go out in the world and function like a professional.

"Are you there, Miss Golden?" Skylar asked.

"I can't promise anything, Skylar," Reese finally said, her heart drumming. "I'll try my best, though."

"Oh, thank God!" Skylar sniffed. "I live up at Wild Creek Ranch near Sage. Can you come here? That way you can see Daisy's room. I haven't touched a thing since the kidnapper crawled in through the window and took her."

"I'll come there tomorrow, if that works," Reese said, her mind whirling at the idea of going out on a limb to help Skylar after six months of self-imposed isolation. "Is 10 a.m. a good time for you?"

"Perfect, I'll see you then," Skylar said. "I see your retainer fee on your website and I'll send it through Pay-Pal right away."

"I appreciate it," Reese said. "And please, call me Reese."

"Thank you so much," Skylar said. "You have no idea what this means to me."

Reese clicked off her cell phone, sighed, and said to the spider, "Skylar Ellington has no idea what this means to me."

TWO

It RAINED MOST of the night. Now, morning mist drifted in veils, like long, thin ghosts hugging the prairie landscape as Reese Golden drove her rebuilt Ford Bronco, which she'd nicknamed "Betty," toward Wild Creek Ranch, which was located about a mile from the town of Sage.

She'd never visited Sage before, so this would be a first. Like many of the small towns located around Wyoming, she believed it possessed its own unique character. Some places were famous for special restaurants or maybe they featured old hotels known for ghostly activities. Further north, around Yellowstone National Park, towns boasted of their breathtaking views and tourist attractions.

What was Sage's claim to fame? If she were visiting for fun, she'd look forward to finding out. Since she'd be conducting an investigation, that was out of the question. She'd be too busy looking for Skylar's little girl.

Who had taken her and why?

It boggled her mind to think of someone harming a child. If luck were on her side, she'd actually find Daisy alive. She hoped and prayed for that outcome.

As the miles passed, the monotony of driving across the vast prairie became tiresome. Reese adjusted the radio to find a talk station—something to keep her awake. She twisted a knob on the dashboard, frustrated to hear only static.

Looking up, she spotted a herd of pronghorn antelope

crossing the road smack-dab in front of her. Just in time, she pressed on the brakes and slowed to a stop, watching as the tan and white animals bounded across the asphalt.

The five deer-like critters hoofed it through the sagebrush and continued on their way, the horned buck in the lead. A couple of does stopped to nonchalantly chew prairie grass alongside the road.

Reese felt fortunate she hadn't plowed into the beautiful creatures. Resuming her journey, she focused on the asphalt cattle trail before her. Her musings turned to the impending meeting with Skylar Ellington.

She could only imagine how devastated the young woman must be, and she sympathized with her. Although Reese didn't have children, she understood the pain of losing a beloved family member.

During her career as a police officer, children's kidnapping cases always broke her heart. The first 48 hours were vital in trying to find the little one.

Unfortunately, weeks had elapsed since young Daisy had been taken. The chance of finding her alive wasn't good. Unease sifted through Reese, then she pushed it away. It was important for her to remain practical and professional.

She glanced at her watch, satisfied she'd arrive at the ranch in time to make her 10 a.m. appointment with Skylar. In her quest for caffeine, she'd brought along a Starbucks mochaccino, which she sipped at right now.

Accustomed to the flat, rolling prairie around Meadowlark Valley where she'd grown up, this area took on the appearance of a different planet. Colorful rock formations and unusual twists of the land piqued her curiosity, reminding her of an old Star Trek episode where Mr. Spock and Captain Kirk had been chased around by monsters on an alien planet.

Clouds skittered apart and sky arched overhead like a giant blue canopy. Clear radio stations were as rare as diamonds, despite Reese's search attempts. Time passed in a haze of crackling static and humming car tires, so she plugged in an old cassette tape featuring '80s country music.

When her exit appeared, she wheeled down a winding gravel road surrounded by tall grass and summer wildflowers that dipped and waved in the breeze. Sunlight painted the distant mountain peaks with an otherworldly glow.

Reese turned off her air conditioner and rolled down her window. The silence, marked only by the buzz of insects, awed her. She marveled at the country panorama, legendary for cowboys, rodeos and buffalo. A sense of peace and calm came over her. Her breathing settled, almost as though she'd walked into a yoga class.

Several low, rolling hills brought her face to face with split rail fencing that stretched as far as the eye could see. A large log entry gate supported by stone pillars and a sign emblazoned with "Wild Creek Ranch" announced she'd arrived at her destination.

Nestled in a lush valley, a large, old-fashioned ranch house with a wraparound porch sprawled like a sleeping giant. Juniper bushes, orange daylilies, pink coneflowers and rambling roses hinted that a gardener tended the home with a loving touch.

A red barn and several outbuildings perched nearby. A couple of grazing horses and a few cows dotted the emerald green pastures. Leaning out of her truck window, Reese snapped some photos with her cell, then approached the gate. It was unlocked and both sides had been propped open. Slowly, she drove through the entrance and toward the heart of the ranch.

In her mind's eye, Reese evaluated where a kidnapper might have hidden, waiting for the perfect moment to slit Daisy's window screen in the middle of the night. He or she must have studied the lay of the land and made plans about where they would take the child.

Newspapers articles and other information Reese had researched online yesterday reported the police and other officials hadn't found many clues. And the kidnapper hadn't left any ransom notes.

Once again, that struck Reese as odd. If Daisy wasn't kidnapped in order for someone to demand ransom, why was she taken?

In the coming days, she planned to scrutinize every possible reason someone might have abducted the little girl. Also, she would narrow down the suspects who could be responsible.

She had every reason to believe the police had done a thorough investigation when the kidnapping occurred. What did she think she could find all these weeks later?

Hopefully an angle that law enforcement never thought of pursuing.

Her truck jerked, vibrated, and moved forward unevenly. She'd just driven right into the world's largest pothole. *And now I've got a flat tire.* Gripping the steering wheel, she maneuvered the Bronco onto the road's shoulder.

Crap.

Her appointment with Skylar was only a few minutes away. She slid out of her truck, her grandfather's boots crunching on the gravel. He hadn't been a tall man and he'd worn a size eight, which fit Reese perfectly.

In honor of him, she'd adopted the footwear when he'd passed away last year. He'd walked a lot of miles in the old leather, and now she was the one doing the walking. Knowing they had once belonged to him made her feel protected—almost as though he was nearby looking out for her.

Looping her purse strap over her shoulder, she headed toward the front of her truck. With each step, sharp rocks tortured the soles of her worn boots. Next to the hood she stopped and leaned over to examine the tire. A nail protruded from the synthetic black rubber.

She glanced around, noting the other nails that made a wide swath across the road. She could almost believe they had been scattered to cause damage to a vehicle.

Is someone sending me a not-so-welcome message?

She shook her head. Surely no one had done it on purpose. Most likely the nails had fallen out of someone's truck. That's all.

Suspicions fading, she resumed her walk toward the ranch house. The sun's rays beat down on her head and perspiration dotted her brow. Dust seeped into her favorite gold jackalope T-shirt, and clung to her skin. Her legs felt like roasted hot dogs inside her jeans.

By the time she reached the ranch house and rang the doorbell, she figured the wind had made a mess of her shoulder-length, dark brown hair. What a great first impression she would make.

No one answered the door on the first ring, so she tried again. While she waited, she took pictures of the colorful flower gardens.

"May I help you?"

Caught off guard, Reese spun around, taking note of the tall man who stood there, his Stetson brim shading his eyes.

"I have an appointment with Skylar Ellington this morning." She slid her phone in her purse.

"She's not home right now, but I'm her brother, Chance."

Reese frowned. Had Skylar forgotten their meeting? That was hard to believe, especially considering how she'd pleaded with Reese yesterday to help her.

"Do you know when she'll return? I'm here to visit with her about Daisy. I'm a private investigator."

He shook his head. "Whoa, she never mentioned anything about that."

"She hired me to look into the kidnapping."

He folded his arms across his chest. "The police issued an Amber Alert and they're doing everything they can to find her. I don't see how you can help."

"Maybe I can come up with some new leads."

"I only see how my sister is about to become disappointed all over again. She's wasting her money."

"It's too bad you feel that way."

Daisy's uncle was sure touchy about Reese being here, but she could sympathize with him. It must be awful to have a family member missing and feel helpless to resolve the situation. Especially when it was an innocent child.

"I think it's crazy," Chance growled. "My mother and sister are both in agony. What more can you do to find Daisy that we haven't already been doing?"

"Since Skylar's my client, I'd like to speak with her," she returned in a firm tone.

Coldness emanated from his eyes.

She reached inside her purse and fished out a business card.

Handing it to him, she said, "Are you certain your sister didn't mention our appointment today?"

"Reese Golden of Golden Private Investigations," he read aloud. "And you're from Meadowlark Valley?"

She nodded.

"Well, Ms. Golden, I'll let her know you stopped by."

"Do you know when she'll return?"

"When she returns."

Chance obviously didn't intend to give Reese the satisfaction of a real answer.

"No worries. I'll catch up with her later."

She stepped off the porch and walked down the gravel driveway. After changing her tire, she'd head into town and find a place to repair the flat. Then she'd settle into her hotel room and go over the ideas she had about looking for Daisy.

THREE

DETERMINATION SURGED THROUGH Reese as she jacked up her truck, unscrewed the lug nuts, and removed the old tire. She braced herself, gave another gigantic effort, and managed to fit the spare on the hub.

"Pffew!"

She'd just finished fastening the lug nuts when she heard tires crunching gravel. Brushing hair out of her eyes, she turned to see Chance Ellington driving toward her in a big maroon pickup truck.

Peachy.

Did he come out here to gloat? As Ellington climbed out of his truck and walked toward her, she knitted her brows.

"Watch it," she said, her hands on her hips. "There are nails scattered across the road."

"What the hell?" He moved around picking them up. Finished, he dropped them in his pocket and brushed his hands on his pants.

She relaxed, and some of the stiffness drained from her shoulders.

"I'll have this handled in a jiffy," he assured her.

She shook her head. "It's all taken care of, Mr.—"

"Chance," he corrected her.

"Chance," she repeated. "It's nice of you to offer your help but I'm fine."

Ignoring her protest, he double checked the lug nuts

and dusted off his hands. He placed the punctured tire and the jack in the Bronco's cargo area and closed the door.

"You're right, you're all set."

"Thanks," she said.

Reese sensed his distrust. Did he think she was taking advantage of his sister by giving her false hope about finding Daisy? This wasn't the time or place to lose her temper. She knew better than to piss off a client or their family members.

Chance leaned back against his truck. "I realize maybe I'm coming off as overbearing. But my little sister is young and naïve. I've always believed it was my job to protect her."

"I understand," Reese said. "I don't blame you for feeling that way."

He scowled down at the dirt, but didn't comment.

"Look, Chance, I'm not here to cause your family grief," Reese said, trying to be patient. "I only want to find Daisy. I think we both want that."

He met her gaze again. "Sorry to come off like a jerk."

"Let's work together on this, okay?"

"Sure," he said.

She smiled. "Now, tell me, where can I can have my tire fixed?"

"Rusty's. It's on the corner of Main Street next to the hotel. The only hotel."

Must be the Buffalo Mountain Inn, she thought. Yesterday, she'd Googled the town of Sage and had already secured reservations for a room.

He touched his hat. "Have a good day, ma'am."

Chance sauntered back to his truck, climbed in, and drove away.

Reese got in her truck, closed the door and headed toward Sage. When she arrived at Rusty's Auto Repair, which she couldn't miss due to the large red lettering in the front window, she parked, and entered the shop.

"Sorry, ma'am, we're about to close for the day," a guy at the front counter told her in an apologetic tone.

"Darn, I've got a flat tire I need fixed." The man's name tag identified him as Rusty.

"In that case, no problem," he said. "I'll personally see to it that it's patched up and ready for you in the morning. Is 8 a.m. a good time for you to come and get it?"

"That's perfect, Rusty," she said, relieved as he took her truck key and wrote up her order. When he handed the paper to her, she felt like she'd made progress. She'd have her truck back in time to drive out to the ranch tomorrow.

"See you in the morning," she told Rusty.

"You bet," he said, smiling.

Walking outside to the Bronco, she scrounged around in the back and collected her duffel bag.

"Hmm," she muttered, realizing it weighed heavier than usual. Undoing the zipper, she looked inside and groaned.

Instead of grabbing her things before she left home, she'd grabbed a nearly identical bag of full items one of her neighbors had asked her to take to Goodwill. None of these things would fit her—especially not this.

She looped a finger around the strap of a large cup bra and held it at arms' length. "Wow."

After stuffing the lacy lingerie back in the bag and rezipping it, she slung her purse over her shoulder, then grabbed her laptop. She walked toward town, which fortunately wasn't very far.

When she noticed a library, she stopped and asked for permission to hang up a couple of posters, which she removed from her purse. She'd designed them with a photo of Daisy Ellington that Skylar had emailed. She also left posters at a bank and a convenience store.

Hopefully, the reward of $15,000 for solid information that might lead to Daisy's whereabouts would entice someone to come out of the woodwork and start talking. When Reese had talked with Skylar on the phone yesterday, that was the amount the young mother wanted to offer.

Approaching the white, columned hotel, she stopped to read a historical marker. It said the Victorian era retreat had originally been a hunting lodge during the days of President Teddy Roosevelt, who had stayed here a few times.

Now the place hosted events like business retreats, special dinners and wedding celebrations. Reese could only imagine the romantic photos brides and grooms could count on with such a charming setting.

Bushes rattled and she looked around, but she didn't see anything. Maybe it was the wind, but no, that couldn't be the problem. It wasn't whipping around like typical Wyoming weather.

Barking and snarling, a scruffy dog about the size of rabbit came out from behind a terra cotta planter bursting with red geraniums. If the ankle biter hadn't been so cute, in a fierce sort of way, she would have been scared.

"It's okay, pooch," she said in a soothing tone. "I honestly don't bite."

The dog continued making a ruckus as it guarded the sidewalk.

"Amazon, where are you?" Someone called. "I can hear you. Hurry back here where you belong, naughty girl."

The dog whirled around and scrambled lickety-split

through the shrubbery. The scruff monster raced toward a house where a lady in a long skirt stood at the front door.

Chuckling, Reese headed into the hotel. After checking in at the front desk, she walked up a broad staircase to her room. A white ruffled cover adorned the bed and flower-sprigged wallpaper covered the walls. Lacy curtains allowed sunlight to flood the space and a thick, room-size carpet covered wooden floorboards.

"Comfortable and quaint," she murmured. "Just what the doctor ordered."

She took a shower and washed off the combination of road dust and perspiration. Wearing the soft hotel robe, she sat on the bed, reached for her cell phone and called her friend Kiki.

Kiki Morningstar, Meadowlark Valley's premier holistic guru and owner of a new age shop called The Celestial Eye, had been one of the first people Reese befriended when she moved back home to Meadowlark Valley. They'd both attended the local high school and had been in the same graduating class, although they weren't friends back then.

In a very uncharacteristic move, Reese had gone into The Celestial Eye to look around. When Kiki greeted her, she'd offered Reese a tarot card reading. The cards revealed she would meet a new friend, and she had. Now the two jogged together each morning and had lunch frequently.

Soul sisters, they called themselves.

"So, you made it up to the ranch without driving off a cliff?" Kiki asked when she picked up.

"I did. But I wound up with a flat tire. And I forgot to ask Mrs. MacGillicuddy if she'd watch my cat. He'll be fine for a couple of days, but can you stop by and take care of him after that? I'm not sure how long I'll be here."

Kiki chuckled. "You bet. Me and Mr. Bojangles will bond some more. He's got quite the personality. By the way, what do you think of Skylar Ellington? I looked through the online newspaper archives and her daughter's kidnapping was featured for days. People said she acted like she was hiding something from the police."

"I pulled up some articles online and read them yesterday," Reese said. "People like to gossip and they can be so cruel."

"You've got that right," Kiki agreed. "Some folks claimed they figured Skylar did something with her kid so she could lead a party girl lifestyle. What do you think?"

"I haven't met her yet—apparently she forgot our appointment today. But when I talked with her on the phone, she sounded young and scared. And how can you blame her?"

"I can't," Kiki said. "And I can't imagine what it would be like to lose a child. It would be especially devastating to have one abducted by a stranger."

"It would be horrifying," Reese agreed. "Skylar's brother claims he didn't know she'd hired me and he was not happy when I showed up at the family ranch to talk to her."

"What happened?"

"Let's just say he didn't invite me in for lemonade and tea cakes."

"That must annoy you, right?"

"I think he's just worried about his sister. He admitted he's always been overprotective of Skylar. But I can tell that he's hurting, too."

"No matter how you look at it, this case won't be easy," Kiki said.

"I'm sure Daisy's kidnapping has been hard on the entire Ellington family," Reese said. "But I will need their cooperation in answering my questions. I believe that's the key to finding out what happened to the little girl."

"Maybe you'll actually *find* her," Kiki said.

"That would be a miracle."

"Have faith in yourself, Reese. You're good at what you do."

"Thanks for the vote of confidence, my friend," Reese said, feeling a surge of determination coursing through her. Skylar was counting on her to do her best, and she planned on doing exactly that.

"Seriously, you can do this," Kiki pressed. "I know in my heart that you'll come through. You always have and you always will."

Right after she hung up with Kiki, Reese's phone rang.

"Golden Private Investigations," she answered.

"I'm so sorry forgot about our appointment this morning," Skylar said in a frustrated tone. "I got thrown off one of our horses and broke my ankle. My mom took me to the hospital and I forgot all about you coming."

"I'm sorry to hear that," Reese said, aware how traumatic incidents can do a number on your memory. "I think I upset your brother, though."

"Oh, pish. I told him you were coming, but he was acting like the overprotective, bossy big brother. He's always been that way, but these days he's doubled his efforts. I explained to him why I hired you. He's worried, though."

"That's obvious. But I promise, I'll do my best to find Daisy."

"Thank you so much." Skylar took a ragged breath. "Can we meet again tomorrow at ten?"

"That's fine. See you then."

After Skylar's call, Reese leaned back on the bed. She needed to dress and go on a walkabout to hopefully find a store. A toothbrush and toothpaste were in order, along with a hair brush. She glanced at her jack-alope T-shirt, spotting wrinkles on the mythical Wyo-ming rabbit with antelope horns. Maybe she should buy a couple of tops, too.

She noted a small desk located along one wall—the perfect place to set up her laptop. After scooping up the Toshiba, she stood, walked over and plugged it in. Perus-ing the knotty pine wall, she chose the perfect location to arrange her suspect board. The large window next to it would provide plenty of light.

To start the board, she tore off a sheet of paper from the hotel note pad sitting on a night table. After writ-ing on it, she scrounged through her purse, and located a small safety pin.

"Missing, Daisy Ellington, age four," she said as she stuck the sheet on the wooden wall. "Little sweetie, your mama misses you. And I promise to move heaven and earth to bring you home."

FOUR

REESE DRESSED IN her dusty clothes and ambled out-side. In the gathering evening dusk, she strolled down Wind River Street. A typical small western town rose up around her with several false-fronted buildings perched along sidewalks. Newer brick edifices were sprinkled into the mix.

Towering cottonwood trees, their leaves rustling, cre-ated a giant green canopy. Her gaze alighted on a place called The Spotted Horse Mercantile, a country store housed in a large red building. She crossed the street and went inside.

A bell on the door tinkled as she entered. Shelves filled with farm equipment, horse tack and miscella-neous items like shoes, scarves and handmade jewelry dotted the area. A long glass and wood showcase held old-fashioned candy and other sweets. An elderly gentle-man stood behind it, tapping on a cash register.

As he rang up several items for a woman in shorts and flip-flops, he smiled at Reese. "Howdy there, I'm Sam, the store owner. Let me know if I can help you."

"Thank you." Reese returned his smile and wandered down an aisle. In the corner of the store, she found a section with ladies' clothing. Relieved she wouldn't be wearing her dusty clothes much longer; she perused her choices.

Before long, she'd selected new underthings, a couple of tops and two extra pairs of jeans. She'd be traipsing around Wild Creek Ranch with its jagged mountains and rolling hills, and it would be nice to have some outfit changes.

Passing by an aisle displaying office supplies, she picked out a plastic organization tote and filled it with masking tape, black felt tip pens and yellow sticky notes.

Darkness engulfed the room.

A large hand clamped over her mouth and an arm tightened around her waist, dragging her backward. She tried to scream, but a palm smashed her lips against her teeth and she could only moan.

Ragged breathing, stale from tobacco, brushed past her face as a raspy voice said, "Leave town. Before you wind up hurt."

Though caught off guard by the attack, sanity soon took hold of Reese. She stomped down hard with one of her boot heels. To her relief, it connected with a foot.

Reese's attacker yowled.

The arms that held her captive shoved her into what felt like a mannequin. She tumbled headlong into the figurine, crying out as she crashed. When she hit the floor, the clothes and office supplies flew from her grip.

Aching all over, she managed to stand and look around. She couldn't see much in the inky gloom. Her attacker must have fled, despite a wounded foot. Apparently, somebody knew she was here to look into Daisy's kidnapping.

He or she wanted her gone.

The lights came back on, and Reese blinked to adjust her vision.

"I can't believe someone had the nerve to attack you in my store," Sam said as he rushed down the aisle toward her. "Are you all right?"

"I'm fine," she said, brushing off her clothing.

She noted the mannequin had survived her awkward swan dive without breaking. The figurine's western-style clothing was askew, but it wasn't damaged.

"I'm calling the police." Sam hurried back to the counter. "Can't be havin' my customers attacked."

Reese gathered the clothing and office supplies, then carried everything up to Sam, who ranted on his phone, gesturing wildly.

"Your purchases are on the house," he said as he hung up the receiver, which belonged to an old-fashioned black handset.

"Seriously, you don't have to do that," she said.

"I want to," Sam insisted as he placed everything in a plastic store bag.

As they waited for the local law enforcement, Reese and Sam discussed the incident. They ruminated over the fact that the attacker must have known the store's lay-out well enough to know where to switch off the lights.

Before long, the front door opened and a man in a tan police uniform walked in. The officer said something into his two-way radio, which squawked back at him, then he approached the counter.

"Howdy, Officer Savage," Sam said.

"Hello, Officer," Reese said.

"You must be the lady who was attacked," he said to her in a deep, serious tone.

She nodded. "Yes, and my name is Reese Golden."

"You got here pretty quick," Sam said to Officer Savage.

"It's a quiet evening. Except for this. I'm sorry for the trouble, ma'am. Sage is typically a nice, welcoming town."

From his pocket, Officer Savage pulled out a notepad and a pen.

"Some jerk turned off the store lights, then attacked Reese right down there." Sam pointed toward the disheveled display.

"Ma'am, are you all right?" Officer Savage looked her over with his brown eyes.

"I'm fine," she said, smoothing down her hair. "Just a bit shaken."

He squinted at her cheek. "Got a scratch on your face."

"No big deal," she assured him.

"I can take you to the hospital and—"

"No, I'm all right."

He nodded. "Do you feel like you're in danger of being attacked again?"

"No. I'll be more watchful now."

"Are you visiting someone or just passing through Sage?"

Reese reached in her jeans pocket and handed Officer Savage one of her business cards. "Skylar Ellington hired me to try and find her daughter."

Officer Savage read it, nodded, and tucked it away. "It's been weeks and weeks since she was kidnapped. My unit did everything we could to find her."

"I want to dig deeper into the case," Reese said, hoping Officer Savage wouldn't take offense.

"Believe me, we conducted a thorough investigation," Officer Savage said, his gaze unwavering. "Nothing panned out."

"I'm sure you understand grieving parents never give up hope, even when cases go cold."

He nodded. "Be careful."

"I was with the Denver Police Department for 10 years, Officer Savage. I'll be fine."

"Good to know," Savage said. "For little Daisy's sake, and the Ellington family's, I hope you find some answers.

I don't believe you'll discover much, though. As they say, we left no stone unturned."

"You never know."

Officer Savage asked her to explain everything she could remember about the attack and wrote down her statement, then Sam's. Unfortunately, since the lights had been turned out and it had happened so fast, neither Reese nor Sam could relay any specific information. Neither had been able to determine whether the person had been male or female.

"I'm 5'8" and I believe the attacker was taller," Reese added. "He or she had bad breath. Like a chain smoker or someone who doesn't like brushing their teeth. I stomped down on the person's foot and they took off."

"Got it," Savage said as he jotted down another note, then handed Reese his business card. "Call me day or night if you need anything. Meanwhile, I'll be on the lookout for suspicious activity."

"Thank you," she said. "I plan to stop by your office and visit with you about Daisy's case as soon as I can. I've got lots of questions."

"Not a problem," he told her. "Nothing would make me happier than finding that little girl."

Turning to Sam, he said, "I'm going to have a look around here if you don't mind."

"Whatever you need," Sam said.

HIS BLACK POLISHED boots clunking on floorboards, Savage checked out the door located on the side of the store. He opened it and looked out. "Appears the intruder entered this way."

"I always keep that locked," Sam said, his bushy brows drawn together.

"The lock's jimmied. Better secure it with a deadbolt. We don't want something like this to happen again."

Sam shook his head. "I've owned this place over 20 years and no one's ever messed with that. What's this town comin' to?"

"You've had lots of clerks helping out at your store, haven't you, Sam?" Savage asked.

"Yep, lots of high schoolers." He opened his eyes wide. "Dang, any of those kids would have known about my side door and where the light switches are located. Think one of them might have done this?"

"It's possible," Savage said.

"Damnation," Sam muttered, scratching his head. "You know, this town is scarier by the day. People running around doing all sorts of crazy, stupid things. I remember when little Daisy went missing. Folks talked about how her mama might have gotten tired of taking care of the kid and did something to her."

"Gossip, that's all it was," Savage said. "We didn't find any evidence to support that theory."

"It's funny you guys couldn't find anything."

"That happens more than you know," Savage said. "It's one of the downsides of this job. We'd prefer to find the bad guys right away."

"Hard to believe the kid disappeared without a trace. And she's such a cute little thing. Curly dark hair and big blue eyes." Sam tsk, tsked. "A real shame."

"You two have a good day," Savage said.

"Thank you," Reese said.

"Appreciate it," Sam added.

After Officer Jeremy Savage left, Reese picked up her sack and headed back to her hotel, ruminating over what she'd heard about Daisy.

Blessed with an active imagination, she'd begun to

formulate another theory about what might have had happened to the little girl. If Daisy had an accident and someone was trying to cover it up, that may be why there hadn't been any ransom notes or kidnapper calls. Could be somebody in town knew exactly what had happened.

She had to find out who.

Meanwhile, since her attacker had warned her to leave, someone obviously wanted to keep her from discovering the truth.

FIVE

CLUTCHING A FRUIT BASKET, Reese stood on the Ellingtons' front porch the next morning. The apples and oranges weren't much in the way of apologizing for yesterday's confusion with Chance. Oh well. The small grocery store in downtown Sage didn't carry a large assortment of hostess gifts, so this would have to do.

Anxious to begin her investigation, she rang the bell. A dog barked, then a tall young woman wearing jeans, a T-shirt, and a flower-sprigged apron opened the door. Her blond hair had been styled in a curly, shoulder-length bob and she bore a sad, haunted expression.

Glancing down, Reese noticed the cast encasing one of the young woman's feet, and the fact she leaned on crutches. A Golden Retriever stood beside her, growling.

"Rocky, stop making such a fuss." The woman patted the dog's head and the mutt fell silent, pink tongue hanging.

"Skylar?"

The woman smiled. "You must be Reese."

"I am."

"Please, come in. Sorry about yesterday." Skylar nodded toward her foot. "I feel like such a klutz. I've ridden horses all my life, now look at me."

"Accidents happen." Stepping inside, Reese noted the antique furnishings and faded floral wallpaper. The hardwood floors were worn, no doubt from generations of foot traffic. Plants burst with green in every corner. Moreover, something smelled scrumptious.

"Thanks for the fruit. You can leave the basket there." Skylar inclined her head toward an entry table.

"This is a peace offering since I upset your brother yesterday," Reese said as she set it down.

"He'll live. My brother has always been protective, you know? Too protective, as a matter of fact."

The Ellingtons' front room reminded her of her grandmother's cozy parlor, and a sense of familiarity settled over her. In here, a person could relax with a cup of tea, enjoy a good book, and forget their troubles.

But never your missing child.

Skylar made her way to a couch, propped her casted foot on a coffee table and leaned her crutches against the cushions. "Please, have a seat. I can't thank you enough for coming. My mom and my brother think I've lost my mind, but I need my baby back, you know? I can't sit around doing nothing."

"I understand," Reese said as she settled in a rocking chair. "Of course you want to find her."

Closing her eyes, Skylar rested a hand on her chest. "I can feel in my heart that my child is alive. It's like I have this psychic connection with her, you know?"

Reese nodded. "I've heard of things like that—the bond between mother and child."

"Exactly." Skylar's eyes opened. "At night, when I dream, I hear her whispering to me. 'Mama, I'm here… Mama, come find me, I want to come home.'"

A sob caught in her throat, and she wiped away a tear. "I feel like I'm living in a nightmare."

"I sympathize with what you're going through," Reese said.

She'd worked with anguished parents with missing

children and she knew they went through hell. Many had expressed the desire to stop living if anything had happened to their child.

Reese wanted nothing more than to solve the mystery of what had happened to Daisy and remove the case from the books. Best case scenario—she'd be able to bring the little girl home.

Skylar held her hands against her face, her shoulder shaking as sobs wracked her body. "I just want all of this to stop. I want my daughter home. I want to go back to the way it was."

"I understand how difficult this is," Reese said, her heart squeezing.

Finally, Skylar removed her hands, revealing a puffy, tear-stained face. She offered a shaky smile. "Wh-where do we start?"

When the floorboards creaked, Rocky barked and bounded from the room, his toenails scraping the floor.

"Oh, Rocky," Skylar said, then cleared her throat. "Crazy hound. He barks at the wind. This old house has a lot of nooks and crannies. And creaks."

Chance sauntered into the living room, Rocky padding alongside him. He sat down on a loveseat.

Reese preferred interviewing family members separately so she could listen to each person's recounting of the incident without coaching from the sidelines.

"Speak of the devil," Skylar said. "Here, no doubt, is the cause of the creak. My brother, Bigfoot himself."

"Ha, ha," Chance shot back as he as he stretched out his long legs. Hands resting in his lap, he absentmindedly twirled his thumbs. "Skylar figured you'd want to look around the place, so she enlisted me to be your tour guide since she's a gimp these days."

"He's such a loving sibling," Skylar teased, then her

expression turned solemn and a lone tear streamed down her face. She wiped it away quickly, and straightened her shoulders, as if realizing she needed to pull herself together.

Reese removed a small journal and a pen from her purse.

"Let's go back to the evening Daisy disappeared," Reese said. "Skylar, I want to start with what you remember. Who was in the house at the time?"

"Just me, Chance and my mom."

"What was the weather like?"

"It was warm and calm with a bright moon," Skylar said.

Easy for a kidnapper to see without a flashlight.

"And the last time you saw Daisy?"

"When I put her to sleep in her toddler bed. She wasn't happy about it, but eventually she settled down and quit crying. She had to learn to sleep on her own, you know? I'd spoiled her by allowing her to stay in my bed."

"I understand," Reese said.

Rocky padded over by Reese and nosed her hand. She put down her pen and rubbed the top of his furry head. The dog closed his eyes, obviously enjoying the attention.

"Rocky, come here, boy." Chance whistled, and the dog trotted over beside him. "Sorry, he's a real slobber hound."

"No problem. I love animals. Okay, Skylar, when did your realize Daisy was gone?"

"Daisy woke me up a few hours later with her fussing. She was having a hard time adjusting to sleeping in her own room." Tears glittered in Skylar's eyes as she appeared to be recalling that night. "When I heard a thump, I thought she'd rolled onto the floor and hurt herself. Half asleep, I headed down the hall to her room.

I woke up fast when I saw she wasn't under the covers, which had blood on the sheets. The window was open and the screen had been ripped apart. I was horrified! I fell on my knees and screamed, then I ran to look outside, but I didn't see anything…wait, actually I remember something now."

Chance leaned forward; brows raised inquisitively.

"What?" Reese asked.

"I was so upset that night so I wasn't thinking straight when I talked with the police. Now I remember lights on the back road that runs by our property. They didn't last long, though. There was a glimmer, then it went dark."

"Good, Skylar, that's really good. What else happened?"

"After that, everything was a horrible blur." Skylar buried her face in her hands and her shoulders trembled.

Reese continued to jot down information. "What about the blood? What did the police say about it?"

"Turns out it was from an animal." Skylar shook her head. "Why would the kidnapper smear animal blood all over?"

"It was most likely a trick to make the police follow a certain course."

"Like what?"

Reese didn't want to upset Skylar even more by explaining how law enforcement might consider Daisy had been killed, rather than abducted. At least until they had analyzed the blood and discovered it belonged to an animal.

"It doesn't matter," Reese said. "Let's focus on what we know. I'll follow up with local police to look at Daisy's case files. Meanwhile, what do you recall about their efforts to find Daisy?"

"They set an Amber Alert right away," Skylar said.

"They searched our house from top to bottom, grilled my mother and brother and our neighbors, searched our property with dogs, and pawed through the garbage dump. My mom, Chance and I, along with neighbors and friends, scoured the area for days looking for her."

"Did the police search your outbuildings?"

Skylar nodded. "I'm pretty sure they did."

Chance nodded. "Yes, they did."

"The police never discussed any persons of interest or suspects?"

"There was a registered pedophile living in the area, and they questioned him, but ruled him out."

"Did they say why?"

"No."

Reese made a note to see if the man still lived in the area because she wanted to talk to him.

"I read some newspaper articles online about the kidnapping, and they mentioned there weren't any ransom notes at the time of the kidnapping. Have you received any since that time? Maybe calls from the kidnapper?"

"No," Skylar said. "We never heard a word after Daisy disappeared. But I set up a website so people would hopefully report if they see or hear something. I constantly send out fresh posters to towns around the state. In fact, I need to put up some new posters in Sage."

"I spread some around town yesterday hoping we might receive a tip from a concerned citizen." Reese looked over at Skylar's brother. "Chance, when was the last time you saw Daisy?"

"When Sky got ready to put her to bed," he said, a distant look in his eyes. "I gave Daisy a big ol' kiss, and she giggled like a silly head."

"What else?"

"Pretty much what my sister told you. When she

screamed, Mom and I came running into Daisy's room. I went out and looked around before the police came, but I didn't find a thing. I've been going crazy since Daisy went missing. I'd like to kill the son-of-a-bitch who took my niece. And if I ever find him, he's a goner."

He clasped his hands together, as though he was choking someone. His eyes gleamed with deadly conviction.

"It's understandable you'd feel that way," Reese said. "But more violence doesn't solve anything."

"Can't help it," he growled. "He or she deserves to die."

"Do you recall the police finding any distinctive tire tracks outside around the house?" Reese wanted to change the subject. Daisy deserved justice, but Chance's threat to kill the perpetrator didn't help.

"No," he said. "We have so much traffic on the roads around here, nothing stood out. I remember Officer Savage mentioning that since there hadn't been any recent rain or snow, they couldn't make out anything specific in the dirt."

"Reese, what have you heard about Daisy's case?" Skylar asked. "I mean, it made big waves around here. People blamed me that Daisy went missing. Said I was a bad mom. Accused me of killing my daughter and hiding her body."

"I heard about it when it happened," Reese admitted. "There were a few articles in my local newspaper about the kidnapping. And I researched a few things online after I talked to you yesterday."

"Do you suspect me like everyone else?" Tears glimmered in Skylar's wide eyes.

"I've seen a lot in my experience as a police officer," Reese said. "And I know better than assume anything until the facts are in. It's not fair."

"I appreciate that," Skylar said.

"What about Daisy's father?"

"I don't know him," she said.

Reese quirked a brow.

"I mean, well, it's hard to say. He's just a guy I met at a club one night. I never even knew his name. I know that's bad, but I was 18 and those were my crazy days, as my mom calls them. She said I was young and naïve."

"Did you meet the guy here in Sage?"

"No, I was working in Jackson Hole that summer. Some girlfriends and I went up there after graduation. Mom says I got caught up in the Jackson Hole lifestyle. It's so different than our quiet little town."

"Do you remember the name of the place where you met him?"

"Um, yeah, it was called, The Hideaway Bar."

"Was the guy a local or a tourist?"

"I don't know. I, I didn't ask."

Chance shook his head. "I swear, Skylar, you're the most ditzy—"

"Chance," Reese said, noting Skylar's tearful expression, "blaming your sister isn't going to help us find Daisy, okay?"

He grumbled under his breath.

As Reese jotted down notes, she listed Daisy's mystery father as a suspect. She just needed to find out who he was.

Nancy Drew would have known how to handle this. As a kid, Reese had loved her mystery-solving books. When the world sucked and life couldn't become any worse, Nancy always saved the day.

Nancy might be a storybook character, but right now, Reese needed to channel her persistence. This case tugged at her heartstrings. What if the police and other agencies had missed a vital piece of information? With her fresh perspective, she might find the missing clue that would solve the case and bring Daisy home.

Skylar looked into space. "You know, the police pawed through the local landfill. That's one of the gross things—they thought maybe I had smothered Daisy and threw her in the trash. They had other terrible theories, too. Like, that I'd sold her to human traffickers or traded her for drugs—and I'm no junkie, believe me."

"Police witness some gruesome stuff," Reese said. "They don't rule out anything."

If Reese had worked Daisy's case, she'd have considered all the same ideas. Standard operating procedure, by the book, and all that. She recalled Officer Savage saying, "We left no stone unturned."

However, being on the other side of an investigation would make the process different. Victims often felt intimidated. Endless questioning wore them down until they feared they'd done something terrible in their sleep, but had no waking knowledge.

Skylar had perhaps been unprepared for single motherhood. In a small town like Sage, Reese had no doubt that neighbors had gossiped about her irresponsible and careless behavior. In the court of public opinion, Skylar had been deemed guilty by her neighbors when Daisy went missing.

During her online research yesterday, Reese had found miscellaneous newspaper articles about Daisy's kidnapping. From those, she'd gleaned as much information as possible, considering she no longer had police resources at her disposal. Talking with Skylar today had launched a plethora of fresh ideas about what leads to pursue.

"We had search teams and candlelight vigils and I even went on some local TV stations to plead with anyone who might have taken Daisy," Skylar added. "A few talk shows contacted me to appear and discuss what happened. Mostly, people continued to blame me."

"People are sometimes thoughtless, Skylar. I haven't experienced what you have, but I can sympathize with what you've gone through."

Skylar took a trembling breath. "I sure hope you can help, Reese. I know I'm obsessing, but Daisy's my child, you know? How do I let go of that?"

"You can't," Reese said. "No one should expect you to."

She exchanged glances with Chance, hoping he understood better why his sister had hired her.

Losing a child would be like your heart had been ripped from your chest. Things would never be the same after that. Life would become clouded with doubts and insecurities.

If Skylar had done something to Daisy, she wouldn't be searching so desperately to find her. Meeting the grieving mother in person helped Reese see the case in a new light, and she honestly wanted to do everything in her power to find Daisy.

Had the police made Skylar out to be the enemy, instead of enlisting her help? That could have prejudiced them against the case. Reese's dedication to finding the truth may bring new evidence to light.

"I can't promise anything," Reese told Skylar. "But I'll do my best."

"That's all I can ask," Skylar said. "And just so you know, Daisy's an extremely bright child. The Sage daycare center, Little Lambs Learning Center, tested her. They said they believe she's gifted."

Reese jotted that in her notes.

"I'll have to say she is smart as a whip," Chance said, his eyes filling with tears. "At four, she can already read and write and she can do simple math like nobody's business. It amazes me."

"Grandma Ellington was a smart lady," Skylar said, sniffing back sobs. "Dad said her teachers believed she could have gone to college to be a doctor or a scientist, but she chose instead to marry and raise a family. Which isn't surprising, since that's typically what women did back then. Mom's side of the family are all intelligent and accomplished, too. Between them and the Ellingtons, Daisy could be our little genius. She learned to walk at eight months old and she talked clearly by the time she was one. She's inquisitive and loves putting together jigsaw puzzles, which I think most kids don't care for. Daisy never seemed to require the same amount of sleep that other kids need. I believe that's one of the reasons I had trouble getting her to stay in her own bed. She wanted to be up playing with her toys, exploring outside or hiding in one of her secret forts."

"Daisy also takes after you, Skylar, because she picks up ideas quickly," Chance reminisced, his voice taking on a faraway quality. "She already understands that Santa Claus and the Easter Bunny aren't real, but it didn't bother her when she found out the truth."

"When did that happen?" Skylar asked.

"Last Christmas," he said. "She kept badgering me about it, and I finally told her. It didn't make sense to keep that from her any longer."

"What did she do when you explained?" Skylar's brows rose.

"She smiled and said she thought it was great that adults were so clever they could fool children into behaving by telling them fairy tales." He laughed, but a sob caught in is throat and he looked away. "God, I miss her."

"Me, too," Skylar said. "It's like Daisy has an old

soul, she seems to just know things. I believe she has this ability to understand life in a way most adults don't. I miss her too, and I want her home where she belongs. I need her home."

When Skylar buried her head in her hands again and sobbed, Chance walked over and patted his sister's shoulder.

Tears welling in her own eyes, Reese noted on her paper that Daisy had gifted abilities and a high intellect. She cleared her throat and said, "I'd like to speak with your mother. Hearing her account about that night would help."

"My mother's health isn't good these days," Chance said. "After Daisy went missing, it went downhill. She doesn't want to become caught up in another fruitless search for her granddaughter."

"It's her heart," Skylar explained. "She's on medication, but we don't want to upset her."

"That's unfortunate," Reese said. "It might help for me to hear what she remembers."

"I'm sure nothing more than we've told you," Skylar said. "Let's leave Mom out of this for now. Later, I'm sure she'll talk with you. She's upset I called you in the first place. She is afraid to get her hopes up about you finding Daisy, then, if it doesn't happen, she fears being disappointed all over again."

"I plan to prove your mother wrong," Reese said firmly. "One more thing, have either of you told anyone about me coming here?"

"No," Skylar and Chance said, almost at the same time.

"Why do you ask?" Skylar wanted to know; her eyes narrowed.

"I stopped by the mercantile in Sage yesterday and

somebody switched off the lights and attacked me. I didn't pick up on much except the stale smell on their breath. Do you have any idea who might do something like that?"

"No," Skylar said.

"Did you call the police?" Chance asked.

"Yes, and Officer Savage came over right away. He took statements from Sam and I, and said he'll watch for suspects. I think somebody doesn't want me here looking into Daisy's disappearance. Do you have any ideas who that might be?"

Skylar and Chance looked at each other and shook their heads.

"Do you have any enemies you can think of? Someone who is jealous of you for some reason? Someone who wants something from you?"

"No," Skylar said.

"Nope," Chance added.

"These days, I stick around home mostly," Skylar added. "I help around the ranch. I don't feel like being social."

"I'm about the same," Chance said. "I take care of the small amount of livestock we own and handle day-to-day maintenance. I teach at the local high school during the school year, but there's no one there who has any beefs with me. At least that I know about, anyway."

"This could be in your past," Reese said. "Maybe someone insists on holding a grudge."

"Oh, my Lord, does that mean someone around here took my little girl?" Skylar fisted her hands, her expression fierce.

"God help them if I get a hold of 'em," Chance growled.

Reese figured Skylar must have plenty of social network connections. It was possible she'd talked to someone about hiring Reese to investigate Daisy's case, but didn't remember doing it.

Whatever had happened, she wondered who might want to prevent her from investigating Daisy's disappearance. Had she kicked the hornet's nest?

"I'd like to take a look around now," Reese said, rising. "Let's start with Daisy's bedroom, then yours, Skylar."

"I'll wait right here while Chance plays tour guide," Skylar suggested. "I'll only slow you down if I try to limp along."

SIX

"SORRY FOR CATCHING you off guard yesterday," Reese told Chance as they walked down a hallway.

"I was worried about Skylar. She took a nasty fall. And, like I said, I got protective of her. She's upset about Daisy, and she doesn't think straight sometimes. She gets emotional."

"She's a grieving mother, so of course she'd be emotional."

"Well, yes, I agree. I'm a wreck, too. And so is my mom. But I couldn't believe Skylar hired a P.I. She's gonna tap out her trust fund if she doesn't watch out."

"If your child was missing, would you worry about money?"

Chance opened a door and stood aside; his expression pensive. "Yeah, you're right. I wouldn't. And come to think about it, I'd clean out my account, too, if it would help Daisy. I'm just worn out from the police and the FBI never coming up with anything, you know?"

"I imagine it would be heartbreaking."

Chance motioned for her to enter. "Nothing's changed in my niece's bedroom since that night. Sky can't stand the idea of anyone touching even one item."

As she entered, Reese pulled out her phone and snapped photos. The room stood like a shrine to the missing little girl. The walls broadcast a bright pink color, as did the curtains and the juvenile-print quilt hanging on the wall over the small bed. A rocking chair and a dresser filled one corner and a toy shelf sat nearby.

Giant pink rose appliqués covered one wall, along with Daisy's name, painted in hot pink. A pink, furry rug nestled across the floor. Reese walked to the window— the old-fashioned tall style. She noted the torn, flapping screen, big enough for an individual to enter through. Said individual could have easily grabbed the child, jumped back onto the porch and headed off into the night.

In her mind's eye, she saw someone doing exactly that. Daisy would have been screaming, but when Skylar came into the room, she hadn't heard her daughter crying. More than likely, the kidnapper had a vehicle waiting with which to whisk away the little girl.

"It was hot that day, so we had the window wide open to catch the cool evening breeze," Chance said. "I wish we'd have invested in air conditioning. Then this would never have happened."

Reese inspected the area under the bed, rifled through the closet, and got a general feel for the room's layout. She picked up a few toys and examined them, then opened the dresser drawers, noting the clothing organized in neat stacks.

It bothered her to think that Skylar's child had been alive and well one day, missing the next.

A bulletin board held photos of the ranch, members of the Ellington family and several were of a small girl with a large grin and curly dark hair. She pulled one off of the corkboard. "Daisy, right?"

He nodded.

"May I take this? It will help me."

"Sure. Skylar said to let you take whatever you need."

She tucked the photo in her purse. "I'd like to see Skylar's room now."

Chance led her down the hallway and opened another door. This room was painted a blue-gray color. The old-fashioned sleigh bed displayed a purple bedspread and purple drapes framed the window. Comfortable and inviting, and nothing looked amiss.

Reese snapped more photos.

She decided her penchant for scouring the area in a missing person's case came from her time with the Denver Police Force. She bit her lower lip, remembering how much she'd loved her work.

The next room she and Chance visited was the den. She studied the book shelves and the shaggy, furry heads of wildlife mounted on the wall.

"I sure hope we can find Daisy." Chance leaned against the door frame; his arms crossed over his chest. "That little girl means more to me than my own life. I've helped take care of her from the time she was born."

"I can tell how much you love her."

"Since Daisy's dad wasn't in the picture, I tried to be the father-figure in her life. But I'm tired of never finding any answers about what happened."

"Speaking of fathers, did Skylar ever say anything to you about Daisy's?"

"Not much. I know, it's crazy."

"She never even tried to find him when Daisy was born?"

"No."

What if Skylar did know him, but she didn't want him in the picture? Reese digested that information. Maybe there was bad blood between Skylar and Daisy's dad. Had he decided to exact revenge on Skylar by taking the baby?

Chance ran his hand through his hair. "I don't understand how, after all these weeks, you'll be able to uncover any more clues about Daisy's disappearance. I'm sure the police and the other law enforcement agencies checked out every possible idea."

"I handled my share of missing person's cases when I was a police detective," Reese said as she met Chance's gaze. "I might find something another investigator missed. Or I might think of a different angle to pursue and uncover a new suspect. There's plenty of evidence when kidnappings occur, it's just that not all is clear during the initial search."

"I realize that. I'm just… I don't know what I feel."

"Sad? Hurt? It's okay. No doubt it tore apart all of your lives when Daisy went missing."

He strode over to the window and looked out, but remained silent.

Reese turned to study the animal trophies again, aware that many people found it difficult to express themselves after tragedies. They often bottled up rage and anger inside of themselves. Chance was apparently having issues, too, so she decided to change the subject.

"You're a hunter?"

He nodded. "Dad taught me when I turned 12. Haven't done much lately, not since he passed from a heart attack two years ago. That's my elk head over there, and there's my pheasant. Dad shot the mountain lion."

"By the way, how big is your ranch?"

"It covers a little over 100 acres," Chance said. "We can have a look at any areas you'd like to see."

"The kidnapper could have used back roads, and hidden on your ranch somewhere until the heat died down. Especially if he's someone local and is familiar with your place."

"True," Chance said. "I'd never considered that before."

Reese needed to head over to Jeremy's office to take a look at Daisy's case files. There might be something in them that could tip her off with new clues.

When they entered the foyer, Chance started up a broad staircase, motioning for her to follow. "This place has nine rooms. Four bedrooms, two downstairs, and two up. We have two bathrooms, a kitchen, dining room, and the front room. There's also a screened-in porch on the back of the house and an attic storage space."

He opened a bedroom door. The interior was decorated with flowered wallpaper and held an older style bed covered with a patchwork quilt. The hallway bathroom featured a claw-foot bathtub and a silver radiator.

Reese snapped photos, making no comment as she took it all in. There were plenty of places where an inquisitive four-year-old could have wandered. Had she hurt herself somehow, maybe by falling down the stairs? Had someone disposed of her body? It didn't seem to be a likely scenario.

"Thanks for showing me around," Reese said.

Chance ushered her back down the stairs and they entered the dining room where a large farm table, big enough to seat 12, dominated the space.

After taking more photos, she noticed a painting over a carved buffet that featured a colorful sunrise over mountains, with frontier-style buildings clustered in the forefront. A ribbon of water ran through the middle of the town, its banks dotted with piles of dirt. Miners hunkered over the blue depths.

"That's a unique piece." Reese studied the composition, finger placed in the middle of her bottom lip.

"My Aunt Polly painted that," he said. "She lives up in Jackson. Skylar visited her a couple of times the summer she worked up there. It was right after she graduated from high school. That fall, she came home pregnant."

Reese's interest piqued. Had Aunt Polly met Daisy's father at some point? Maybe she could shed some light on who he was.

"Skylar didn't stay at your aunt's place?" Reese asked.

"No, Sky and her girlfriends shared an apartment."

Reese made a note to ask Skylar about her roomies, then her gaze drifted back to the painting. "I love the ebb and flow of the colors—the rich browns and greens on the landscape set against the backdrop of the peach and pink sunrise."

"You sound like you know a thing or two about art," he said.

"I love it. It was my college major for about a minute before I switched to law enforcement."

"Aunt Polly is talented; I'll give her that. She married some rich guy and hobnobs with the upper crust of Jackson. Movie stars, real estate moguls—you know the type. She encourages them to donate to her charitable causes. That makes them feel better about their gobs of money."

"The wealthy one percenters, eh?"

"Exactly. She loves entertaining the beautiful people in her million-dollar house with the million-dollar views."

Reese could only imagine Aunt Polly's fabulous soirées and upscale gatherings held in the wealthy tourist ski resort. For someone like Reese who stretched pennies until her next payday, that lifestyle didn't exist.

Glancing at Aunt Polly's painting again, Reese asked, "Is this a real place?"

He trailed his hand down the painting's gilded frame. "It's Lucky Gulch, and that's Wild Creek running past the buildings. My dad's grandfather got in on the gold rush up there. Later on, he went into ranching and bought property, including the land the town is on."

"Interesting," Reese said.

Chance rubbed the back of his neck. "It was abandoned in the early '40s when the gold vein tapped out. Only a few ramshackle cabins are left, a couple of old saloons, a store and some of the miners' homes. We use one as our hunting cabin."

"Have you been up there recently?"

"No," he said. "It's been a while since any of us have visited. After dad died, none of us felt like going up there."

She followed Chance as he walked out onto the porch, opened a door and strode into the sunlit yard.

SEVEN

REESE SCOURED GRASSY knolls and scrub brush, looking for any scrap of evidence. Since the kidnapping occurred weeks ago, she didn't expect to find anything. Still, she didn't want to pass up the chance to inspect the area.

One of the gnarled cottonwoods held a tree house, so she set aside her purse and climbed up the ladder to look around the structure. She found it empty, except for leaves and twigs.

"My sister and I used to spend hours playing up there," Chance called up to her. "Daisy loves playing in it, too. Or, she did…" His voice trailed off.

Making her way back down the tree, she noticed a flash of pink nudged into the trunk base. Using her fingernail, she dug out a broken baby pacifier, the plastic nipple worn and cracked.

Chance took it from her, and his face drained of color. "This is Daisy's. It's probably been here for years. I thought the police searched this area."

"They're not perfect," Reese said as she brushed her hands on her jeans.

"What do you suppose it means?" Chance handed the pacifier back to her.

"If the police didn't find this, it could mean they missed other important evidence."

"Damn," he muttered. "I hate to hear that. It makes me mistrust them big time."

"I'm sure they did their best. But if your local police

department is like most of the places I'm familiar with, they are understaffed and underfunded."

Grabbing her purse, Reese followed Chance as he sauntered between tufts of tall, tasseled grass and headed toward a large red barn. Weathered and faded by the sun, it dominated the pasture.

Reese snapped some photos, then caught up with Chance and asked, "You're a teacher, right?"

"Yep, I teach history at Sage High—specifically, the U.S. Constitution and the Founding Fathers. Also, how our state government operates. There's more, but that mostly covers it."

"Are your students bored? I hated history."

"They're more interested than you'd expect."

"It takes a special individual to work with young people."

"Or a crazy person," he said, chuckling, then he quickly sobered.

"I got awful grades in history," she admitted.

"Those who do not learn history are doomed to repeat it."

"Catchy quote."

"I don't recall who said it, but I believe it's true."

"Have any of your students, or their parents, made threats against you or your family?"

"Never. My students are good kids. So are their folks."

"You've never had to reprimand anyone?"

"Oh, I've had to pull some of them aside on occasion and have strong words about their grades or their behavior. Nothing's ever been so dramatic that one of them would want to kidnap my niece."

"Think about it," Reese said. "It may not have been obvious to you, but it could have been overwhelming for them."

"I'll mull over the idea."

Reese snapped some more pictures of the barnyard area, pockmarked with ridges of dried mud. Surrounded by split rail fencing, the weathered barn had seen better days. It needed a new roof and a fresh coat of paint, but the weeds and bushes around it were neat and trim. A windmill stood nearby, whipping around in the breeze and making a clacking sound.

Chance held the large wooden barn door open for her. She entered the darkened area, watching as dust motes fluttered through shafts of sunlight. All of the stalls stood empty. Hay scattered across the floor and the room reeked of dirt and musty manure.

"The ranch used to be more operational, back in the day. Now things are mostly quiet and we only keep a few animals."

She stumbled on a loose floorboard and quickly righted herself.

Chance shot her a concerned look.

"It's dark in here," she said.

"I've been meaning to nail the floor down again. It's hazardous in certain places, so watch out." His lips twitched, and he asked, "You ever been in a barn before?"

"Newer ones, yes. Never one this old. I grew up in Wyoming, but I don't consider myself much of a country girl, you know what I mean?"

"Yeah, I get it."

Reese eyed the interior. Dust motes danced on shafts of late morning sun streaming through the small windows along the front wall. Snapping pictures, she explored nooks, crannies and cupboards. Hay piled in drifts across the worn floorboards, and several bales of the dried yellow grass were stacked against one wall.

An ancient green tractor sat in one of the stalls, a

couple of rusty tin buckets lined a shelf, and a milking stool hung on the wall beside a wood oxen yoke. A pair of cow hobbles sat on a wooden table.

Nothing looked out of order, and Reese didn't find any secret compartments where a kidnapper could hide with a screaming child while police scoured the area.

She jumped when a barn cat appeared. The furry critter strutted back and forth, her belly sagging between her legs. Reaching down, Reese stroked the tabby's soft fur.

"Well, look who's here. It's Miss Kitty," Chance said as he walked up beside her. "We wondered where she'd disappeared to."

Growling, the cat jumped to the top of a stack of wooden crates and snaked her tail over her head. Then she pounced into the hayloft and scurried into the shadows.

"She's beautiful."

"She's independent, like all of our barn cats. She goes off on her own a lot, but she usually shows up at dinnertime. She hasn't come around for a few days, though."

"I love her name. It's very...creative."

"Daisy named her," he said. "That cat strutted into the barnyard one day, pleased as punch, and made herself welcome. No one around these parts claimed her, so we let her stay. She's a great mouser." He paused a minute. "I bet she delivered her kittens, and she's hidden them up in the loft."

"The loft, I forgot to look up there," Reese said.

He nodded toward the half-floor located above them. "We'll have to go up that old ladder for a good look-see. You okay with that?"

"Sure." Reese set aside her purse and walked over to the ladder where she began climbing, testing each wooden rung for sturdiness. When she reached the platform and stood, she noticed the cat burrowing into a nest of hay. More bales rested along the walls and dry stubbles were piled here and there across the floorboards. A large square opening dominated one of the walls—most likely where farm hands chucked hay bales to the ground.

Chance climbed up and stood beside her. "Anything catch your eye up here?"

Reese shook her head.

He approached the pile of hay where the cat had disappeared. Hunkering down, he gently moved aside the yellow straw, revealing a litter of kittens resting on a threadbare red and blue blanket. Curled around her sleeping kittens, one of her paws resting on a small furry body, Miss Kitty watched the humans with wary green eyes.

"Adorable," Reese whispered. She leaned over to see better.

The cat continued to observe Reese and Chance with an unwavering gaze. Her tail switched back and forth as the kittens roused and began to suckle.

"Time to get to get work again," she said. She walked toward the ladder and began to descend.

Chance followed.

"You don't have to show me around anymore," she told Chance. "If you are okay with it, I'll walk around the property on my own."

"My chores are done for the day," he said. "I'm fine if—"

A shot rang out, whizzing past Reese. She looked down to the main floor, spotting someone all in black with a matching hoodie ducking behind a large barrel full of shovels and pitchforks. She swore the figure possessed a man's typical build.

She scrambled back up the ladder and into the loft.

Chance pointed toward a stack of hay bales and they hunkered behind it.

"What the hell's going on?" Chance whispered.

"It could be the same person from the store." Reese tensed when she heard heavy footfalls approaching the loft.

"We're sitting ducks," Chance muttered.

Reese patted a hay bale. "How heavy are these?"

"Maybe 50, 60 pounds."

"Help me push this," she whispered.

Chance nodded, and with their combined strength, they shoved one of the rectangular objects to the loft edge. Hearing the footfalls stop, Reese peeked out from her hiding place and glanced down. Mr. Hoodie stood by the ladder, reaching for the rungs.

She nodded at Chance. Sharing the burden, they pushed over the hay bale.

A thump sounded, along with a loud grunt. Then something scraped across the floorboards. Reese scrambled over to look, noting the hay bale had hit its mark. Mr. Hoodie was stretched out on the floor and the gun had flown from his hand.

She started down the ladder, followed by Chance.

As her feet hit the floor, Mr. Hoodie scooted from beneath the bale and stood. He looked around, spotted his gun and lunged toward it.

Chance took long strides toward a cabinet, pulled out a shotgun, cocked it and aimed at Mr. Hoodie, who managed to grab his weapon before he headed out the door.

Reese snatched her purse and followed the intruder into the barnyard. Her stomach churned with anger as she watched the guy clamber onto a motorcycle and roar down the road.

Whipping her keys out of her pocket, Reese ran to her

truck and jumped in. Chance slid in the passenger side, resting his shotgun on the floorboards.

Revving up the Bronco, Reese tore down the road. It didn't take long to catch up to the motorcycle. She gripped the steering wheel with white knuckles, her mind clicking as she memorized the license plate number; 3-2151.

"Bastard," Chance growled.

"It's got to be the same person who attacked me in Sage. I got a better look at his build. I'm pretty sure it's a man."

Mr. Hoodie turned off onto a dirt road and roared away.

"Hang on," she told Chance as she headed after the bike.

Chance grabbed the off-road handle as she navigated the bumping, winding road, wincing as it narrowed.

"Damn," she said through clenched teeth.

"This old truck is great," Chance commented.

"Betty has a souped-up engine. Comes in handy in my line of work."

"Betty?"

"Betty the Bronco. Named her that a long time ago because my grandmother loved the cartoon character Betty Boop. Grandpa taught me how to drive on her and we rebuilt her together."

When the truck hit the mother of all pot holes, she lifted up in her seat. Her teeth clanked like porcelain dishes. After catching her breath, she focused on the road again. Mountains rose in the distance and rocky, sagebrush-dusted plains surrounded them.

Zig-zagging over hills and valleys, the motorcycle continued traveling north. Mr. Hoodie kept glancing back at the Bronco, as though he found it impossible to believe someone continued to follow him. At some point, he'd donned dark motorcycle goggles, so Reese couldn't define any facial features.

The mountains encroached the road and jagged bluffs jutted from the ground. After one more look at the Bronco, Mr. Hoodie steered his motorcycle between two narrow rock outcroppings and down another path, impassable for a vehicle.

Reese pulled off the road and stopped. She climbed out of the truck and hurried over to get a good look at the motorcycle's escape route.

"Damn it," she said, scuffing a rock with the toe of her boot. Shading her eyes from the bright sun, she watched the bike zoom down the path into tall evergreens, disappearing from sight.

Chance came up beside her and rested a hand against one of the red rock outcroppings. "I got the license plate number."

"Yep, I got it, too. Let's head into Sage and ask Officer Savage to run the number through the DMV. Based on what just happened, I think he needs to have another look at Daisy's case."

EIGHT

WHILE CHANCE CALLED Skylar to let her know what was going on, Reese drove down Main Street toward a small, brick building with a sign that read, "Sage Police Department." It was huddled between Gene's Greasy Spoon and Rarin' Roger's Pawn Shop.

After pulling her truck in a spot next to the one stamped, "Chief's Parking Only," she and Chance entered the building. A green plastic and chrome couch, along with two matching chairs and a dusty plant, decorated the room. A scratched wooden coffee table held a pile of dog-eared magazines.

She and Chance approached the reception window. Behind the glass, a small communications area displayed equipment along the walls, along with TV monitors and other office machines. A dispatcher sat at a counter next to a phone and a computer featuring two large screens.

Solid offerings for a small-town police office, Reese noted. That must mean SPD officers had possessed the right resources to conduct a thorough investigation into Daisy's disappearance.

"May I help you?" the dispatcher asked, looking up from a file on her desk. Her drab gray hair and black clothing contradicted her bright smile.

"We'd like to talk to Officer Savage, if he's available."

"Let me check to see if he's at his desk." After sliding

a pair of glasses up the bridge of her nose, she placed a quick call, then said, "He'll be right out to talk with you."

"Thanks," Chance said.

A few minutes later, Savage entered the reception area. "Hello, Reese," he said, hands placed on his hips. "Chance, I haven't seen you in a while. What brings the two of you here today?"

"There's been a shooting at my ranch. No one was hurt, though," Chance quickly added. "Some fool decided to trespass in my barn and try to pick us off."

"The shooter took off on a motorcycle and we followed it as far as we could. I need you to run the license plate," Reese added, realizing she'd made more of a demand than a request. "Please."

Savage raised his brows, then ushered them back to the patrol officer area, indicating they should take a seat on the chairs by his desk. He walked around and sat in a cracked leather chair.

Another police officer wearing a tan uniform sat at a desk in a corner, talking on the phone. She glanced over at them, then resumed her conversation.

"You two aren't the law around here," Savage growled. "You did a dangerous thing chasing after that guy. Or was it a guy?"

"I think so," Reese said. "He wore all black with a black hoodie. I think it was the same man who attacked me the other day at the mercantile. Which leads me to believe he has something to do with Daisy's disappearance or at least has vital information. You need to start active investigation into this lead."

"Whoa, there," Savage said. "We have a few procedures to follow. Let me check out this new information, then I need to talk to Chief Miller. He'll have to authorize resuming investigations, but he's gone for the next week."

"Bunch of bullshit red tape," Chance snarled.

"In this police department, we follow regs," Savage said.

Reese placed her hands, palms down, on Savage's desk and leaned forward. "You do what you have to. Believe me, I understand procedures. But be quick about it. This is a child's life we're talking about. I want to find her, so *I'm* following up on this lead."

Savage leaned forward and glared at her. "You do that. Meanwhile, be careful not to break your neck or cause any trouble while you snoop around."

Grabbing a piece of paper and a pen from Savage's desk, she wrote down the motorcycle license plate number and pushed it toward him.

"At least run this."

Savage took the paper and logged into his computer. He clicked computer keys and entered the plate number. A few minutes later, he frowned, looked at Chance, and said, "Says here the motorcycle is registered to Matthew Ellington."

"It can't be!" Chance said. "That motorcycle is locked in a shed up at our hunting cabin."

"Apparently not anymore," Reese said. "You said it's been a while since anyone in your family checked on things up there."

"Damn it," Chance said.

Reese glanced at Savage. "I'd like to see Daisy's case file."

"The Chief—"

"Never has to know," Reese said. "You said he's not here today, right?"

"Come on, Jeremy," Chance said. "We're talking about my niece. Give us a break, huh?"

A muscle twitched in Savage's cheek. He stood,

walked over to a file cabinet and pulled out a thick manila folder. He sat it on the desk and glanced over at the other officer, who was now huddled behind her computer, typing away on the keyboard.

"I'm going to grab a cup of coffee," Savage said. "You two want anything?"

Reese and Chance shook their heads.

"I'll be back." He nodded toward the file and walked down the hall.

Reese slid the manila folder into her lap, glancing over to make sure the other officer hadn't noticed. As Chance looked on, a worried expression on his face, she thumbed through photos, interviews and SPD reports. She read through the important information, gleaning enough to develop some ideas. Using her cell phone, she took pictures of various items.

"Typical stuff here," Reese whispered to Chance. When a photograph of a footprint in the dirt appeared, she looked closer, noting the hiking boot brand: *Timber Ridge, size 10.* She pulled it aside, then sifted back through photos.

"Got it," she muttered, finding the one that pictured Daisy's mussed bed and a dirty footprint on the pink carpet. *Timber Ridge* sold very expensive boots and other outdoor gear.

At the sound of a throat clearing, she noted Savage sauntering toward them, obviously giving her time to return things to normal. She slid her phone and the photos inside her purse, thankful she preferred handbags big enough to tote a kitchen sink.

After shoving file contents back into the manila folder, she slid it on Savage's desk. *Crap.* It looked like a bomb had exploded among the pages. When she leaned back in her chair, so did Chance.

Savage entered the office and stood by them; arms folded across his chest. He shot a quick glance at the folder, nodded, then met Reese's gaze.

"Anything else I can help you folks with today?"

"We're good," Reese said. "You'll ask your chief about checking into Daisy's case when he returns, right?"

"I'll mention it. He's a good guy, he'll probably authorize us to open the case again."

"Have a good day, Officer Savage."

Savage nodded at Reese. "Same to you."

Reese and Chance left the police station and walked down the sidewalk toward her Bronco.

"Aren't you worried Savage will notice those photos are missing?"

Reese chuckled. "I doubt he'd care. I'm sure he'd like this case solved, too, and to bring Daisy home."

"How will a photo of a footprint help find her?"

"I don't know, but I didn't think I should rule it out," Reese said as she slid into her truck and shut the door. When Chance had settled in, she added, "One of those pictures shows a high-end brand of hiking boot. The sole didn't look worn. That tells me the owner recently purchased them and had big bucks to throw around. A minor detail right now, but it might be important later."

"If you say so."

"By the way, how well do you know Jeremy Savage?"

"I've known him since we were kids. He graduated from high school the year before me. Why?"

"I don't believe this is the case, but I hope he's not the type to sabotage Daisy's investigation. He might think it would compromise the Sage Police Department's integrity if they failed at finding Daisy."

Chance's piercing blue eyes widened in surprise.

"No way, man. Not that guy. He's like a Boy Scout

and always has been. He's so squeaky clean and by the book he'd make you puke."

"Just making sure I know who I'm dealing with here."

Reese started her truck and backed out of the parking spot. "I need directions to your family's cabin. Also, keys for the door and the shed, though it's most likely open since someone's riding around on your dad's motorcycle."

"I'll do you one better. I'll drive you up there." Chance glanced at her; his expression lined with determination.

"Thanks, but you don't have to do that," Reese said, preferring to do the detective work herself. Having family members along on a case wasn't part of her process. "I've taken enough of your time."

"Nah, I won't be real busy until school starts up in the fall," Chance said. "I'd do anything to help find Daisy."

Reese realized she wouldn't change his mind, and she didn't feel like arguing. "You know the lay of the land. That'll prove helpful."

"Don't forget, I've got this, too." Chance patted his shot gun.

"Hopefully we won't need it."

NINE

"TURN HERE," CHANCE SAID, pointing toward a side road. "It's a quicker route to drive up the mountain."

Reese wheeled onto the gravel pathway.

Chance's cell phone rang, and he fished it out of his pocket. "Hi, Skylar. We're headed up to the cabin. Someone broke into the shed and stole Dad's motorcycle and… what's wrong?"

Reese noticed the alarmed expression on Chance's face.

"Oh, my God. Is he—"

"What's up, Chance?" Reese whispered.

He pointed back toward town, and Reese did a U turn.

"We'll be right there," Chance told his sister and pocketed his phone. "Somebody hit Rocky. Mom and Sky are at the vet clinic with him."

"Oh, no," Reese said.

She followed Chance's directions. After she parked, he jumped out of the truck and she followed, managing to keep pace with his long strides. At the low white building, he opened the front door and held it for her.

Inside, Skylar and an older woman with short, feathered blond hair, who must have been Chance's mother, sat on a black vinyl couch. Skylar's crutches leaned against a coffee table. The two ladies glanced up, faces grim and tear-streaked. Chance walked over and hugged them both, then sat next to his sister.

"Rocky must have gotten out of the fence and wandered down the road. The driver who hit him just took off," Skylar said.

"Loser," Chance growled.

"Adam Jenkins called me and told me what happened," Skylar said. "The driver went out of the way to hit Rocky."

"Did Jenkins see what kind of vehicle it was?" Reese asked.

"No," Skylar said.

Reese frowned. This could have been an accident. Or it could be another attempt to intimidate the Ellingtons. Was someone trying to send them a message to stop checking into Daisy's kidnapping? Or some heartless person could have swerved to hit Rocky, finding a cheap thrill by hurting a helpless animal.

"Adam loaded Rocky in the back of our Traverse so we could bring him here," Skylar added.

"Good old Adam," Chance said.

"Yep," Skylar said. "You can always count on him."

"Mom, this is Reese Golden, the private investigator Skylar hired." Chance nodded toward Reese.

"I'm Leyla Ellington," she said as she stood and shook Reese's hand.

"It's nice to meet you, Mrs. Ellington," Reese told her.

"Please, call me Leyla." She clasped her hands, white showing on her knuckles.

Why did Leyla behave so standoffish and distant? Reese's earlier concerns that the Ellington matriarch might be hiding something prickled her senses. Did Leyla have a secret? Or maybe she preferred privacy and didn't like anyone digging into the family's affairs. Hard to tell, at this point.

"Reese is doing an awesome job," Skylar said. "I have this feeling she's going to find Daisy."

"I'm only being thorough," Reese said, fearing the chance of finding the little girl was slim. Nevertheless, she intended to work this case until she hit the proverbial brick wall, or until she found Daisy.

"Have a seat," Leyla said. "It might be a while before Rocky comes out of surgery."

"I should go," Reese said, hesitating. "I've got work to do."

"Hang out with us," Chance said.

She knew she should be writing up reports and adding sticky note clues to her suspect wall. And, admittedly she felt out of place. Yet, because Chance had been helping her, she decided to stay. She settled in a chair with chrome arms.

Silently, she observed the Ellingtons' family dynamics, picking up on snippets of conversation and observing body language.

Leyla sat with crossed arms—a closed book. Skylar gestured and talked a lot, enthusiastic, outgoing and hopeful. And yet, she maintained an aura of sadness that Reese sensed came from her anguish about Daisy. And Chance—well, he was steady as a marble statue.

"Rocky looked bad," Skylar told her brother. "Dr. Connor's not certain how he's going to fare because of his age."

Chance ran a hand through his tousled hair. "I sure hope he pulls through."

"We all do," Leyla said.

"That old mutt is like family," Chance said. "Hell, he is family."

Reese had never owned a dog, but she'd enjoyed her grandparents' pooch, Paddy. Because her mother, her brother and she had lived with her grandparents, she'd grown up around him. He'd slept at the foot of her bed each night and greeted her with licks on the face when she came home from school.

Her grandparents had doted over that scruffy hound and spoiled him rotten. She knew people got completely attached to their pets. Since the Ellingtons continued to suffer from Daisy's kidnapping, losing the dog would be rough.

A woman, appearing to be in her late thirties, entered the waiting room brushing off her white overcoat. Everyone turned to look at her with expectant expressions.

"How is he, Dr. Connor?" Chance asked.

"Rocky made it through surgery." Lines of weariness showed at the corners of her eyes, and her dark red hair fell loosely from her bun. "All we can do now is wait."

Each Ellington family member sighed with relief.

"Thank you, Dr. Connor," Leyla said in a solemn tone. "You don't know how much we appreciate this."

"You can all come in and see him briefly if you'd like," Dr. Connor said as she walked over and held open the door to her surgery.

Skylar grabbed her crutches, rose, and limped toward Dr. Connor. Chance took his mother's arm and walked with her. He glanced over his shoulder at Reese. She shook her head and patted her chair arm. This should be a family moment and she didn't want to intrude.

After they left, Reese flipped mindlessly through a magazine to pass the time. She didn't absorb the words or the pictures. A million theories about Daisy's case cluttered her mind, and she swore under her breath.

What am I doing here? I should have gone back to my room to document my suspicions and theories. To satisfy her churning mind, she pulled out her phone and used the notes app to write down her ideas.

A short time later, Leyla and Skylar exited the recovery room, sniffling and wiping away their tears. Chance followed; his expression sober.

"I'm going to take Mom and Skylar home," Chance told Reese. "It's touch-and-go with Rocky. Dr. Connor said she'll call us if there are any changes."

Reese stood, checking her watch to see it was after 6 p.m. "It's late. Let's head up the mountain tomorrow."

"Good idea. The road will probably be a mess," Chance said. "We haven't maintained it in ages."

"Skylar," Reese said, "before Chance and I leave tomorrow, I want to talk with you about something."

"How about now?" Skylar suggested. "I'm starved. We can head over to the Horseshoe Bar and Grill."

"I'll take Mom back home, then I'll meet you two there," Chance said.

"Maybe your Mom wants bite to eat, too," Leyla said, sounding miffed.

"Sorry," Chance said. "Didn't mean to speak for you. Do you want to go with us?"

"No, I don't," Leyla said with a chuckle. "I'd rather go home. I just didn't want you kids to think I'd become too feeble to think for myself."

"Mom, that's never going to happen," Skylar said.

Everyone walked out of the clinic; Skylar a bit slower as she maneuvered her crutches.

"I'll meet you ladies in an hour," Chance said as he took Leyla's elbow and steered her toward a large white vehicle.

TEN

LATER, REESE SAT in Sage's country western honkey-tonk, drinking a beer as she waited for Skylar to come back from the rest room. She glanced around, listening to the band. *I must stick out like a broken toe*, she thought, noting people's stares.

Her western-cut shirt, jeans and boots were similar to what everyone else wore. She should have fit in, but the locals continued to give her sidelong glances, apparently doing their best to size her up.

Who's she? Where's she from? What's she doing here?

A strange face in a small town.

She could almost hear their voices riddled with curiosity and suspicion. It was obvious citizens in the small town of Sage, Wyoming, kept close tabs on newcomers.

Nobody here knew her name, though, or maybe they did? Was there someone here in the bar who wanted to stop her from investigating Daisy's kidnapping? Or to stop the Ellington family from finding out what happened to Skylar's little girl?

Gossip spread like wildfire in small towns. By now, she had no doubt that most of the residents had discovered her reasons for being here. Could be they were afraid. If the Ellingtons had lost a child, others might fear suffering the same fate. They might fear having their little ones fall prey to a similar kidnapping. They wouldn't want to be reminded about that awful time when one of their own went missing.

Shaking off her unease, Reese scrolled through her cell phone messages without digesting the contents. What should be a friendly place didn't feel so friendly right now. The stares bored holes into her, making her feel like she was from outer space. Somewhere along the line, had she turned into a purple alien with giant eyes and floppy antenna?

Looking up again, she took stock of her surroundings. Cow skulls with horns, horse shoes and coiled ropes decorated the walls along with several rusted ranching and farming implements. Lantern lights suspended from the ceiling gave off a soft glow. There were even honest-to-goodness batwing doors—exactly like the ones you see in old western movies—gracing the restroom entryway.

She found the hand-painted signs hanging on the barnwood walls clever. One said, "Yee Haw," while another boasted, "I'm here to kick ass and drink whiskey." The cutest one, in her opinion, declared, "Rise and shine, mother cluckers."

"Sorry it took me so long," Skylar said as she plunked down in the chair across from her and leaned her crutches against the wall.

"You're doing good," Reese said. "I'd fall flat on my face if I tried to use crutches."

"It's a fine art," Skylar said as she sipped her beer.

Reese observed how people stared at Skylar and whispered to each other. Did they realize how obvious their gossiping was, or did they care? Reese was insulted on her client's behalf.

"I know, they look at me like I've got a scarlet A on my shirt," Skylar said. "It's unnerving. How can I defend myself when they've all decided I'm guilty of doing something to my daughter?"

Skylar hadn't had an easy time since her daughter went missing. No wonder she stayed close to home these days, Reese thought.

"What questions do you have for me?" Skylar asked.

"I'm curious about the summer you spent in Jackson," Reese said. "Where did you work?"

"I waitressed in a little restaurant called the Black Diamond," Skylar said. "Boring work, low pay."

"Did you have any trouble with the customers or maybe the staff?"

"No. I did learn my lesson to never wait tables again. That's backbreaking stuff."

"Chance mentioned you had roommates."

"Me and a couple of my girlfriends decided after graduation we'd spend the summer working up there. We rented an apartment. It was supposed to be this big adventure, but I got a big dose of reality instead."

"Why do you say that?"

"Three girls living in a small place? Hah! That totally sucked. Audra spent like two hours primping every morning. And Nina was such a drama queen. Everything that happened to her was like the end of the world. She should be in my shoes right now, missing her baby girl." Skylar chewed on her lower lip for a moment. "She thought she had problems."

"You still having bad dreams?"

"Yes. In them, Daisy keeps insisting that I need to find her." Skylar sobbed, pulled a tissue from her purse and dabbed her nose.

"Do you believe Audra or Nina would want to hurt Daisy?"

"No way. I mean, we griped at each other but that's all."

"What about Daisy's father?" Reese realized that was

a sensitive topic, but it was a possibility he might hold the key to Daisy's disappearance.

"What about him? I told you I met him at the bar and I don't…" she cleared her throat. "I was too drunk to think about asking his name. Believe me, I'm ashamed to tell you that."

"Did Nina and Audra go out with you? Maybe they remember something."

"They did, but I've lost track of them. Nina took off for college the fall after graduation. And Audra moved away with her boyfriend."

"Tell me what you do remember about the guy."

"He was hot, as in, off-the-scales-on-fire hot. He had dark hair and dark brown eyes. We danced and we hit it off. After a couple of drinks, we, uh, we must have gone back to his room."

"Must have?"

"That would be the natural progression of things, right?"

"You don't remember?" Even with too much alcohol in her system, Reese could recite basic details of her one-night stands.

"The booze made my head fuzzy," Skylar admitted.

"Did he buy you a beer? A mixed drink?"

She frowned. "Wait, I think I ordered a Fuzzy Navel."

Had the guy slipped something into Skylar's drink?

"Skylar, this is important. Did you black out?"

She nodded. Pressing her face in her hands, she leaned her elbows on the table and sobbed. "That's why I don't remember. He must have spiked my drink. I never should have gotten so plastered. I've regretted that night for a long time."

"You were young, and anyway, it's not your fault— never think that. It sounds like he took advantage of you."

Reese's heart broke as she watched Skylar sob. On top of everything else, the poor girl had possibly been raped.

"Don't tell Mom or Chance, okay? They'll know how stupid I was. I'd never live it down." Skylar folded her hands on the table as she took a deep breath and composed herself.

Reese reached out and patted her arm. "They'll put the blame where it belongs. On that guy."

Skylar shook her head. "You don't know my mom. And Chance would hold it over me the rest of my life. He bosses me enough as it is."

"What can you tell me about the next morning?"

"I woke up all alone in a strange motel. It was awful. At first, I couldn't remember how I got there."

"You should have reported what happened to the police, Skylar."

"I just couldn't. And I was so ashamed." She sighed heavily.

"Wyoming has no statute of limitation on rape. It's not too late to report it to the cops."

"No way," Skylar said. "I'd sound like a straight up fool. I don't even remember the dude's name."

"You have every right to enjoy a night on the town," Reese said.

"Yeah, I know," she said miserably. "But I should have been more careful."

"Maybe you could talk with somebody. It would help. Do you want me to help you find a therapist or a counselor?"

Skylar's eyes went wide. "I've already talked with a therapist and they just prescribed medication for my anxiety. I really needed it to help for a while, then I tapered off."

"I'm so sorry for all you've had to suffer," Reese said.

She now had a better understanding of why Skylar's memory had so many holes in it. She'd been through some very difficult experiences. And now with her daughter missing, it added more concerns for the young mother.

"Promise you won't say anything to anyone about this," Skylar pleaded.

Leaning back against her chair, Reese said, "Of course not. It'll stay between us. But I do have one more question."

"Whatever you need."

A waitress brought their meals, and Reese's stomach growled. It smelled scrumptious, but her appetite was dampened by Skylar's chaotic circumstances. She waited until the server left before asking her, "Do you recall the name of the motel?"

Skylar perked up as she grabbed a French fry and began to munch. "The Rawhide Motel. My head was pounding like crazy, but I checked it out before I left. It was a cheap, hole-in-the-wall dump outside of town. Why does that matter?"

"It may, or it may not," Reese said as she pulled a pad from her purse and jotted down notes.

"Good news, ladies," Chance said as he sauntered toward them and sat down at the table. He grabbed one of Skylar's fries and shoved it in his mouth.

"You're welcome," Skylar shot at him.

"Whatever," he responded. "The vet called. Rocky's awake and drank some water. It appears he's going to pull through."

"Yes!" Skylar said, her face brightening. "I'd miss that old hound if he hadn't survived."

Reese was glad Skylar had something positive to focus on now, rather than her troubling memories. She also appreciated Chance's timing. If he'd shown up earlier, Skylar wouldn't have shared vital information about what happened in Jackson.

Now, she needed to start sorting through all of the leads. First on the list was to search Chance's hunting cabin for possible clues.

ELEVEN

"FIND ME..."

A child's crying awakened Reese.

She sat up, threw off the covers and wiped a cold sweat from her brow. Her dream affected her as though it had been real—a dark haired little girl standing in the mist calling out to her. Obviously, Skylar's plight had begun to eat at her and the ghostly image had to be Daisy.

Usually, her nightmares were about being shot and the painful aftermath. Not this one.

The room burst with a pale violet glow as dawn slid past the curtains. Crawling out of bed, Reese showered and dressed. Down in the lobby, she grabbed a cup of coffee from the breakfast bar, along with a banana. When her cell buzzed, she checked to see Chance had texted. He was already waiting outside.

Grabbing her purse, she tossed her trash and headed out of the hotel. She spotted Chance immediately parked next to the curb in his huge, rumbling truck. No wonder he'd insisted on driving. Compared to her old Bronco, his behemoth could handle any rough, uneven roads.

She crawled in the truck and said, "Good morning."

"Mornin'," he said.

She watched the passing landscape—rolling prairie that erupted into foothills and grew into mountains. Sagebrush and rocks covered the area, but it soon transformed into steep terrain.

The truck hit a rough spot and she grunted as her

shoulders jerked, and her body swayed. Some people might find this bumpy, off-road travel thrilling, but not Reese. Like a demon, Chance kept going.

"Are you okay?" she asked him, her jaw dropping as the truck dipped.

He nodded. "I'm just pissed."

"Care to explain?"

"Who in God's name had the nerve to kidnap my niece? And why? The more I think about it, the angrier I become. It makes me feel so, so... I don't know."

"Vulnerable?"

"Yeah, I guess that's it."

"You have every right to feel that way."

When Chance drove around a rock outcropping, the trail almost disappeared. Chewing her lower lip, Reese reached for the truck's grab handle.

He furrowed his brow. "C'mon, where's your sense of adventure?"

"I forgot to pack it," she returned.

"I've seen your feisty side, lady. You are no shrink-ing violet."

Reese wasn't certain if Chance had just paid her a compliment or if he'd accused her of being too aggres-sive. Regardless, she took it as the former. That didn't make her feel any safer as he drove the truck up a hill, perilously close to the edge of the road.

A rock wall rose vertically on the left side. To the right, a steep cliff dropped into a canyon divided by a ribbon of blue water. Trees and scrubby green bushes dusted the boulders and rocks, their roots clinging to random patches of dirt.

Reese's heart pounded like a Kabuki drum.

"You don't look so good," Chance said, giving her a once-over.

"I don't feel so good," she responded, her breath uneven. "I'm not a fan of heights."

"You'll live."

Reese frowned. What if the truck slipped? She envisioned it rolling down the mountainside, slamming against jagged boulders. With the vehicle crushed like a tin can, how could she or Chance survive?

Did I honestly need to come up here? Hopefully it will be worth it.

She double checked to make sure she'd fastened her seat belt. Then her mind sent her a rabid thought. What would it be like to die hanging upside down, belted into the demolished truck?

Who knows if she and Chance's bodies would ever be found, let alone be recovered? Reese glanced over her right shoulder. That rugged creek below could wind up being their watery grave.

"You said the road might be bad, not that there wasn't one."

He chuckled. "That's why I wanted to drive."

"Well, thanks for that," she said. "I think."

When Chance sneezed, Reese squeaked in alarm.

He gave her a discerning glance. "What?"

"Keep both hands on the wheel, please."

"Yes, ma'am," he returned.

Reese sucked in a ragged breath, then released it. Maybe if she focused on something else besides the canyon, she could calm down. She glanced at the thick clouds gathering in the gray sky. Several drops of moisture splattered against the truck's windshield, sliding down the dusty glass.

Great.

"I never even thought to check on the weather," she said. "It looks like we're in for some rain."

"I looked at the AgWeb this morning. It is supposed to drizzle this afternoon, but the storm should blow out by evening."

Talking about the weather relaxed Reese. For a second, she released her hold on the grip handle. From the corner of her eye, she noticed a white, shaggy creature perched atop a boulder. Sporting long, thin horns, it looked almost mythical.

Chance must have noticed the creature, too.

"It's a mountain goat," he said. "We're in their territory."

"Amazing how it managed to climb up there."

"They're sure-footed. That's why tracking them is complicated."

"You've hunted them?"

"My dad got a license to hunt a trophy billie one year. I was only along for the ride."

Reese wrinkled her nose.

"I know, you don't like it. The Wyoming Game & Fish Department controls the hunting licenses to keep the populations stable. Think of it as a humane way to prevent animals from starving during the winter if food is scarce."

"I suppose."

"Both my dad and my grandfather hunted enough game to keep our freezer stocked all year."

"Mmm." Reese considered what it would be like to eat Bambi. The idea sent a shiver of disgust up her spine. She didn't like consuming anything with eyes in the first place, yet she liked cheeseburgers way too much to give them up.

"What do you think our pioneer ancestors did to keep themselves fed?"

"They hunted," Reese said.

"Exactly."

Though it was a different way of thinking to her, she supposed everything Chance said made sense. At least for him. In her world, the only thing she hunted were the spiders that invaded her office.

"Does Skylar hunt, too?"

"She's a better shot than any of us. She can blast a peanut off a tin can from a good distance."

Reese laughed, envisioning Skylar with a rifle.

"Out here, we learn gun safety from the time we're little. We have a healthy respect for firearms."

He drove around a corner and romped on his brake, staring at a pile of rubble up ahead. "Damn. I was afraid we'd run into a rockslide."

Reese leaned forward to study the dirt, rock and branches strewn across the road.

"Should we turn around and go back?"

"Nah, I'll clean it up. This isn't a huge mess, so it shouldn't take long."

He climbed out of the truck and went around to the bed. Removing a pair of leather work gloves and a shovel, he tromped toward the debris pile. After sliding on the gloves, he dug into the mess and began tossing aside shovelfuls.

Reese rooted around in the glove box and discovered another pair of gloves. She put them on, noting they were way too large, but what the heck. This wasn't a fashion show. And she sure didn't want to sit here while Chance did all the work.

Hopping out of the truck, she walked over to stand beside him. "How can I help?"

He glanced over at her, grinning at the oversize gloves. "Thanks, but I can handle this."

"Seriously," she said. "There's got to be something I can do."

"Fine," he said. "How about you toss aside any larger rocks and branches you can lift?"

Reese set to work immediately, bringing sweat to her brow. She sorted through everything and tossed debris off the cliff, watching it spiral through the air down into the canyon.

She leaned over and wrapped her gloved hands around another large rock. At the sound of rattling, she glanced to her left. Coiled on the ground in front of her was a brown snake marked with a scaly diamond pattern. It watched her, its pink forked tongue flicking in and out.

"Chance," she murmured, her heart racing.

"You tired already?"

"There's a rattler. A b-big one."

He turned around. Noticing the reptile, his eyes opened wide. "Don't move."

"I'm not planning to do the Macarena," she whispered.

Chance moved slowly toward her and in one fluid movement, scooped up the rattler with his shovel and hurled it off the edge of the road.

"Holy crap." Reese took a shuddering breath.

"I bet that rattlesnake was as scared as you," he said.

"I think it wanted me."

"Rattlesnakes don't hunt people."

"True," Reese said, thinking of someone kidnapping Daisy from her bed. "Only people hunt people."

TWELVE

Once they'd cleared the road, Reese and Chance resumed their journey. The truck shimmied when it hit a rough spot. She grunted, her shoulders jerking as she swayed from side to side.

"Man, I'd rather have a root canal than go off roading again," she said.

Chance grumbled something under his breath.

To her relief, the road widened, giving the truck a wider berth. The cliff leveled out and the gulch turned into a bowl-shaped valley. Sagebrush-covered hills stretched into the distance, and a small town came into view along with a bubbling creek. Thick, dark clouds cast an enormous shadow over the deserted shacks and ramshackle log cabins.

Relaxing her coiled muscles, Reese wondered what it had been like to live up here so far from civilization. It must have been lonely. Hell-bent on becoming rich from panning gold, she supposed sometimes people replaced their common sense with fanatical determination.

"It is remote up here."

Chance gave her a sidelong glance. "Folks had to have a lot of grit."

"I'm sure. It couldn't have been an easy life."

Chance rubbed the back of his neck. "Gold lured folks like proverbial moths to a flame. I figure they had to be half crazy."

They both nodded.

"Even if they didn't strike it rich, they had schools, churches, stores, hotels, banks and blacksmiths," Chance said. "All the comforts of home. Including outlaws, just like the jerk who broke into my shed."

"Bad guys are like cockroaches. They'd survive a nuclear holocaust."

"No shit." Chance drove past more crumbling buildings and parked next to a wooden bridge spanning a churning waterway.

"Is that Wild Creek?"

"Yep. You want to have a quick look around town before we head over to the cabin?"

She nodded. "Might as well."

He jumped out of the truck and she got out, too. They walked through the center of town past crumbling water troughs, broken hitching posts and abandoned wagon wheels. Tumbleweeds dotted the deserted streets. Reese scanned the area for clues that someone had recently been here. There didn't seem to be any indication, however.

"The mine was active for about forty years," Chance told her. He pointed toward a large hill covered in pine trees and scrubby underbrush. "See that long building with the smoke stacks?"

Looking into the distance, she scanned the large, low-slung structure that stretched down the mountain.

"That's the mill where the guys processed gold from the Daisy Mae Mine," he said.

"Is your niece named after the mine?"

He nodded. "Mom and Skylar thought of it."

"It's cute." Reese reached into her pocket, pulled out her cell and snapped photos of the buildings.

"By the time the Depression rolled around, everyone pulled up stakes and moved away. That's the price of progress." Chance propped one of his boots on a tree stump. "Things change. Life moves on."

His expression darkened, and Reese sensed what was on his mind. "You're thinking about Daisy, right?"

He met her gaze, his expression grim. "I want to beat the living tar out of whoever took her."

"I'm stubborn, and I don't give up easily," Reese said. "I'm going to do my best to find some answers for your family."

He nodded.

As if trying to remind them of their mission and urge them to move on, the heavens opened, and fat raindrops splashed their faces.

Chance looked up at the swollen sky. "Looks like we're in for it. We'd better head to the cabin."

After they returned to the truck, Reese wiped moisture from her face with her sleeve. Chance started the engine and drove over the bridge. He continued up a hill and turned into a gravel driveway, then parked in front of a tin-roofed log cabin fronted by a wide porch.

Rain pelted them as they left the vehicle and hurried toward the door. Reese frowned. The lock had been jimmied.

"Shit," Chance said. "They got in here, too."

Inside, the place looked like a herd of wild horses had stampeded. Food wrappers, boxes and tin cans were strewn across the floor. Trash covered the tables and other furniture. Someone had made a hot mess of the place, but a pair of hiking boots drew Reese's attention.

She walked over, picked one up and read the label. *Timber Ridge, size 10.*

"I can't believe it. The person who broke in left their boots," Chance said as he began stuffing garbage in a large black trash bag.

"Right, and not just any person," Reese said. "I think it was Daisy's kidnapper."

Chance stopped and stared at her. "How do you know?"

"This is the style and size of hiking boot in the picture I took from Daisy's case file." She held up a leather boot.

Chance walked over and took it from her. He gripped it until his knuckles turned white.

Reese retrieved the boot from him and set the pair aside. "This is a huge break. I'll take these to Officer Savage. He can turn them into the crime lab and have them processed for DNA."

"How long will that take?" Chance's face lit up.

"Depends on how backlogged they are."

"I hope they aren't too far behind on their workload."

"Did the police come up here after Daisy went missing?"

"No. None of us ever thought to mention the cabin. There was so much going on. I could kick myself for not thinking of this place."

"It's okay, we're checking it out now. Who knows about your cabin up here?"

"Just my family."

"You've never brought friends to hunt or camp?"

"No."

"What about Skylar?"

He shook his head. "Dad didn't want us to bring anyone else, just in case they broke a leg or an arm and decided to get sue happy."

"Somehow, the kidnapper learned your family had this cabin."

Swearing, Chance started reaching for more trash.

"Wait," Reese said. "Let me sort through everything first. Clues, you know."

"Uh, sure. I didn't think about that."

Reese began digging through the drifts of rubbish, handing it over to Chance to toss if she deemed it useless. She uncovered some cracker boxes and other children's food containers. Under a couch cushion, she found a small pink blanket.

Chance grabbed it and held it against his chest. "It's Daisy's favorite," he said in a raw voice.

"The kidnapper must have kept her here for a while," Reese said. "He or she must have wanted to wait until the heat died down from the Amber Alert. Or until…"

"Until what?"

"It's hard to say."

"I can't imagine who would do this to our family. Or why." Anguish lined Chance's expression, and he looked pale. "Daisy was up here all that time! And the kidnapper didn't even ask for a ransom. We'd have paid it, too."

"Don't draw any conclusions yet," Reese said. "Until we know otherwise, Daisy could be out there, waiting to be found."

"God, I hope so."

AFTER GOING THROUGH the cabin, Reese found children's books and a few toys. Someone had made sure Daisy was well fed and entertained, so that was positive. She gathered items she considered evidence and put them in a large brown paper shopping bag that Chance gave her.

They searched the shed, which had indeed been broken into. Chance cursed when he noted his father's motorcycle was missing, even though they both knew it had been stolen.

"I can't believe I didn't recognize the motorcycle when we were following that guy," Chance grumbled. "The bike is unique, in fact vintage—one of a kind."

"Uh, news flash, he'd just shot at us. I think we were both in a state of shock," Reese said. "No one expected it."

"True," he said.

"When was the last time you saw the motorcycle?"

"A couple of years ago, maybe, could be longer." He swore. "The jerk who took the motorcycle must have hot-wired it."

"Interesting," Reese said. "I didn't realize you could hotwire those. But I honestly don't know much about motorcycles. Or hotwiring."

By the time they got back to the cabin, they were both soaked. Chance grabbed a couple of towels from a cupboard and handed one to her. Drying off, she looked out the window and shivered—not just from the cold weather, but from the idea of how cold-hearted people could be.

For some reason, she sensed Daisy was still alive. But where was she and who had taken her? And why? She realized she kept posing those questions to herself over and over. But it would bother her until she could come up with some answers.

"A little bad weather and it turns frigid real fast this far up in the mountains." Chance gathered a few chunks of wood from a pile in the corner.

Reese rubbed her arms to generate warmth. "Hard to believe it's August."

"No kidding." He strode toward the stone fireplace, hunkered down, and began stacking logs on the hearth. He dug out long wooden matches from a tin container and used one to light the wood, then coaxed flames into life.

As the room's temperature rose, Reese relaxed. On one wall, a red sign with white lettering said, "Welcome to the Moose Lodge." An elk head with a set of large horns graced another wall, along with a pheasant sporting a long tail. On another wall, a large metal tub suspended from a hook.

A colorful woven rug covered the floor next to a worn leather couch that displayed a granny square afghan. An antique wooden rocking chair perched beside the fireplace where Chance used an iron poker to nudge several fiery, sparking logs.

A wooden trestle table with matching benches dominated one corner. Next to it sat a black, old-fashioned black stove. A short counter holding a sink and a hand pump nestled beneath several shelves containing plates, bowls, pots and pans. Next to that stood a tall, wooden cupboard painted an eggshell color.

Red-checkered curtains lined the windows, a framed map of Wyoming and a couple of paint-by-number artworks decorated the walls. Next to the door were a couple of antique oil lamps, wooden walking sticks, a fur-covered stool and a wooden wall rack holding an antique fishing basket, hats, shawls and overcoats.

The place offered comfortable accommodations, albeit dusty and musty smelling from lack of use. The idea someone had been hiding Daisy up here puzzled Reese. Chance said only family members knew about the cabin. Obviously, someone else did too. How did they find out about it?

Chance's crackling blaze sent fingers of warmth through the room. Reese's gaze drifted toward a doorway to another room containing a brass bedstead covered in a worn red, yellow and brown quilt. The covers were twisted in a heap, revealing someone had slept there.

She envisioned Daisy curled up, sleeping, missing her

family. *Find me*, Reese imagined her saying, just like the little girl in her dream had urged.

"I'm looking, kiddo, I'm looking," she whispered.

THIRTEEN

AN HOUR LATER, the rain stopped and sunshine filtered through gray clouds. While Chance rustled through cupboards and chests, looking for more indications that Daisy had been held in the cabin, Reese went outside.

She trudged through tall grass and wildflowers up a hill, spotting a narrow wooden outhouse. The half-moon cut out gracing the door intrigued her. What purpose did it serve? Maybe to allow light inside the little shack? In the dead of night, however, only a shaft of pale moonlight would shine through.

Stepping inside, she wrinkled her nose at the stale odor and frowned at the wooden bench seat. Now wasn't the time to be picky about where to relieve herself, so she took care of business and headed back out into the fresh air.

She walked down to the creek, mesmerized for a moment by the swirling water. It appeared to be running high, since it spilled over the banks. Crossing over the bridge into the old town, she enjoyed the sun's warmth as it spread golden fingers over the rooftops. Steam rose from the damp streets, soaked cabins and buildings. Chimneys that hadn't held fires in decades released wisps of white moisture into the atmosphere.

During her quick explorations, she checked out the crumbling school and the church, an old bank and a couple of decrepit homes. Back outside, she took a picture of a daisy sprouting through a wagon wheel and the rusted red pump in front what must have been an old gas station. Shards of dirt-encrusted pottery and colored bottles were scattered in the alley behind a restaurant.

There were no signs the kidnapper had taken Daisy anywhere besides the cabin, so she headed back. As she tromped along, a ghostly little girl's image appeared in the distance.

Find me, she said.

Blinking to clear her vision, knowing her mind was playing tricks on her, Reese passed through a grove of trees. She climbed toward to the cabin, which perched on higher ground. A cloud blotted out the sun, and rain began to drizzle again, then it became a steady downpour.

By the time she reached the abode, she was wet again. When she walked inside, Chance gave her a critical once over.

"I know, I look like a drowned rat," she said.

Lips pressed into a firm line; he tossed her the towel she'd used earlier to dry herself.

"Thanks," she said, patting her hair with it.

"I didn't find anything else in this mess," Chance said, looking around at the disarray. "Just dust and dirt that I'm doing my best to clean up. The mouse traps did their jobs, too."

With a broom, he swept up a pile of debris into a dust pan. He dropped the contents into a large black trash bag.

"No other traces of Daisy?"

Chance shook his head.

Reese began picking up empty cans and boxes, which she also tossed into the trash bag. She decided they'd found all they were going to, and they might as well be on their way. The weather had decided to turn wild outside, though, and rain pounded on the tin roof.

"That's a wicked downpour settling in," Reese commented.

"It can get pretty intense up here in the mountains," Chance agreed.

"You've seen it get bad like this before?"

"Tons of times. One minute it's a gentle rain, the next, it's deadly." He closed his eyes for a moment, then looked at Reese. "You know, it just kills me to know the kidnapper held Daisy here, practically right under our noses. I've gone over and over in my mind ideas of who may have brought her here. And why he grabbed her from our house. It's creepy."

"He even knew where Daisy's bedroom was located, which leads me to believe he's been watching the family. Possibly even knows your family well."

Chance held his head in his hands. "This is making me crazy. Until we get Daisy back home where she belongs, me and Mom and Skylar are all going to be out of our minds with worry."

"At least we found evidence that whoever took her is taking care of her," Reese said. "I know it's hard, but keep trying to think about who would want to take her."

"That's constantly gnawing at me, and it doesn't make any sense," Chance said, then sighed heavily. "The kidnapper didn't ask for money or anything. Why would someone take a child?"

Lightning flared outside and the interior of the cabin illuminated with bright light. Another crack of thunder exploded.

"There are other reasons," Reese said quietly. "But let's hope it's none of those."

Chance walked over to a window, staring through the waterfall of moisture covering the windows. Reese came up behind him, noting, with dismay, that the entire landscape had become a massive blur. She had a good idea how tortured he felt right now, but it was difficult to offer tidbits of wisdom that would alleviate the pain.

"You can't see a thing out there," Chance said. "So much for weather reports. I thought this storm was supposed to pass quickly."

"It doesn't appear to be ending anytime soon, that's for sure."

"Look at the bridge—it's nearly covered by the water now. It's crazy."

Reese stepped in front of another window and glanced toward the wooden passageway, noting the swirling current that threatened to cover it completely. Stretched beyond it, the road they'd arrived on had been pounded into a muddy mess. Their chances of leaving that way didn't look good.

"Is there any other road out of here?"

"Nope."

"I suppose it wouldn't be a good idea to go out in this mess right now anyway," Reese said with frustration. "I've gotten stuck in this type of weather. You have zero visibility because the windshield wipers can't keep anything clear."

"Yeah, I've run into that, too. It's best to stay put till this weather passes, especially considering that road isn't in the best condition anyway."

"True," Reese said, recalling the steep, pot hole riddled path they'd taken up here.

Chance studied the sky, his brows furrowed. "When the storm settles down, we can head out. Until then, we'll hang tight."

Peachy, Reese thought. As much as she wanted to follow up on the new leads about Daisy, she knew it was for the best.

FOURTEEN

ALTHOUGH REESE WAS anxious to return to town and get busy working on the new developments of this investigation, rain continued to cascade in heavy sheets across the mountain. She glanced frequently out of the window, watching the storm water hammer the churning creek. The gloomy gray sky augmented the depressing scene. It was only late afternoon, but the gathering darkness made it seem as though night had settled.

"Even if the storm stops, the creek might not go down till tomorrow," Chance warned as he glanced out the other window again, then met her gaze.

"Great," Reese said, not happy that her search had come to a temporary halt. "I'm sure you've seen this happen before since you've stayed up here during hunting trips."

"That's a fact," he said. "I'm anxious to get going, too, but at least I managed to call my mom and Skylar to let them know we're stuck up here."

"It's good you got through to them," Reese said.

"A true miracle since the cell service is spotty on this mountain," he commented. "Sometimes it works, sometimes it doesn't."

Reese smoothed down her hair, noting that with the moisture, it was doing its typical frizzy, kinky, curly number. Like she'd stuck her finger in a light socket.

Chance stuffed kindling into the stove and used a wooden match to light it. Then he pumped water from the sink into a tin coffee pot. He paced until the liquid began to boil, then from a can, he poured dark granules into the brew.

"Cowboy coffee," he told Reese when he looked up. "It's not fancy, but it hits the spot."

"No doubt," she commented.

He reached for a cheese and crackers snack pack on the table and handed it to her. "It's not much, but it'll tide us over. While you were exploring the town, I got them out of the stash in my truck."

"I've got an emergency bag in the back of my truck, too." She opened the cellophane, removed a cracker and munched on it. "Thanks. In this country, you never know when you might need some supplies."

Chance grabbed another cheese and cracker pack, opened it, and munched until it was gone. Then he began opening cupboard doors, looking inside. He seemed restless and agitated as he paced around.

"There's lots of nonperishable items missing around here," he growled. "Canned goods and the like. At least we know the kidnapper kept my niece well fed."

"Again, that's a good thing," Reese said.

"Even though he ought to be shot for taking Daisy in the first place," he added.

He took out two thick crockery mugs from a cupboard, filled them with coffee, and handed her one. They both sipped the brew in silence.

Before long, gathering darkness filled the small cabin. Chance lit two old-fashioned kerosene lamps, but it was dim and did little to dispel the gloom. Rain still pounded mercilessly on the roof. Standing vigil at the window every now and then, Reese noted that the bridge over the creek was now completely under water with only the railings visible.

It was apparent they wouldn't be leaving any time soon, not with the bridge in its current condition. She struggled to tamp down her impatience.

"Tell me about your niece," Reese suggested, thinking that would pass the time and she might learn something useful. "Special or cute things she does. Her favorite activities—you know."

Chance sat his large frame down in the rocker and began talking about Daisy, occasionally sipping his coffee. He talked about how from the time she was born, his niece had changed his world and filled it with joy and happiness.

Reese felt so sorry for him and the entire Ellington family. The loss of Daisy must weigh heavily on all their minds and the stress must be crushing. What a blow they must be suffering from, living with the fact that someone broke into their house and snatched Daisy like a thief in the night.

From her experience, Reese knew most people want to believe they are immune from such tragedy. An event of this magnitude drove home the fact that none of us are. The sobering reality oftentimes destroyed people's spirits, and she couldn't blame them for being so upset.

Moving away from the window, Reese sat down on the sofa and continued listening, only commenting here or there to clarify what she'd heard. After a while, weariness settled into her and the rain drumming on the roof lulled her into a relaxed state. Yet, she continued to stay alert, hoping to glean any information about the little girl that might be of importance.

"Minnie Mouse is Daisy's favorite cartoon character," Chance said with a sad smile. "When she was really little, she called her 'mi mouse.' It was so cute."

"What about food? What are her favorites?"

"M&M's," Chance supplied. "She loves those. When she was two, she used to call them M-ah-noose. One time she kept asking for them and nobody knew what she wanted, but I figured it out."

"Uncle Chance to the rescue," Reese said. "That's so cool that you understood what she was saying."

"Man, I'm wiped out," he said, his voice cracking with emotion. He pushed up from the rocking chair, walked over to the window and glanced out. "It's still coming down hard."

He walked over to a large plastic container, reached inside, and lifted out two blankets. "Stretch out on the couch there if you'd like and I'll grab some shut eye in the chair."

He handed her one of the blankets and took one for himself.

"I'll take you up on that," she said, hearing the weariness in her voice as she wrapped the cover around her shoulders.

With a sigh, she closed her eyes and leaned back into the cushions. Despite all the thoughts running through her mind, despite her eagerness to resume work on Daisy's case, a troubled sleep claimed her consciousness.

FIFTEEN

A LOUD CRASHING noise awakened Reese. She sat straight up, confused for a moment, then realized it came from outside, where a crescendo of thunder had sounded. A weird, eerie blue light also flickered around the room.

Perched on the edge of the rocker, Chance wiped the sleep from his eyes. "Reese, what's wrong? Are you all right?"

"I'm fine. The weather woke me." She blinked several times as the strange illumination faded from the cabin's interior. "It's so loud up here in the mountains."

He cocked his head and looked around. "It must have hit somewhere pretty close."

"I hate rain storms," she murmured. "They make me nervous and I think they bring bad luck my way."

He chuckled. "That's only your imagination. It's just nature—raw and simple."

"I'm not imagining things," Reese said, recalling incidents in her life where bad weather had defined the outcome. She wasn't superstitious, but still, it bothered her.

Chance stood and eased toward the window, where dawn had begun to lighten the horizon. "A storm is just a storm. It doesn't foreshadow anything bad or good."

"I'll try to remember that," Reese said.

"I'm pretty certain we can head back down the mountain soon. The storm isn't as intense now, and the visibility is better."

"What does the creek look like?" Reese walked over

and glanced out the other window. It overran the banks, but its wild churning had settled and the bridge surface was visible again.

"Another hour or so and we'll be good to go." Chance went back to the rocking chair where he sat down and closed his eyes.

Reese headed over to the couch and settled in. She studied the dying fireplace embers for a while, then did her best to get a little more rest, too.

THE SOUND OF Chance rustling around brought Reese to full awareness. With her knuckles, she wiped the sleep from her eyes. Figuring she must look like the ghost of Christmas past, she got up and grabbed a makeup bag from her purse.

Digging through the contents, she located some toiletries to freshen herself. She brushed her hair—which must look like a tumbleweed—and applied gloss to her dry lips.

Making her way to the window, she observed the gray pall shrouding the sage-dusted countryside. Rocks and boulders glistened with a wet sheen and chocolate brown mud covered bare patches.

Veils of mist drifted above the drenched log buildings and streets of Lucky Gulch. The town looked more deserted than before, if that was even possible.

"You about ready to go?" Chance asked.

"Yes, I am."

When her phone chimed, she pulled it from her purse, noting it was a text message from Jeremy.

Got some info for you on Daisy's case. Stop by my office to talk.

Thanks, I'll be by later today, she texted back.

After dropping her cell back into her bag, she decided

Chance had apparently been up for a while because he'd set the shopping bag full of evidence on the table, along with his truck keys.

She honestly felt sorry for him. He tried to put on a brave face, but she knew, deep down, he was a wounded man, hoping to find his young niece. The entire Ellington family was counting on her to come up with some answers about Daisy's disappearance, and she felt the weight of responsibility on her shoulders.

Renewed confidence surged through her. With the evidence they'd found up here, she believed she'd be able to piece together some solid clues about where to search for the girl.

"By the way, you snore like locomotive," Chance commented. "Just thought you should know."

"It's a talent," Reese shot back.

"That's one way to look at it," he said.

"Do you think the heavy rain caused any problems for the locals?"

"I'm sure the ranchers farther down the creek got their pastures watered well."

"I'll be glad to get back to work," Reese said. "I've got a ton of things to do, including taking that evidence on the table to Officer Savage so it can be processed."

"Let me know if I can help do anything," Chance offered. "If it will help find Daisy, I'm all in."

"Sure," Reese said, glancing at the mussed bed in the other room. "Shoot, I never looked in the bedroom, so I'm going to check it out now."

"Good idea," Chance said.

As she walked into the area with the bed, Chance followed. It wasn't a big room, but he searched on one side as she searched the other. There really wasn't much to see, but Reese looked over the night stands, the dresser and shook out the bed covers.

When she lifted a pillow, a coloring book and several crayons were revealed. The theme of the book was zoo animals, and Reese flipped through the image-filled pages, which were nicely shaded.

On the back white cover was a drawing of a person with slits for eyes and a large round mouth. Beneath it were the words, BAD MAN.

Reese handed the book to Chance. "I think Daisy drew us a picture of her kidnapper."

He glared at the drawing. He didn't say anything, but Reese had a good idea what he was thinking.

They went back into the front room and Reese dropped the coloring book into the bag of evidence. She picked it up along with her purse.

Chance removed a heavy-duty padlock and key from a cupboard, then walked to the front door and held it open for her.

Stepping out onto the porch, she breathed in the cool mountain air. It smelled fresh and clean, and she felt ready to start another day of searching. She watched Chance close the cabin door and click the padlock on a metal hasp.

"While you went to check out the town yesterday, I put a lock on the shed and got the cabin ready to lock up, too." He slid the key into his jeans pocket. "We don't need unwanted visitors snooping around the place again."

"Good idea," she said.

She climbed into the passenger side of Chance's truck and buckled her seat belt. He jumped in on the driver's side, started the engine, and pulled away from the cabin. As he drove down the hill, Reese glanced around at the wet landscape.

Clutching the grab handle, she winced as they bumped across the muddy creek bank and over the wet bridge, noting the swirling depths still nearly touched the wooden planks, but the water looked much less agitated than it had yesterday.

The ghost town buildings were soaked and puddles pockmarked the land. For decades this little town had been untouched by man, but Mother Nature had left her mark on it last night, that was evident.

"I hope our trip up here gave you a few ideas about where to look for Daisy," Chance said, giving her a probing glance.

"We definitely found some good evidence," Reese said. "I've got some ideas of leads to follow. Thanks for coming up here with me."

Chance stared at the road; deep lines etched into his grim expression. "This is the hardest thing I've ever gone through in my life, you know, having my niece taken like this. The waiting and the wondering—it's killer."

"I can only imagine," Reese said.

At least she knew what happened to her loved ones, Reese thought. It would be difficult to sleep at night if their whereabouts remained a mystery. Yet, that was what the Ellington family had been dealing with for weeks now. God help them.

She fell silent during the trip back down the mountain.

A few miles away from the ranch, Chance's cell phone rang. He answered it on his truck speaker. "Hello?"

"Chance?" Skylar sounded upset. "Are you all right? What's going on? Your phone kept going to voicemail."

"You know cell service is touch-and-go up at the cabin and I was lucky I got a call through yesterday afternoon to let you and Mom know about the storm."

"I know, I know," Skylar said.

"We had to wait for the bad weather to pass before we could hit the road," Chance added. "We're almost home how."

"I know but—"

"Reese and I found some of Daisy's things at the cabin," Chance said. "It looks like someone broke in and kept her up there."

"Oh, my poor baby," Skylar said, alarm flaring in her voice. She broke into sobs and added, "If we'd only known…"

"It looks like whoever took her there was taking good care of her," Chance quickly supplied.

"But they had *my* little girl," Skylar cried. "How dare they take her?"

"Who, besides our family, knows about our cabin?" Chance asked. "I've never told anyone. Have you?"

"Geez." Skylar was silent for a few seconds, then admitted, "I know Dad forbade us to bring friends, but I did take a boy up there once."

"Who?" Chance demanded.

"I don't remember his name. It was so long ago—I was 15. That was so stupid of me. What was I thinking?"

"Obviously, you weren't," Chance said. "How did you get up there?"

"I drove our old Jeep," Skylar said. "Dad was teaching me to drive on it. There are no cops on that old dirt road, so I wasn't worried about not having a license yet."

"Try to remember the boy," Reese said, her radar on full alert. "Did he go to your school?"

"I'm pretty sure he went to Sage High," Skylar said, sniffling. "I'll keep trying to come up with his name. But listen, Chance, Mom's in the hospital. I'm here with her in the ER."

Chance swore under his breath. "What happened?"

"She got dizzy and couldn't see well. I rushed her here. The doctor says it was a minor stroke. But I'm… I'm worried sick."

"Where were you when it happened?"

"At the gas station by the interstate. Mom was rambling about seeing Daisy when she nearly passed out." Skylar sniffled again. "Hurry."

"On my way." Chance disconnected his phone and glanced over at Reese. "I'm heading to the Sage Hospital."

"I'll walk to my hotel," she suggested, not wanting to disturb the Ellington family during a health crisis. She hoped Leyla would be okay, and that she hadn't added to the Ellington matriarch's illness by churning up the circumstances surrounding Daisy's disappearance.

"No, come with me." Chance ran a hand through his hair, his eyes brimming with concern. "If Mom and Skylar found out something important about my niece, you need to know."

IN THE HOSPITAL emergency entrance, Chance explained who he was and a nurse in dark blue scrubs led him and Reese through a pair of double doors and into an examining room. She felt out of place, just like she had when Rocky got hit, but even more so.

With her crutches leaning in a corner, Skylar sat in a chair beside an examination table where Leyla lay resting against a pillow. The two talked in low tones, but Leyla's halting speech and pale face indicated her poor health. An IV dripped clear liquid through a tube attached to her arm.

"Chance," Leyla said in a thick voice when she looked up and saw her son.

He hurried beside the bed and gripped her free hand. "Mom, how are you feeling?"

"Better. B-but scared."

Reese sat in one of the plastic molded chairs, trying not to draw any attention to herself. This had to be a difficult time for Chance and his sister. They'd already lost Daisy, they didn't want to lose their mother, too. It would be like experiencing a double whammy to the solar plexus.

"They took Mom in for a CT scan and the doctor has ordered a ton of lab tests," Skylar said. "They'll let us know what they think is going on."

"Did he give you any ideas?"

"Her blood pressure was too high," Skylar said. "We have to wait to find out more. For now, the doctor said it's good we headed straight to the hospital."

"Thank God," Chance said.

"We stopped...for gas," Leyla said, her eyes wide as she looked back and forth between her children. "I saw... thought I saw...D-Daisy."

Skylar patted Leyla's hand. "I think that's what made you sick, Mom. Don't talk about it now."

"No," Leyla said firmly. "You t-tell...them."

"We can't have you upset again," Skylar warned.

"Isssh okay," Leyla said. "Please."

Skylar sighed. "Mom and I were at the Quick Fill gas station. I was pumping gas and she went inside to buy some gum and a couple of sodas. When she came out, she believes she saw Daisy in the back seat of a red Mercedes-Benz. They made eye contact, and Mom said the girl stared at her hard, like she recognized her."

Leyla nodded and said, "Yes."

"Are you sure you weren't imagining things, Mom?" Chance asked.

"She wasn't, because I saw them, too," Skylar said. "I wasn't paying that much attention at first, though, because I was cleaning the windshield."

"Huh," Chance said, folding his arms across his chest.

"Was anyone in the car with the girl?" Reese asked.

"A white-haired older woman sat in the passenger seat," Skylar said. "A guy with a long gray pony tail came out of the store, got in the driver's seat, and drove off before we could do anything. Otherwise, I'd have come unglued. I'd have ripped that car apart to get Daisy out of there."

"And did you see the license plate number?" Reese's pulse shot up.

"Mom couldn't see the full information, but she's sure it started with the number 22."

"Did you recognize the adults?" Reese asked.

"No," Skylar said.

Leyla shook her head.

"Teton County license plates start with 22," Chance said in a solemn tone.

Jackson Hole was located in Teton County, Reese recalled, her investigative antennae waving. The city where Skylar had met Daisy's father.

Was there a connection? Had Daisy's father learned of her existence and decided to take her? Could the little girl be alive and well, living just north of here?

She walked over to the end of Leyla's bed and gripped the railing.

"I'm so sorry this happened," she told Leyla, doing her best to let the elder woman know how much she sympathized with her plight.

The news about a possible Daisy sighting caused a tingle to travel up her spine and into her fingertips. There was no need to raise everyone's hopes, when this information only provided a small lead. Nevertheless, Reese felt optimistic, however she looked at it.

"Docs say…I'll be…okay," Leyla said, sharing a trembling half smile.

"With some lifestyle changes," Skylar said. "No more fatty steaks and we're both going to start exercising together. You'll also be spending a day or two here for observation and after that, you'll receive physical therapy."

Leyla nodded.

Skylar met Reese's gaze. "Mom and I really think it was Daisy in that car. What can we do about it?"

"Well, I'm going up to Jackson to follow up on it," Reese said. "It's definitely worth looking into. By the way, was the man you saw taking anything back to the car? A pack of cigarettes, chips or a snack of any sort?"

Skylar nodded. "M&M's."

Reese and Chance looked at each other and smiled. Skylar caught on too, and she laughed until tears filled her eyes.

"M-ah-noose," they all said at the same time. Daisy's favorite treat.

SIXTEEN

AFTER VISITING LEYLA at the hospital, Reese rode with Chance back to her hotel. He parked, and she began to slide from his truck.

"Hey," he said, gazing at her steadily.

"What's up?"

"I appreciate all your hard work to try and find Daisy. I'm sure you know how much it means to us to bring her home."

"I most definitely do," she said. "You, your mom, and your sister have been under immense pressure for weeks now. I'm sure it's been grueling. And I promise to do my best to find her."

"If you find her, we'll owe you big time."

"It's my sincere hope, Chance, that will be the outcome. Will you be prepared for whatever truth I may uncover?"

He inhaled deeply. "I have to be, don't I?"

"I know you'll be there for your mom and Skylar to help them through any emotional roller coasters."

"Of course," he said. "They're my family."

Reese looped her handbag over her shoulder and grabbed the large brown shopping bag full of evidence they'd found at the cabin. "They're lucky to have you, Chance."

Chance nodded. "I'm lucky to have them."

"Do me a favor, keep working with Skylar to see if

she can remember the boy she took up to the cabin. I believe that will be important."

"I'll do that."

Reese jumped out and closed the passenger door. She headed into the hotel and passed through the lobby where people sat reading in the reception area. At the desk, a couple was checking in for their stay. When she reached her room, she unlocked her door and started walking in, but felt her boot kick something. Glancing down, she noted an old alarm clock laying catawampus.

She froze, heart hammering. Seconds passed as she looked for any telltale wires or explosive devices. It appeared the clock was just a clock, and she released a deep breath. Setting aside the evidence bag, she picked up the ticking timepiece, and read the note taped to it.

Your time is running out. Leave before it's too late.

Brow furrowed; she noted the scribbled, spidery script slanted backward. By her guesstimate, whoever wrote the warning had been trying to disguise their handwriting so it couldn't be analyzed. However, there might be fingerprints on the tape.

Reese put the clock inside the evidence bag and carried it inside her room, locked her door, then placed everything on the bed. Her next stop was the bathroom, where she shed her clothes, turned on the shower and stepped under the hot, steamy spray.

She had plenty of leads to follow, she just needed to use gut instinct to decide which one to start on first. And that instinct told her to follow up on the potential Daisy sighting.

After her shower, which improved her mood, she wrapped up in the hotel robe and padded barefoot out to her evidence board. She used her own hieroglyphic shorthand to write on several sticky notes, which she put on the wall in her own crazy organizational system.

To her, it made perfect sense. To someone else, well, she'd wish them luck on trying to figure it out. That was the beauty of her crazy handwriting. No one could decipher it but her.

She dressed in clean clothes, then texted Jeremy to make sure he was in his office and not out on patrol. He texted back, telling her he was there, so she grabbed the evidence bag and headed downstairs. The Sage Police Department wasn't far, so she walked toward it, hoping whatever he'd texted her about would be groundbreaking.

"WHAT DO YOU have for me?" At the station, Reese dropped into a chair beside Jeremy's desk and put the bag next to her feet.

"I'm going for a coffee break," Jeremy announced to the other police officer seated at a desk in the corner. He stood and motioned for Reese to follow.

Outside, he took her elbow and walked beside her toward a small café's seating area. A greeter seated them at a black wrought iron patio set and offered two menus.

"No thanks, just two cups of coffee," Jeremy said, then looked at Reese. "Do you want anything else?"

"No," she said.

When the greeter disappeared, Reese met Jeremy's gaze.

"What's the mystery?" she asked.

"No mystery, I just wanted out of the office," he said. "There are lots of big ears around there and the Chief hasn't authorized us to start actively investigating Daisy's case again. He's still at a safety convention in Cheyenne, so his mind is preoccupied."

She leaned forward, propped one elbow on the table surface and rested her chin in her hand. "What did you find out?"

Right then, a smiling waitress in tan slacks, a white shirt and a red apron stopped by and filled their coffee cups.

"Anything else, folks?" she asked.

"Thank you, no," Reese said.

Jeremy waited until the waitress had left, then turned back to Reese. "I got a call on the SPD's anonymous tip line. The individual said Audra Woods is back in town. I think it's possible she may know something about Daisy's kidnapping."

"Audra's one of the friends who went with Skylar up to Jackson to work, isn't she?"

"Yes. I checked it out and she's staying with her mother. They live at 210 Dormer St."

"I'll pay Audra a visit today—hopefully she's home." Reese scooted the evidence bag toward Jeremy. "Whoever took Daisy held her at the Ellingtons' hunting cabin in Lucky Gulch for a while. Chance and I found all of this up there."

"Lucky Gulch?"

"It's an old ghost town on the Ellingtons' property."

Frowning, Jeremy scrounged through the bag. "Look at all this stuff! The family never mentioned their cabin when we were looking for Daisy."

"Chance said they never thought about it because they were so upset. They haven't been up there in a couple of years, not since his dad died. Chance thought only family members knew about it."

"Apparently someone else does if they used it as a hideout," Jeremy said, holding up the alarm clock with the note taped on its face. "What's this?"

"I found it outside my room this morning. Sweet, huh?"

"I don't like this, Reese. This warning is a bad sign. You'd better back off. Let the SPD take it from here."

"I'm not going to because this is my job," she said. "Besides, I'm not the type to be easily frightened."

"You're telling me," Jeremy said.

"Skylar said she took a boy up to the Ellingtons' cabin when she was 15, but she doesn't remember who."

Jeremy shook his head. "Wow, that's another piece of evidence my guys could have used."

"I know, it's frustrating. Hopefully she'll remember more."

"That would help," he said. "I'm certain the Chief will want to start in on Daisy Ellington's case. It's really heating up."

"Right, and I've got work to do." Reese put money on the table and stood. "My treat. Thanks for your help."

"Okay," Jeremy said.

Reese nodded at the evidence bag. "You'll want to check the items in there for fingerprints and DNA."

"Of course," Jeremy said as he picked up the bag and rose.

"Sorry," she said. "Old habits, you know? I appreciate you helping me."

"We'd like to find the kid, too. Nothing would make us happier." He walked with Reese toward the sidewalk, and they stopped beneath the branches of a large cottonwood tree. "Stay safe. You don't carry a gun, do you?"

"I'll be fine," she said. "There's a reason I don't like firearms, but I'm pretty good with my right hook."

Jeremy shook his head. "You really ought to carry protection. At least some pepper spray."

"I mostly perform federal background investigations. I don't usually need one."

"Why don't you like guns?"

She sighed. "I screwed up. I accidentally shot someone."

"What happened?"

Reese's memory transported her back to that time in her life. She shivered, and said, "My partner Harry and I answered a domestic call. The perp was beating up on his girlfriend and we got into a scuffle with him. Somehow, the perp got Harry in a chokehold and held a gun to his head. I thought I had a clear shot." She shook her head. "Turns out I didn't. My bullet grazed Harry's face and the perp's bullet hit my shoulder."

"You took down the bad guy, didn't you?"

"Yes, my bullet hit the perp in the chest and he went to jail for domestic battery. But Harry's bullet graze caused him a lot of trouble and he went through several reconstructive surgeries. His wife, who used to be a good friend of mine, now hates me. That's why I left the DPD. That whole episode haunts me."

"Reese, you saved Harry's life."

"That's what he said, but I don't care. I'll always feel responsible for his pain and suffering."

"You should stop beating yourself up."

"Yeah, well, that's my prerogative."

"It's too bad you gave up your career. You must have been one hell of a cop."

"I gave it 10 years of my life. Made detective, even."

"It's a shame when we lose good officers." He pressed his mouth into a firm line. "Watch your six, okay?"

"Yes, Officer," she replied.

"I'd like to take you to dinner tonight," he added.

While Jeremy's offer seemed tempting, she didn't

want to become caught up in any emotional entanglements. They complicated things and she was determined not to get distracted from this case. The Ellingtons were counting on her.

"I've got a lot of work to do, but maybe another time," she said. "Rain check?"

He looked determined. "Tomorrow night, then?"

Like a dog with a bone, he refused to let go of the matter. It wouldn't be easy to put him off and truthfully, she disliked doing it.

"It depends what I'm working on," she said. "How about I call you and let you know if I can make it?"

"Roger that." He picked up the evidence bag. "I'll start processing this."

"Appreciate it."

Jeremy sauntered down the sidewalk toward his office. He turned and waved at her, then went inside.

Reese pulled out her cell phone, plugged 210 Dormer St. into the GPS and noted the address was only a couple of blocks from here. Readjusting her purse on her shoulder, she headed toward the address.

Hopefully, Audra would be willing to talk with her.

SEVENTEEN

SWEAT PEPPERED REESE's brow as she plodded up the hill. Despite the fact she was an avid jogger, the incline was steep and her lungs felt like they would burst. Her favorite exercise was jogging around the lake in Meadowlark Valley Park, which was near her house. Apparently, she wasn't as in as good shape as she'd imagined.

When she reached Audra's house, she caught her breath, noting the cottage's faded pink shingles. Once upon a time they must have been a vivid hue and the yard most likely had been in better condition. Along with the worn exterior, the yard was littered with a couple of old appliances, rusty metal outdoor chairs, numerous terra cotta pots full of dead and dying plants and heaps of trash.

Birds chirped in the trees and a soft wind brushed past her face as she walked by a battered yellow Volkswagen Beetle parked in the driveway. Stepping up on the porch, she raised her hand and pressed the doorbell. No one answered. Reese almost rang again, but she heard sounds of movement, so she stepped back.

A very pregnant young woman with cropped orange hair opened the door. A couple of silver studs pierced her brow and one forearm bore a barbwire and butterfly tattoo.

"If you're sellin' something, I don't want it," she said, chomping hard on her gum.

Reese handed her a business card. "I'm investigating Daisy Ellington's disappearance," she said. "You're Audra Woods, aren't you? Can we talk?"

"I'm Audra, but I don't know nuthin' that would help you." She shoved the card in her dress pocket. "You wasted your time coming here."

"Let's talk anyway. Please."

She narrowed her gaze. "Did Skylar send you here? How did she know I was home?"

"Skylar didn't ask me to come."

"Look, I'm sorry about what happened to her kid. I was in California with my boyfriend Frankie when it happened, but my mom told me everything. I feel bad, but I can't help you."

Audra began to close the door, but Reese placed her foot on the threshold and prevented it from shutting.

"Don't do this. Please. Talk to me."

Audra pinched her brows together, and she looked ready to tell Reese off for being annoying and pushy.

"You and Skylar were friends. You hung out," Reese pleaded. "You might not think you have anything to say that will help me find Daisy, but let me decide that. Okay?"

Audra didn't shut the door, but an angry expression remained on her face.

"Think about Skylar and what she's gone through to try and find out what happened to her child." She glanced at Audra's bulging tummy. "What if someone took your baby? Wouldn't you move heaven and earth to look for it?"

Tears sprang to Audra's eyes. At last she opened the door and stood aside. "The place is a mess, but we can sit at the kitchen table."

Reese entered the small house, taking note of the magazine and newspaper stacks, mountains of boxes and clothes and other items. Pictures hung crooked on the panel walls. It looked like a bomb had exploded. It was dusty, musty and smelled like old cat litter. Somewhere in that mess, Reese could make out a couch, a recliner and a TV.

Audra walked toward an old vinyl and chrome dinette set located beyond an arched wall. Reese followed her into the dining area, which contained more dead and dying plants, stacks of books and piles of old records. They both pulled out chairs and sat down.

Reaching out, Audra swept greasy fast-food containers, wrappers, fries and other leftovers onto the floor. Two cats sat on a kitchen counter full of boxes and dishes, staring at them, their tails switching back and forth across food crumbs. Two more hunched atop the cupboards. Reese figured mice didn't stand a chance of surviving with the feline patrol prowling through this disaster area.

"I know, it's bad in here," Audra admitted. "My mom's kind of a hoarder."

Kind of?

"No worries," Reese said.

"I'm helping her clean up, but it's not easy. She hates letting go of anything. But I can't have my baby crawling around in this filth. People from our church are coming with a crew this weekend to help us haul stuff away and scrub the house."

"That's good," Reese said.

"I can't believe I got myself knocked up like Skylar. Speaking of Sky, I don't know what I can tell you about her, except that we were friends in high school."

"Did you hang out with a lot of the same people?"

"Yeah."

"I understand you went with her up to Jackson Hole to work the summer after you graduated from high school."

She nodded. "We both waitressed at the same restaurant. Nina did, too. We were like The Three Musketeers for a few months."

"Skylar said you and Nina went to The Hideaway Bar one night to party."

"We did," Audra said, staring into space as if remembering events. "Wow, that was an intense time."

"Do you remember seeing the guy Skylar left with?"

"Well, let me think about that." Audra closed her eyes for a moment, then said, "I do remember seeing her leave with a man. An older guy."

Reese sat up straighter. "Did she introduce you to him?"

"No, I just remember her waving to me once when they were dancing."

"Do you recall what he looked like? Features? Hair color?"

"Damn, he was hot. I remember wishing he'd asked me to take a spin."

"Okay," Reese said.

"Oh, features." Audra closed her eyes again briefly, then said, "Um, he had dark brown hair."

"That helps—"

Audra slapped the table, fraying Reese's nerves so much she nearly jumped out of her chair.

"I remember him from somewhere else. Where was it?" Audra chewed her lower lip, then met Reese's gaze. "Aunt Polly's party! He was there and she introduced him to us."

This bit of new information interested Reese. Skylar had never told her about a party she attended at her aunt's house. "Do you remember his name?"

Audra closed her eyes, seemed to be thinking hard, then opened them again. "No, I don't."

"Thanks for trying, Audra."

"I do remember that during the party he was just hanging around, drinking and mingling with the guests. Skylar's aunt, Polly Ellington Beech, is a huge social butterfly. She married into big money, so she only invites millionaires and billionaires to her parties. That woman entertains to impress the big dogs so they'll donate to her favorite charities."

"You think the man who left the club with Skylar is wealthy?"

"I suppose so. Otherwise, I don't believe he'd have been invited."

True, Reese thought. "Do you remember what charity Polly was promoting that night?"

"Hmm, I think it was either the free medical clinic in Jackson or the animal shelter. Or maybe both."

"Thanks for your help," Reese said. "I appreciate you talking to me."

"Why is any of this important?"

"I'm not sure. But it's good information."

Audra pressed her hands to her swollen tummy and leaned forward. "Do you think you'll really be able to find Skylar's kid? My mom told me the local police and even the FBI couldn't find her."

"There's always hope. No one found…" Reese trailed off, not wanting to say the last word in her head. But Audra must have sensed what she'd been about to say, because her gaze narrowed.

"A body," she supplied. "I watch lots of them crime shows after work. That was when I lived in California, though. I need to find a job in Sage, but my mom said since she's working, I should stay home with the baby for a while."

"That sounds like a reasonable plan," Reese said, wondering why Audra had chosen to tell her so many details about her life. Then again, once people warmed up to her, they often felt comfortable sharing personal information.

Maybe something in Reese's eyes let people know she wouldn't judge. In her work as a private investigator, the trait would serve her well. That is, if she took on any more cases beyond the federal background investigation business she'd been handling up until now.

Audra leaned back in her chair. "My mom told me people in town thought maybe Sky had done something to her baby."

Reese raised her brows. "Did she say why people thought that?"

"Mom said the police thought Skylar could have been more cooperative. One theory was that she had accidentally done something to Daisy, so she was scared to say anything."

"Or she may not have been forthcoming with information to the police because she remained in shock from the trauma of losing her child," Reese suggested.

"Could be," Audra agreed. "In fact, that's probably more like it. I've always liked Skylar. She's a good person. Maybe a little naïve and sheltered by her family, but I always enjoyed her as a friend."

"What other theories did locals mention?" Reese asked.

"It may be farfetched, but some folks thought Skylar sold Daisy to a human trafficking ring. Hard to believe that sort of crap exists in Wyoming, but it does."

"Why would they think that?" Reese asked, aware

of the problem and hating that it tarnished the state's reputation.

"Mom said people thought maybe Skylar needed the money for drugs, but I don't think she uses. Or at least she didn't back then. Besides, Skylar always had money to blow for whatever she wanted."

"Why do you say that?"

"Sky's granddaddy was a bigtime rancher and was rolling in the dough, so the family always had plenty. She was spoiled rotten and always got what she wanted." Audra snorted in derision. "You can tell by the looks of my house that I wasn't raised with no silver spoon in my mouth. I have to work my ass off for everything I earn."

"That's how the real world works for most of us," Reese told her. While she could understand Audra's frustration about money, she realized the young lady had turned the interview into a pity party for herself.

It wasn't that Reese didn't feel sorry for her, it was just that life is about making good choices and it didn't appear Audra's were very wise. While the girl had landed in difficult circumstances, she was the only one who could take the steps to improve her condition, which it sounded like she was doing.

"Thank you so much for taking the time to talk with me," Reese said as she stood.

One hand pressed into the small of her back, Audra kept pace beside her as they headed toward the front door.

"Have a good day and I wish you all the best," Reese said as she walked out onto the porch.

"I hope you find Skylar's kid," Audra said. "It sucks that she got kidnapped."

"It does," Reese said. "But I'm doing my best to find some answers."

As she went down the steep sidewalk toward town, Reese had a good idea where those answers might be.

All signs pointed to Jackson.

EIGHTEEN

BACK AT HER HOTEL, Reese headed up the stairs toward her room. She processed everything Audra had told her and tried to fit the pieces into the puzzle that had formed in her mind. After checking out of the hotel today, she'd head up to Jackson to launch another branch of her investigation.

She pulled out her cell and began to dial Jeremy to let him know she couldn't go to dinner. He didn't answer, so she left him a message.

Moaning and wailing pierced the air, then voices rose in argument. Reese listened closer. Unable to make out the heated conversation, she picked up the pace and hurried toward her room.

When she rounded a corner, she saw an elderly woman gesturing wildly and shouting at a hotel staff member. A too-large sunflower-print dress and a ragged purple poncho draped her thin frame. Snarling, she kicked him.

As her worn leather sandal made contact with his shin, the man stepped back, wincing. He pointed at the stained canvas shopping bag that had fallen on the carpet. Its spilled contents included oranges, apples, bagels, instant oatmeal packets and slices of bacon.

"You're out of control!" the staffer growled. "Isn't it enough that we let you take all the food you want? Now you're talking like a crazy fool."

"I'm telling the truth, Amos," the woman said in a

miffed tone. "You might think I'm a looney old woman, but I see things other people don't because I'm invisible."

"Huh, you're invisible?" Amos scratched his head. "That's a new one."

"People never know I'm around. And I saw the boy-man who went in there and killed Gayle." She pointed at Reese's room; her ragged fingernail ringed with dirt.

Amos turned toward Reese. "Sorry for the disturbance, ma'am. Can I help you?"

"That's my room," she said.

The woman, whose straight white hair had been pulled into two long pig tails, met Reese's gaze, her ice-blue eyes wide. "The boy-man killed Gayle in there. I heard everything. It was awful, I tell you. Just awful."

"Ma'am, this is only crazy Kora," Amos said. "Please don't be alarmed. She's, well, she's having a bad day."

"I can tell."

Kora stuck out her tongue at Amos.

"If you'd like, you can go downstairs to the breakfast bar and grab yourself some coffee," Amos told Reese. "I'm sure by the time you return to your room this matter will be settled, right, Kora?"

He tried to pull on Kora's arm and she yanked it away.

"Stop manhandling me," she shouted. "You have no right to treat me that way."

"This is private property. And you're stealing again." He nodded down at the food.

"Carl always lets me have whatever I want." Kora held her head high in the air and sniffed. "Call him. He'll back me up."

Amos gripped the old woman's arm again. "Please, Kora. You're making a scene and it's upsetting hotel guests." He glanced at Reese. "Carl has warned you about doing that. He might be your nephew, but he's the manager of this hotel and he's given the staff strict instructions to escort you from the premises if you cause trouble."

"Hmmph," Kora said as she jerked away from Amos and folded her arms across her chest.

"Let me talk with her," Reese said.

Amos shoved his hands on his hips. "Be my guest, but she's bullheaded. Carl's aunt is, um, eccentric. She tends to embellish things."

Kora made a face. "What the fuck does *embellish* even mean?"

"It means, oh never mind," Amos said.

"Oh, piss off you little dick head," Kora said.

Reese smiled at the old lady with her best let's-settle-this-matter face. "Kora, what is this about? Who killed who?" She leaned over, picked up the canvas bag and tucked the spilled fruit into it. She handed it to the old woman, and patted her hand. "I believe you did see something."

"Thank you, dearie," Kora said, giving a huge smile that revealed she was missing one front tooth.

Reese nodded at Kora encouragingly. She'd dealt with many homeless individuals while working her beat in Denver. There were plenty of reasons why they wound up on the streets—mental health issues or possibly bad luck.

And Kora was right—people often discounted them, which is why they witnessed things others didn't. She always found it worth her time to stop and listen to them.

"It was that bastard again—the boy-man. I saw him up here when he left that alarm clock and later when he was skulking around with a knife. I was hiding behind that huge-assed plant over there, watching when he broke in," Kora pointed toward a large Schefflera down the hall. "And he stabbed Gayle."

"I'm sure she's fine," Amos insisted.

"Who is Gayle?" Reese looked back and forth at Amos and Kora; brows raised.

"One of our hotel maids," he said.

"How about we have a looksee," Reese said, tensing when she noticed the door to her room had been wedged open. The boy-man, or whoever had entered her room, knew how to jimmy a lock. She remembered her attacker at Sam's mercantile had done the same thing to the store's side entrance. At the Ellingtons' cabin and their shed, the doors had been jimmied, too.

Stepping inside, Reese's nostrils twitched from the coppery scent of blood. She noted a pink maid's uniform had been spread across a chair. Her gaze passed over to the bed where a dark-haired woman stretched out face down. Crimson splotches covered her back and spread to the blanket puddled at her waist.

Reese couldn't tell for certain from this distance, but it appeared she'd been stabbed.

Kora stood behind her, looking over her shoulder. She screeched and began sputtering wildly. "That's Gayle! The boy-man killed her. I told you so! I saw him!"

"Oh, God." Amos winced as he studied the gruesome scene.

"What was she doing in my room?" Reese asked him. She ushered Kora and Amos away from the door.

"Gayle worked two jobs to pay for college," Amos said, running a hand through his hair. "I've caught her napping on the job before. She must have decided to rest in your room today. Carl threatened to fire her if he caught her again. But she didn't deserve this. This is horrible."

Amos's face turned white and he ran down the hall making retching sounds.

"Poor Gayle must have been dead dog tired." Kora said. "She hardly got any sleep. I bet she didn't even hear the boy-man sneak into the room."

"It's possible," Reese agreed.

"Am I in trouble?" Kora asked. "I just wanted people to know what happened. I couldn't leave poor Gayle in here in that condition. She's always been so sweet to me."

"No, you're not in trouble. But the police will want to ask you questions about what you saw."

Kora pressed the canvas bag against her chest, clutching it like a talisman against evil. "I'll tell them everything." She began to pace, muttering to herself.

Reese took her cell from her pocket and dialed 911.

"There's been a murder at the Buffalo Mountain Inn," she told the dispatcher, answering the operator's questions. When the dispatcher said help was on the way, she clicked off and opened her room door to study the murder scene again. It didn't escape Reese's notice that Gayle's hair looked similar to hers—close in length and color. Even their build made them appear similar.

Holy crud.

Had the killer mistaken Gayle for her? That could have been the case because she and the victim looked so much alike, at least from the back. In a flash of memory, she saw the note on the alarm clock that had been left by her door.

Your time is running out. Leave before it's too late.

NINETEEN

THREE HOURS LATER, Reese, along with several hotel guests, clustered in the lobby, watching as uniformed county coroner's assistants wheeled a sheet-covered gurney out of the building.

A crime scene investigator looped yellow "do not enter" tape back around the staircase to prevent bystanders from interfering with the area. A couple more investigators trotted around wearing Latex gloves. A grim-faced police officer stood guard over the activities.

Earlier, Jeremy had taken her statement, along with Amos and Kora's, and he'd also fielded media questions.

A sober atmosphere permeated the hotel and Reese sighed, realizing her room would be blocked off for days since it was a crime scene. It'd be best if she left town and headed up to Jackson to continue her investigation. Her mind burst with potential leads and she wanted to get busy following up on them.

It sucked hanging around here cooling her heels. Nevertheless, she wanted to wait until she could talk with Jeremy again and run a couple of her theories past him.

She plopped down on a green brocade chair and scrounged for the pen and notebook in her purse. From the corner of her eye, she noted the gigantic buffalo head hanging on the wall behind her.

The critter's glass eyes gave the impression of staring into her soul, scrutinizing her. Uncomfortable, she got up and moved over to an identical green brocade chair on the other side of the room. That didn't help. The buffalo eyes continued staring at her in a creepy, judgmental way.

Quit looking at it, dummy.

Reese lowered her gaze, focused on her paper, and started jotting notes. Since she was bored out of her skull sitting here, writing down ideas about Daisy's case would help pass the time.

Number 1: All of Daisy's family members were genuinely remorseful about Daisy's disappearance.

They were all heartbroken. She didn't see a motivation for any of them to hurt the child. If there had been an accident, she believed they would have admitted it and dealt with the consequences.

Number 2: So far, she hadn't discovered any individuals who had an ax to grind with the family. She may have missed something along the way, but right now, nothing sinister jumped out at her.

Number 3: In question, however, was the summer Skylar spent working in Jackson. The party at her Aunt Polly's house, where she'd met Daisy's father, who had possibly spiked her drink her at The Hideaway Bar, piqued Reese's interest.

Yes, the man could have been a wealthy tourist Polly had been cultivating for donations to her charities. If that was the case, it would be impossible to find him and ask questions. However, if he was a Jackson Hole fixture and he frequently mingled with the rich and famous, she could try to track him down.

Number 4: She was very interested in Skylar and Leyla's possible Daisy sighting at the gas station. Especially since the car they'd spotted with the little girl had Teton County license plates. But who was the elderly couple in the car?

Number 5: All the signs pointed toward Jackson, so she needed to drive north to the high-class resort town to conduct some serious snooping.

"I'm done here," Jeremy said as he walked toward her. He held up his note pad. "I've interviewed everybody."

"I believe that knife was meant for me," Reese said as she stuffed her notepad and pen into her purse. She stood, crossing her arms over chest. "Did you notice how much Gayle and I look alike?"

Jeremy frowned. "Yeah, I noticed the resemblance."

"Considering the note on the alarm clock I found this morning, the killer's no doubt been watching my room and waiting for a chance to off me."

"Maybe," Jeremy said.

"I bet he went to the bathroom in the lobby or something like that and didn't see me leave my room earlier," Reese said as she began to pace. "When he broke in, he figured I'd crawled in bed for a nap. Sheesh, Gayle's uniform was laying on that chair. He must have been so bent on murder that he didn't even notice."

"You think the killer is a man?"

"If it's the same person who's been breathing down my neck since I came here, I believe so."

"It's a solid theory," Jeremy said.

"In my line of work, I've seen all kinds of wackos," Reese said. "This dude may not be the brightest crayon in the box."

"Most criminals aren't too smart, as I'm sure you know," he said.

"Poor Gayle. She was in the wrong place at the wrong time," Reese said.

"I sure don't want to have to tell her parents about this." Jeremy scratched his head. "They'll be devastated."

"That's one part of the job I don't miss," Reese said, once again considering how awful it would be to lose a child. It made her consider never having kids of her own. If they wound up hating you for some reason or if something terrible happened to them, it would haunt you forever.

"Right now, Gayle's murder could be related to Daisy's kidnapping case," Jeremy said. "That gives me more leeway processing that evidence you got up at the Ellingtons' cabin. I suspect whoever kidnapped Daisy also killed Gayle."

"Right, and whoever killed Gayle, intended to kill me because I've been digging into Daisy's kidnapping. He thinks I'm closing in on the truth."

"It's a valid idea," he said. "By the way, when you talked with Audra this morning, did she tell you anything that will help?"

"She said she'd briefly met the guy who Skylar left the bar with up in Jackson."

"Daisy's father?"

"I believe so. Audra believes she and Skylar met him at a party Polly Ellington Beech, Skylar's aunt, invited them to that summer. She doesn't remember his name, but she's pretty sure it's the same guy."

"If he had anything to do with Daisy's disappearance, this is big," Jeremy said.

"Which is exactly why I'm headed up to talk with Polly to see if she still has her guest list from that party. I'm banking on the fact she will, since Audra said she solicits donations for charities from the rich society folk up there. About our dinner—"

"Yeah, I got your message. It's not going to work for me, either," Jeremy said. "I plan on working late. After all this, I'll have a ton of paperwork to hammer out and reports to file. Murders aren't frequent around here."

"That's the good thing about small towns."

"This might cause a panic if people come up with the idea a killer is on the loose, targeting young women."

"I sure don't envy you. I stayed late plenty of times when I was a cop. It's not fun," Reese said.

Jeremy's lips twitched. "You're a workaholic, I can tell."

"No, just dedicated, like you," Reese said. "Is it okay if I leave? My room's cordoned off anyway, and I'm anxious to talk to Polly."

He sighed. "Promise you'll be careful."

"I'm familiar with the drill."

"I can tell." He rested his hands on his hips. "Stay in touch. And when you return to Sage, let's have that dinner."

"You can count on it," Reese said.

She headed outside and climbed into her Bronco. The sunset spread vibrant oranges and purples across the sky as she pulled away from the hotel and headed toward the interstate. She'd almost reached the exit when she remembered she had nothing to take with her since everything in her hotel room was behind crime scene tape.

Flipping a U-turn, she drove back down the street toward Sam's mercantile to go clothes shopping again.

TWENTY

REESE PARKED OUTSIDE the store and walked up to the porch carrying her purse and a reusable canvas grocery tote she'd scrounged from her truck. On the porch, she passed by two elderly men in rocking chairs seated on either side of an upright barrel holding a checkerboard. Laughingly, they gave each other guff as they made their moves.

"Good afternoon," she said, nodding at them as she opened the store's screen door.

"Howdy," one said.

The other man smiled and winked.

Inside Sam's place, she noted once again the familiar spicy scent and country flair of checkered curtains and gingham lined shelves. She appreciated the homey atmosphere, wondering if his wife, daughter or possibly a previous owner had set the style in here. With his practical nature, she didn't believe Sam would have a penchant to add the charming decor.

Either way, his wares included a hodgepodge of items; hardware, cookware, western style clothing, toys, puzzles and books, some over the counter medicine and toiletries.

The offerings were endless, and it would have been fun to wander around looking. Instead, Reese gathered what she needed—more personal items, another pair of jeans and a couple of shirts.

At the checkout counter, she placed everything down in front of Sam.

"Women and their shopping," he commented in a good-natured tone.

"Believe me, it isn't by choice," Reese responded with a chuckle.

"How's your investigation coming along? Do you know anything more about what happened to Daisy?"

She shook her head. "I have some leads, but that's it."

"I hope you find her," he said. "It's such a shame she went missing in the first place. Children are gifts from God. I have two daughters myself."

"That's wonderful," she told him.

Sam rang up the price and she paid with her credit card, then put everything in her tote bag.

"Have you had any more incidents like the one that happened when I was here last time?" she asked.

"Nope, nothing so dramatic," he said. "Just a couple of high school punks lifting stuff."

"It makes you wish they'd keep kids in school all year round," Reese said. "They become anxious and bored in the summer, and that's when they stir up trouble."

"True, that," he said.

"Do you have a security system?"

He scratched his balding head. "No, they're too expensive. And I wouldn't know the first thing about installing the contraption."

"It would help if you caught the perps on video, then you could show it to the police. If they hear rumors that you're recording them, maybe the kids will think twice about stealing. You could write off the cost on taxes for loss prevention."

"That's true," he said. "I didn't think of that."

"Tell you what, I'll give you the name of a company I'd recommend. They'll do a free security assessment. In the end, I bet you'll find it worthwhile."

"Can you write it down for me?" Sam handed her a piece of paper and a pencil. "My mind doesn't retain things like it used to."

"Happens to me all the time," Reese said as she made the note. "With that much info crammed in our heads, our brains can't retain it all.

"See you later," she told Sam as she walked out the door, past the checker players and into the parking lot. A light breeze brushed her cheeks as she opened Betty's hatch door, dropped everything in the cargo area and closed it, glad they weren't experiencing typical Wyoming hurricane force wind.

As she walked to the driver's door, Leyla pulled up in the spot next to her in the Ellington family's Traverse. She and Skylar, who sat in the passenger seat, waved at Reese.

"I'm glad I ran into you," Skylar said after she rolled down her window. "I planned on calling you after Mom and I picked up a bag of dog food for Rocky."

"How's he doing?"

"Good, I'm happy to say," Leyla said as she got out of the car and shut her door.

"It was a close call, though," Skylar added.

"What's up?" Reese asked.

"I had posters made at the print shop and I just picked them up. I wanted to bring one to you." Leyla opened a back door on the Traverse and pulled out several magnetic signs bearing Daisy's photo.

The caption read, "Have you seen Daisy?" Below it in large bold print was a phone number.

"These are great," Reese said.

Leyla handed over a sign to Reese, and she attached it on the back of her Bronco.

"I can't believe I never thought of this before," Skylar said.

"Ideas come to us at different times," Reese said. "Especially when you're handling something so emotional—like looking for your daughter."

"Right, right," Skylar said, nodding in agreement.

"I think you've done a great job trying to find her."

"I've tried my best, that's for sure. And I have more good news." Skylar gripped the edge of her window. "I remember who I took up to the cabin all those years ago."

TWENTY-ONE

"WHO?" REESE TOOK a step closer to Skylar.

"This guy who was in my high school biology class—Vincent Warren. Vinny, we called him."

"Does he live here in town now?"

"I'm not sure. I haven't seen him since Daisy was born. In high school he mostly kept to himself, smoking his dad's cigarettes and working on computers. If he's hanging around Sage, he must be keeping a low profile," Skylar said. "Then again, I don't go out much, either."

"What was he like in school?"

"He skulked around the halls in this giant green army coat with a fur trimmed hood. He had a thing for me and he'd follow me everywhere. It used to creep me out when he'd show up, then I finally talked to him. He smelled raunchy and had awful breath. No doubt because he had bad teeth. Anyway, his family life wasn't all that cool."

"How so?" Reese recalled her attacker at the mercantile; specifically, his horrible odor.

"He said his father had pressured him since he was a kid to go to college and make something of himself. His old man wanted him to become a doctor or an engineer. It was like his dad wanted to live out his dreams through his son."

"What did Vinny think about that?"

"It drove him crazy. He only wanted to work on cars."

"What about his mom?"

"She let the old man whip the tar out of Vinny, which

was way too much. She never stood up for him; never tried to stop the beatings. One day she took off and never came home."

"Anything else you remember?"

"I think Vinny wanted something more than friendship with me when we went to the cabin, but we never did anything. He'd brought some weed to smoke. I took a puff or two, but I didn't like it."

Leyla winced and slammed the back door of the Traverse.

"Careful, Mom," Skylar said. "You'll hurt yourself doing that. Take it easy, okay?"

"I can't believe you smoked marijuana," Leyla said with a *tsk-tsk*.

"I was a kid," Skylar said. "I tried the stuff, but that's all."

"You were probably about the only person who was ever nice to Vinny," Reese said to Skylar. "He liked you."

"Hmm," Skylar said. "I've always wondered why he followed me up to Jackson the summer after graduation. I suppose that's why."

"He was there, too?"

Skylar nodded. "I talked with him on occasion. We even met for a Coke once. He worked at a sports store down the street from the restaurant where I worked. He said he was saving money to open his own auto repair shop."

"Where does he live?"

"His family's place is north of town off the interstate, near an abandoned grain elevator. It's an old white farm house with faded green shutters."

"Thanks. I'm going to stop by his house to see if he's there, then head up to Jackson."

Skylar blinked. "What's up there?"

"Do you recall a party you attended at your Aunt Polly's house during the summer you spent up there?"

"Oh, yeah, I remember now. I'd forgotten all about that. Aunt Polly is cool. I had my first beer at that party."

Leyla made a sound of frustration. "Honestly, Skylar!"

"She let you drink? You were only 18. That's not legal." Frustration poured through Reese. Skylar's aunt should have known better.

"I didn't drive or anything." Skylar picked at a finger-nail. "I got a little tipsy and Aunt Polly made me stay at her house that night. How did you hear about the party, anyway?"

"Your friend Audra is back in town. She's staying with her mother and I visited with her earlier."

"That's so neat, I'll have to go see her." Skylar so-bered. "Has she heard about what happened to Daisy?"

Reese nodded. "And she's sad about it."

"Maybe I won't stop by. She surely thinks like every-body else—that I hurt Daisy or sold her or something disgusting like that."

"I don't believe Audra thinks anything of the sort," Reese said. "You ought to visit her."

"We'll see," she said. "Is she with her boyfriend?"

"He wasn't around. There's something else you should know. She's pregnant."

Tears filled Skylar's eyes and she looked down, her shoulders quivering.

"I know how you must feel," Reese said.

"No, you don't," she said in a miserable tone. "You've never been through anything like this. You've never lost a child."

"I lost my mother and brother to a drunk driver. I've hurt, just like you."

Skylar looked up. "Sorry. You didn't deserve that."

"Don't worry about me, Skylar. And don't lose hope. I'm doing my best to find Daisy."

She sniffed and nodded. "I know. And I appreciate your help when everybody else has given up. When Mom and I saw that little girl in the car at the gas station, I swear she looked so much like Daisy that I nearly grabbed her from the back seat and ran."

"I don't blame you."

"Instead, I just froze. I stood there, staring like a stupid dimwit."

"You were in shock, no doubt. Even if she simply had a strong resemblance to our child, it would be unnerving."

"Yeah, that must have been it." Skylar wiped a tear from her cheek.

"Audra said something else that got me thinking, Skylar," Reese said.

"What's that?"

"She said the two of you met a man at your Aunt Polly's party. She believes it was the same man you left the bar with the night you and your friends went out. That's why I'm going up to Jackson. I want to talk with her about her guest list from that night. Maybe she can tell me who he is."

"He doesn't matter," Skylar said, bristling.

Reese quirked a brow. "What if he's got something to do with Daisy's disappearance?"

"How would he even know about her?"

"That's the missing puzzle piece. But if there's even a chance he knows something, I've got to check it out. Text me your aunt's phone number and address."

"Sure, I'll do that. As much as I don't like it, if Daisy's father took her, I have to know."

"I'm going to do my best to find out," Reese said. "And I'm pretty sure I'm on the right track."

"What makes you think that?"

"While I was visiting Audra this morning, one of the hotel maids apparently decided to take a nap in my room," Reese said. "Someone stabbed her to death. Her hair color and length were similar to mine, so I think the killer mistook her for me."

"Oh my gosh!"

"Of course, it's just a theory," Reese said. "But someone, who I believe is also the killer, left a note by my door this morning telling me I should leave before it was too late."

"That poor maid. But th-that must mean…" Skylar's lips trembled and she didn't finish her sentence.

"Yes, Sky, I think it means I'm close to finding out what happened to Daisy."

"I didn't like it when Skylar hired you, but I'm now so glad she did!" Leyla said. "If we can find Daisy, it will be a miracle."

TWENTY-TWO

REESE DIDN'T HAVE any trouble finding Vinny's house, even though it was almost dark by the time she arrived. The weathered farm house sat alongside a service road that exited from the interstate. A large yard surrounded it as well as scraggly bushes and large cottonwood trees that needed a good trim. A skirted trailer sat next to the house with a row of silver-green Russian olive trees between the two.

Once upon a time, before the interstate had been built, Reese imagined the farm would have been about the only sign of life out here, along with the dilapidated grain elevator standing like a silent sentinel in the distance.

The Bronco's tires crunched on the gravel driveway as she pulled up beside the Warren home. Her headlights illuminated pieces of junk that speckled the surroundings—old tires and rims, wooden crates and rusty farm implements.

Located within the brightness, Reese also noted a motorcycle leaning against the garage, which stood next to the house. She slid out of the truck, a dog's loud barking raking against her ear drums.

Glancing at the mutt with its nose pressed against a chain link fence, she murmured, "Shh, now. It's okay."

The mutt, possibly a border collie, barked even louder and growled. Ignoring it, she looked closer at the motorcycle plate. Though shadows had begun to envelop the yard, she could easily see the license number. It matched the one she'd memorized from the motorcycle carrying the man who had shot at her in the Ellingtons' barn.

Something inside of her clicked into place. It appeared the same man, who she felt certain must be Vinny Warren, lived here. Vinny had stolen this motorcycle, which had belonged to Chance's father Matthew, from the Ellingtons' hunting cabin.

Had Vinny kidnapped Daisy. Why, though? According to what Skylar had just told her, he'd been carrying a torch for her for years. It didn't make a lick of sense for him to take her daughter.

Had Vinny left the alarm clock with the warning note? Did he kill Gayle, thinking it was her?

The dog's frantic barking brought her back to reality. She couldn't walk up to the Warrens' door and blurt out who she really was. Nobody would want to talk to her. She hustled to her truck and opened the back hatch.

Scrounging around in stuff she tended to pitch back there, she came up with a Navy-blue blazer and a leather briefcase. After slipping into the jacket, she tucked the notebook under her arm and closed the hatch.

From the glove compartment, she grabbed a pair of reading glasses and slipped them on. Moving aside some papers, she found a hair scrunchie, which she used to pull her hair up into a loose bun.

She walked up on the weathered porch and knocked on the door. *If Vinny's here, I bet he'll be surprised to see me alive.* A few minutes later, a wizened old man leaning on a cane opened up the screen door. He pushed his spectacles higher on the bridge of his nose.

"Eh? What do you want? It's pretty late, young lady. You got the damn dog all riled up."

"My name is Elsie Summers, and I'm from Publisher's Clearing House," Reese lied.

"Numbers Fearing Mouse—is that what you said?" He frowned.

"No, no, Publisher's Clearing House," she enunciated clearly. "I'm here to speak with Vincent Warren. Is he here?"

"Vinny? What do you want with our Vinny?"

"He entered a drawing for Publisher's Clearing House," she said in a louder tone. "And I need to speak with him about it."

"I'm Vinny's gramps but I don't know what you're talkin' about, woman. You ain't makin' no sense."

"Is Vinny here?" she said a bit louder and slower.

The door opened wider and a tall man with dark, graying hair, indicating he might be in his early forties, appeared. "Pops, why don't you go sit down. I'll speak to the young lady."

"Good. Maybe you can understand what she wants." Grumbling, the old guy limped away, his cane thumping on the floor.

"Sorry miss...ah?"

"Summers. Elsie Summers." She swallowed a hiccough. For some reason, whenever she told a little white lie, she would start hiccoughing. Either it had become habit or something weird was going on with her digestive system.

She narrowed her gaze at Vinny's dad. This was the guy who beat the tar out of his kid, according to Skylar. *Scumbag.* No child ever deserved that.

"Miss Summers. Did I hear you say you're looking for Vinny? He's my son."

"Yes, and I need to speak with him personally because he's won one of our prizes."

"Well, well." He stood aside and ushered her into the house. "Let's hear about it."

He pointed toward a living area furnished with a brown couch, and a couple of recliners. Grandpa Warren sat in a padded rocking chair smoking a fat, smelly cigar and staring at a television.

Reese entered the room and spotted the new and quite large flatscreen TV. She couldn't help but wonder who had parted with the cash for such a luxury appliance, considering everything else in here tended to be shabby and worn.

The news program on TV focused on a local woman— Gayle Pendleton, who had been murdered earlier in the day at the Buffalo Mountain Inn. A photo of the victim flashed on screen behind the newscaster as he reported information the police had released regarding the incident, adding law enforcement continued to investigate.

Reese shivered, having seen the murder scene firsthand.

"Please, have a seat," Vinny's father said. "I'm Norman."

"Nice to meet you," she said. "Is Vincent here?"

"He left earlier today," Norman said as he reached for a black remote control and turned down the TV volume. "Took my truck and flew out of here like a bat out of hell."

Of course he did. He'd just killed that poor girl on the TV.

"When do you expect him to return?" she asked, thinking if Vinny knew what was good for him, he'd take off for parts unknown. She didn't think it would take all that long for Jeremy to figure out he was the murderer. If crazy Kora had seen him in the hotel, it was possible others had, too.

"What's it to you, girl?" Grandpa Warren said as he pulled the stogie out of his mouth.

"Dad, Vinny's won himself some more money. He's one lucky fellow."

"Bah, that's a bunch of bullshit," Grandpa said. "You gotta work hard for the things you earn. That's what I think. That boy of yours is too soft."

"Now, Dad, Vinny's doing his best. Remember, he works down at Rusty's garage."

"A few hours a day," Grandpa Warren said with a snort. "What's he gonna do when we're gone? Working part time won't keep him fed, that's for sure. Too bad I don't have my business. He could have run that and made himself a good living like I did. What happened to my business, anyway?"

Norman sighed. "We've been over this before, Dad. People left Lucky Gulch during the war because they shut down the mine and you had to close your store up there. There weren't any more customers."

"Damn it anyway," Grandpa Warren said, his faded blue eyes staring into the distance as though he was re-membering. "People used to come to me for everything, flour, sugar, salt and canned goods. Even the miners got their dynamite from me. I ran an honest, decent opera-tion."

"You say Vinny won something before?" Reese asked Norman, her mind reeling with the revelations these two were spilling without even realizing it.

"Yesiree-bob," Norman said. "A couple of months ago, he won a contest and brought home a huge sum of money."

"Really," Reese said, thinking that's about the time Daisy was kidnapped. "What contest was it?"

"I don't know," Norman said. "He wouldn't say. But he bought us that fancy TV, got hearing aids for my dad and got himself that trailer parked next door. Those things don't come cheap, you know. He bought a few other things, then Dad convinced him to open himself a big fat bank account."

"Rat in the house?" Grandpa Warren said, an alarmed look on his face as he leaned forward in his chair. "Son, did you say we've got rats?"

"No, Dad, I didn't say that. Don't work yourself up." He sighed. "Speaking of hearing aids, I think Dad's need a tune up."

"Or new batteries," Reese said, wondering where Vinny had gotten a windfall of money. Had someone paid him to take Skylar's little girl?

"New batteries!" Norman snapped. He hustled over to open a drawer in a cabinet and pulled out a card layered with tiny silver discs. "Why didn't I think of that before?"

Norman walked over to his dad and helped the old man change out the devices.

"Can you hear better now, Dad?" Norman's brows rose.

"I sure as hell can," Grandpa Warren said, then pointed at Reese. "But who is she?"

TWENTY-THREE

NORMAN ROLLED HIS EYES. "Dad, she stopped by to talk to Vinny. He won a Publisher's Clearing House prize. Don't you remember?"

"Vinny ain't here," Grandpa Warren said in a crotchety tone.

"That's why I'm leaving right now," Reese said, anxious to skedaddle. She'd learned enough about Vinny for now. She walked toward the door and Norman eased alongside her.

"I'm not sure when Vincent will be home," he said, flipping a light switch on the wall. "He didn't say much when he left. Just mumbled that he had something to take care of."

"I'll check back with him another time," Reese said, opening the door and stepping out onto the illuminated porch.

"Do you have a check from Publisher's Clearing House? I could give it to him," Norman offered.

"No, that won't work," Reese said. "According to the contest rules, I have to hand it over to him in person."

"Darn, I see. I hoped I could save you another trip out here."

"Rules are rules," Reese said as she walked down the steps.

"Sure, I understand. Drive safe."

"Thank you and have a nice evening." Reese climbed in her truck and started it. Backing out of the driveway, she flipped on Betty's lights, then removed her reading glasses and placed them on the passenger seat.

Once Norman had gone inside, she flipped off Betty's lights and parked on the road in front of Vinny's trailer. She cut her engine and got out as quietly as she could. She sauntered up to the mobile home and stepped up onto the small porch.

Fortunately, the trailer's entrance couldn't be seen from Vinny's dad's house. She used the flashlight app on her phone to illuminate the door knob. Using the slim blue lock picking tool attached to her keyring, she popped open the front door. The stench nearly overpowered her, but she entered anyway.

Waving around the flashlight, she got a pretty good sense that the place was a pigsty—in fact, that was an insult to pigs. It reeked of staleness. Somewhere beneath piles of magazines and clothes, furniture existed. Food wrappers, beer cans and half-eaten food spilled everywhere. Tin cans full of cigarette butts littered practically every surface. Old and new computers and computer components had been stacked on tables and desks.

She picked up a pair of *Timber Ridge, size 10* boots sitting on top of a coffee table scattered with dog-eared magazines. Reese shook her head. Vinny really liked these boots. When he'd left the pair up at the cabin, it appeared he'd ordered these to replace them.

Doing her best not to breathe too deeply, she stepped through the cesspool and searched all the rooms, snapping cell phone pictures along the way. Everywhere this boy went, disaster followed. The bedroom at the back of the trailer appeared to be where Vinny slept. Of course, it was as messy as the rest of the place, but the walls displayed a unique collage—large photos of Skylar.

They clustered above a small desk in one corner and

across every inch of wood paneling. Above the bed were several larger photos of her. One of those depicted both Skylar and Vincent with a backdrop of tall mountains. It appeared to have been taken in Jackson when they'd both worked up there. Skylar was smiling, but Vinny bore a triumphant grin, as if he'd just won a competition.

She picked up a frame from Vinny's dresser. The photo inside was from a slick magazine page bearing the image of a couple during their wedding ceremony. Over the man and woman's faces, Vinny had placed cut outs of both his and Skylar's faces.

He's obsessed with her.

A cold pit formed in Reese's stomach and she put the frame back. Obsession was dangerous. Could Vinny have done something with Daisy because he wanted the kid out of the way, thinking he'd then be able to have Skylar to himself?

"I've seen enough," she whispered as she made her way from the trailer and hurried out to her truck.

After climbing inside and starting the truck engine, she drove to the service road. Once she reached the interstate, she headed north. Where had Vinny gone? He was definitely a loner. Yet, she wondered if he had a friend or an acquaintance who would let him hide out for a while.

She yawned and blinked. "I need coffee."

Since she wouldn't find a place to fill up on caffeine for a while, she plugged in an old country music cassette tape and began to sing at the top of her lungs.

She figured that ought to keep her awake on the drive to Jackson. No one had ever complimented her on her singing voice. In fact, dogs howled and little kids asked her to please stop, which was why caterwauling in the shower and during long car trips suited her just fine.

REESE RENTED A room at the Rawhide Motel, right outside Jackson. It wasn't in the greatest condition though, and when she placed her canvas bag on the dresser, she noticed a black widow crouched in a corner.

Morbidly fascinated, she watched as it perched in its frothy web between the wooden furniture and the wall. A shiver crawled up her spine.

Vermin grossed her out, mostly those of the eight-legged variety. From the filthy condition of the room, no one cleaned in here on a regular schedule.

"What a dive," she muttered, thinking about the man who had brought Skylar to this motel. "It's quite the no-tell-motel."

By the time she'd reached the outskirts of Jackson, she felt wiped out, so she'd decided this place would suffice. It didn't look too stellar, but sleep was sleep. Nevertheless, it smelled musty in here. The dingy green walls, the dusty furniture surfaces and the grimy bathroom didn't add much more charm.

"To hell with you," she said to the spider. It wasn't going to bother her since it was chilling out, waiting for another hapless insect to trap.

She kicked off her boots and dropped them on the floor. Turning off the lamp, she slid into bed, clothes and all, and closed her eyes. Sleep erased her fatigue and she needed that right now. Tomorrow, she would try to do some good in the world.

Later, when a deep slumber had claimed her consciousness, Daisy appeared to her in a dream. The little girl skipped through a meadow, careless and happy. When she turned to look at Reese, she smiled and tilted her head to the side, her dark curls bouncing.

"Find me," she whispered. "Find me."

TWENTY-FOUR

RUMBLING NOISE AWAKENED Reese the next morning. Confused at first, she thought it might be an earthquake, but the bed wasn't wobbling. She threw off the covers and padded over to the window. Drawing aside the curtains, she saw a woman dressed in a blue jacket and black slacks pushing a large cleaning cart along the sidewalk.

Smoothing down her hair, Reese opened her door and walked outside. "Ma'am," she called to the maid. "Can I talk to you, please?"

The maid nodded and pushed the cart in her direction.

Reese stepped back in her room and switched on a light. The maid, whose name tag said, "Ann," followed her inside.

"Ann, would you do me a favor and give my room an extra cleaning?" Reese pointed behind the dresser. "There's even a black widow spider nest down there."

"This is my first day, I'm sorry the place isn't in good condition." Ann leaned over, examined the area, and winced. Then she ran a finger over the dust on the dresser and looked around. "I see what you mean. I promise I'll take care of this when I reach your room."

"Thank you so much," Reese said. "I imagine this time of the year there aren't many available hotels, and I don't want to move."

"I don't blame you. I'll be by to clean your room shortly," Ann said as she walked back outside and resumed pushing her cleaning cart.

"Thank you," Reese called as she shut the door. She shed her clothes and headed to the bathroom. After a short, but hot and steamy shower, she dried off and combed her hair. Scrounging through her canvas shopping bag, she found a new T-shirt and ripped off the sale tag. This top bore a photo of colorful mountains, and she put it on along with her jeans and boots.

She pulled a couple of twenty-dollar bills from her purse, folded them into a piece of stationery and wrote "Ann" on it. Most people didn't tip hotel maids, but in this instance, she felt compelled. She appreciated that Ann had agreed to do some extra cleaning.

After having breakfast and coffee at the diner next door, Reese called Polly's home phone number, which Skylar had texted to her.

"Hello?" A female answered.

"I'd like to speak with Polly Ellington Beech."

"Ms. Ellington Beech isn't at home right now," the woman said. "But I'd be happy to take a message for you."

"That's all right" Reese said. "Do you know when she'll be home?"

"She's attending the pow wow today, then she's been invited to some art event downtown. It's possible you might be able to catch her at the fairgrounds before she leaves."

"That's helpful, thanks." Hanging up, Reese headed to her truck. By now it was nearly noon and the sun beat down from a brilliant azure sky as she drove toward the heart of Jackson Hole to the fairgrounds. She'd been there a couple of times when her grandparents had driven up here to attend music festivals.

Arriving at her destination, she wedged her truck into a spot as people strolled around the dirt parking area.

Realizing she had no idea what Polly looked like, she texted Skylar and explained she needed a photo of her.

A couple of minutes later, Skylar texted a snapshot of Polly from last Christmas. Reese studied the willowy blond woman decorating a spruce tree. Daisy stood nearby, looking up and clapping her hands.

Aunt Polly looked a lot like Skylar, so it wouldn't be difficult to spot her. Problem was, Reese would have to identify her from amid the huge crowd.

She dialed Polly's cell, but there was no answer.

"Damn," Reese said. Climbing out of the Bronco, she listened to the rhythmic Native American drum beats and flute strains. Enjoying the music, she locked her door and headed toward the activities. Low, green mountains and trees surrounded the horse stalls, arenas, and an exhibit hall.

In a grassy expanse, Native American men, women and children danced and chanted. Their colorful ceremonial regalia consisted of red, blue, yellow and purple. The clothing was fringed, feathered and beaded with cultural patterns and designs. Headbands and headdresses displayed feathers arranged in intricate styles.

Tribal members from the Wind River Reservation south of here offered a beautiful display of culture. Their chants echoed through the area—the language merging with both sharp and mellow tones. Other Native Americans worked in stalls surrounding the dancers, selling traditional food and art items to tourists.

The smells and the sounds were so evocative, Reese felt privileged to witness the performance. She recalled her mother mentioning their family had Native American heritage, but the connection had been lost long ago. No one had ever traced the lineage, but seeing this made her want to dive into the research.

Mulling over the idea, she made her way through crowds, searching for Polly. Groups of children and adults stood watching the ceremony, engrossed. About ready to give up finding Skylar's aunt, Reese finally noticed a couple of ladies wearing jeans and western-style blouses sitting on a low wooden fence. They watched the dancers and chatted with each other.

Reese felt confident the light-haired woman was Polly, but to be sure, she pulled out her phone to check the photo Skylar had texted. She nodded. The woman was practically a dead ringer for Skylar, except she looked older.

Reese walked up to her and smiled. "Excuse me, are you Polly Ellington Beech?"

"That's me," she said as she slid off the fence, then pointed at the redhead who had remained seated. "And this is my friend Fran Keller."

"Nice to meet you," Reese said to Fran.

"Yes, nice to meet you as well," Fran echoed.

"How can I help you?" Polly asked.

"I'm Reese Golden," she said. "I'm a private investigator working for your niece, Skylar."

"Skylar mentioned you were coming up to Jackson," Polly said, raising her brows and giving Reese a once over.

"Good, so you know I'm investigating Daisy's kidnapping?"

"I hate what happened to Daisy," Polly said. "But if you're out to wheedle money out of my niece and fool her into thinking you can find her little girl, I'll—"

Reese held up her hand. "I've been all through the distrust issues with your nephew Chance, and Leyla. I'm not promising anything to Skylar. She contacted me and pleaded for my help. I couldn't turn her down. I want to at least find answers."

Polly sighed. "This whole thing has been a nightmare for our family."

"I'm sure it has."

"It's tragic and strange how Daisy vanished into thin air."

"Maybe not," Reese said. "What would you think if I said she might be in Jackson?"

"I'd say you're crazy."

TWENTY-FIVE

"CAN WE TALK where it's not so loud?" Reese asked.

"Sure." Polly went up to Fran and spoke to her. She patted her friend's hand, whispered something in her ear, then turned back to Reese. "Let's head over this way."

Reese walked with her across the grassy arena and out toward the dirt parking lot. The noise level lowered, so when Polly stopped in front of a van, Reese felt comfortable asking further questions.

"How did you find out I was here?" Polly asked in an annoyed tone.

"I called your home phone and a lady told me," Reese said.

"That Nadine," Polly growled. "I've told her not to answer my door or my phone."

Reese raised her eyebrows.

"Nadine is a sweetheart, and she means well," Polly said. "She dog sits for my standard poodles, Cher and Lady. Watches my house, too. There are professional thieves who skulk around my neighborhood, watching for people to leave. Then they steal us blind."

No doubt, since Polly lived in one of the nicest Jackson neighborhoods, Reese thought. She envisioned a monolithic home with tall windows and stellar views of the mountain landscape. Some of her neighbors could be movie stars and entertainers. No wonder crooks staked them out and waited for opportune times to break and enter.

"You can't be too safe," Reese said.

"True. Especially since my husband passed." Polly glanced at her watch. "I'm attending an art reception, so I need to leave in about 20 minutes. Hopefully this won't take too long."

"I'll be brief," Reese assured her. "I understand you invited Skylar and her friends to a party at your house the summer she worked up here."

"Yes, I did."

"Skylar's friend Audra said you introduced them to one of the gentlemen who was in attendance."

"That was a long time ago," Polly said wistfully. "And I introduced my niece and her friends to many people that night. What's that got to do with anything?"

"Those girls were only 18 and you served them beer. That's illegal."

Polly jutted her chin. "It was on my property."

"Still illegal."

"Whatever," Polly replied. "Are you going to report me to the police?"

Reese shook her head. "No, and I'm sorry to come at you like that. I used to be a police officer and underage drinking gets so many kids into trouble."

The severe expression on Polly's face faded. "That wasn't the brightest choice, was it?"

"Audra said one of the men who had been at your party showed up in a local bar one night when she and Skylar went out. The guy asked Skylar to dance and they left together."

"So?" Polly raised her brows. "It's a free country."

"That's the night Skylar says she…" Reese almost said *was raped* but held back, honoring Skylar's wishes. "Became pregnant."

"Hey." Polly shoved her hands on her hips. "Just what are you insinuating?"

"No offense," Reese said. "My only goal here is to find Daisy's father. I need your guest list from that night."

"Why don't you ask my niece who he is? Wouldn't that be easier?"

"She doesn't remember."

Polly blinked. "Seriously?"

"Apparently she wasn't feeling well," Reese said.

"Poor Sky. Leyla has been so worried about her, although I haven't talked with my sister-in-law for a while. How is she doing? Skylar, I mean. Having a child kidnapped must have devastated her, especially since all these weeks later the cops haven't found her."

"Skylar's doing fine, considering the circumstances," Reese said. "But she'd like to find out what happened to Daisy. Will you help me?"

Polly glanced at her watch again. "What can I do?"

"I need your guest list from the party Skylar and her friends attended."

"All right." Polly sighed as a breeze lifted tufts of her light hair. "I left my purse with Fran. Do you have something I can write on?"

Reese pulled a notepad and a pen from her purse. She handed the items to Polly, who scribbled on the pad and handed it over.

"There's the number of my event planner, Ivan Nesbitt," she said. "He handles all the details for my soirées. I don't have time for that."

"This will help," Reese said, wondering what it would be like to have so much money you could hire people to do everything for you.

"Oh, and tell Ivan it was a party I held in June that year."

"Thanks," Reese said as she tucked the items in her purse.

"Now, I really must run." Polly turned to leave, then glanced over her shoulder at Reese. "Although I believe you have your work cut out for you, it is a shame about Daisy's abduction. I wish you luck finding her. We all want to have her back home where she belongs."

Reese watched Polly walking back toward the arena, her shapely hips swaying, her designer cowboy boots scuffing the grass.

TWENTY-SIX

Reese dialed Ivan Nesbitt's phone number. No one answered, but a voice mail message came on the line.

"Jackson's Black-Tie Events, Ivan speaking. I'm not available at the moment, but please leave a message. I'll return your call ASAP."

Reese left her name and phone number, then hung up.

"Now I just need to find a way to kill time," she muttered as she climbed back into her truck and drove from the fairgrounds. Downtown, she managed to find a parking space. She got soup and a sandwich at a little eatery and spent the rest of the afternoon window shopping.

The stores were cute and trendy, offering a variety of items—all with hefty price tags. Though they were too expensive for Reese's budget, it was fun to look through the quaint shops brimming with handmade treasures. Jewelry stores, candy shops and bookstores offered plenty to keep her occupied.

She found a fine arts gallery and wandered around there, studying the paintings and sculptures. An antique store caught her eye and she meandered through the aisles, enjoying the assortment of furniture from yesteryear.

When her phone rang, she dug it out of her bag and answered. "This is Reese."

"This is Ivan from Jackson's Black-Tie Events. You left a message?"

"Yes. I'm a private investigator working for Polly Ellington Beech's niece, Skylar. Polly gave me your phone number because I need to review her guest list from a party you planned for her about five years ago. It would have been in June; the summer Polly's niece Skylar was in Jackson. Can you meet with me today?"

"My apologies, I'm booked full. In fact, I'm headed for a meeting with a caterer in fifteen minutes and the rest of my week is jam-packed."

"That's unfortunate," Reese said. "I really need to look over that list."

"Summer is an extremely busy time around here," Ivan said. "Actually, to tell the truth, it's always busy." He chuckled.

"I'm trying to find Skylar's daughter. I really need to see that list."

"Hmm, Polly mentioned her great niece's kidnapping a while back," Ivan said, then fell silent. "The police haven't found that poor little girl yet?"

"No. And the Ellington family is desperate by now, as you can imagine."

"Kidnapping is nasty business. Anyone ballsy enough to harm a child ought to be…well, you're not interested in my brand of justice, now are you? Polly's one of my best customers and I'd do anything to help her."

"I'm glad to hear that," Reese said.

"Just so long as this isn't some underhanded way of you purloining Polly's guest list for nefarious purposes," Ivan added in a warning tone.

"Rest assured, it's not," Reese said. "I just want to find Daisy or at least find out what happened to her."

"How about I go through my records and give you a copy of the attendee list? I have dinner reservations at Hayden's Post for this evening at 7 p.m. It wouldn't be a problem to add you, if you'd like to come by and pick up the list."

"Thank you, but I don't want to impose on your dinner plans," Reese said.

"For heaven's sake, it's not an imposition. You do eat, don't you?"

"Well, yes."

"Then come. Besides, I've never met a private investigator before. If you don't mind, I've got a million questions I'd like to ask."

Reese laughed. "My life's not all that interesting, honestly."

"Says you," Ivan retorted.

"All right, then. I'll come. Where is the restaurant, by the way?"

"It's at the Snow King Resort. Best place in town to eat, in my opinion. It's got ambience, fantastic food and views to die for."

"I'll see you later," Reese said as she hung up, envisioning the place must be a ritzy restaurant, where she absolutely could not wear jeans and a T-shirt. She didn't have anything fitting for that kind of joint.

Spotting a charming clothing boutique across the street, she headed out of the antique store and walked toward it. "Holy crap, I hope I don't have to fork over a small fortune for something nice to wear," she muttered.

A couple of people walked past her and stared. Reese gave them both big smiles and they continued on their way. Once inside the shop, she was thrilled to find prices weren't outrageous. She wouldn't have to pay an arm and a leg after all.

She strolled through aisles, turning left and right, disappointed in everything. Shopping was her least favorite activity and she'd had to do too much of that lately.

When she noticed a clearance rack, she made a beeline toward it.

It didn't take long to find a nice, sleeveless blue summer dress in her size. She found some white espadrille sandals and a pair of gold chandelier earrings to class up the ensemble. After purchasing everything at the counter, she carried her bags back to her truck and drove to the motel.

Once inside her room, she smiled at its sparkling clean appearance. Ann, the maid, really had taken to heart Reese's request and the place smelled fresh and lemony. After checking in the bathroom, she noted the clean tiles and shining mirrors.

Now, for the pièce de résistance.

Dropping her purchases on the freshly made bed, she leaned over to check behind the dresser.

"Hah," she said, pumping her fist in the air when she spotted the clean, web-free area.

No more spider. Buh, bye now.

TWENTY-SEVEN

STRIDING INTO HAYDEN'S POST, Reese noted how the uniquely crafted antler chandeliers, airy ceilings and wood beams complemented the rustic atmosphere. The décor included wooden chairs and rustic paneling, all offset with the golden glow from Edison lighting. Jovial banter from the patrons added to the restaurant's comfortable mood.

"Hello, will you be dining alone or will someone be joining you?" The hostess said as she approached Reese. Dressed in fashionable black slacks and a white blouse, she waited for Reese's answer.

"I'm here to have dinner with Ivan Nesbitt," Reese said. "Is he seated already?"

"Yes, and he asked me to watch for his guest. You must be Reese Golden?"

"That's me," she said.

"Come this way," the hostess said as she ushered her past the diners, a large fireplace, and onto the outdoor deck illuminated by twinkling string lights.

Mountain views surrounded the rooftop, the slopes were covered in emerald trees and lush shrubbery. Twilight draped a thin curtain of lavender across the panorama. In the sky, pinkish orange clouds floated like tufts of cotton. Reese took it all in, catching her breath. For a moment, she believed she felt the lightness birds must experience as they soar through the airy heights.

The hostess guided her to a table where two seated men pored over large, leather-bound menus.

"Your guest is here, gentlemen," the hostess said.

A bald man in a dark suit turned and said, "Thank you, Daphne."

As she walked away, both men stood and smiled at Reese.

"I'm Ivan Nesbitt," a balding man said, then nodded at the other gentleman who had dark cropped hair and wore a light suit. "And this is my husband, Hugo Valdez. We are the owners of Jackson's Black-Tie Events."

"It's so nice to meet you," Reese said as she shook their hands.

"Welcome to Jackson," Hugo said with a slight accent as he pulled out a chair for her.

"Thank you," she said as she took her seat.

"It's a lovely night to dine alfresco, isn't it?" Ivan said.

"Definitely," Reese answered.

"Hugo and I have decided on the braised bison, which is what we always have here," Ivan said.

Both men sat down, then looked at each other and laughed.

"Don't mess with a good thing, that's what I always say," Hugo said.

"I totally agree," Reese chimed in.

"Have a look at your menu and decide what you'd like." Ivan poured Reese a glass of wine from a bottle in the middle of the table. "Everything in this restaurant is excellent. And this is our treat."

"You really don't have to do that," Reese said.

"No, we really do," Hugo said. "Ivan tells me you're a private investigator. I imagine that must be fascinating."

"It is interesting," Reese said as she looked over her

menu. She spotted a Caesar salad—her go-to meal for dinner meetings. Perfect.

A waitress came for their orders. The three visited for a short time before their artisan cheese board containing almonds, olives, honeycomb and toasted ciabatta arrived.

Reese enjoyed tasting the Gorgonzola cheese and other items from the appetizer dish. Yet, she wanted to discuss business. Despite the relaxing atmosphere, she remained on the lookout for an opportunity to mention why she was here.

Finally, when the moment arrived, she cleared her throat and said, "About the attendee list from Polly's party…"

"Right here," Ivan said as he reached into a breast pocket in his suit and produced a piece of paper. "My apologies, I got distracted."

When he handed it to her, she looked it over, counting only twenty-one attendees. "For some reason, I imagined Polly's gatherings would have a larger attendance."

"Typically, there are more people at her events," Hugo said. "I remember that evening there was a virtual downpour and we had many cancellations. So, this list only contains the people who actually attended."

"One man passed away before the party." Ivan looked at Hugo. "Manfred Kirk, wasn't it?"

"Right." Hugo nodded. "Heart attack. He was a billionaire and had no one to leave his fortune to."

"Not so," Ivan said. "The animal shelters in Jackson benefitted and so did the University of Wyoming."

"True, true, I forgot he willed the money to the shelters and other humanitarian efforts," Hugo said. "Reese, what exactly did you need the list for?"

Reese had fished a pen from her purse to cross out

Manfred's name. She started to say something but Ivan spoke up.

"Polly's great niece, Daisy, is missing, and Reese is trying to find out who took her," he said.

"What's that got to do with Polly's guest list?" Hugo arched his brows.

"I have reason to believe one of the men at Polly's party that night is Daisy's father," Reese said. "I'm afraid he might have kidnapped her."

"That's terrible," Hugo said. "Poor Skylar."

"Exactly," Ivan agreed. "Her little girl's been missing for weeks. Skylar must be out of her mind with worry."

"No doubt," Hugo said. "Polly mentioned that at some point, didn't she, Ivan?"

"Yes, she did. I always assumed the police had found her, though."

"What can Ivan and I do to help?" Hugo asked.

"Providing me with this list is great," Reese said, tapping it. "I can question the men and hopefully narrow it down to one likely candidate."

"I just thought of something else we can do," Hugo said. "Let me see that list."

Reese handed it to him.

"There are 13 women on this list, so that only leaves seven men," Hugo said. "Did Skylar give a description of Daisy's father? Doesn't she know his name?"

"Skylar doesn't remember that, unfortunately. She only recalls that he had dark hair and was very good looking."

"How odd she doesn't remember his name," Ivan commented, shaking his head.

"No worries," Hugo said. "We can help narrow the suspects from this point."

Reese smiled, amused at how Hugo had lapsed into

investigator language. She appreciated Ivan and Hugo going one step further to help her.

"Right," Ivan said, glancing at the list in Hugo's hand. "Four of the men are married and elderly. If any of them ever had dark hair, it's gone now."

The couple chuckled and high fived each other.

"Iggy Wodehouse is gay, so he's out of the suspect pile," Hugo said. "Besides, he's albino. His skin and hair are as pale as the moon."

"We're down to only two now," Ivan said. "Bobby Nation is a possibility. His grandfather made billions in 'Nation' chocolate bars and other candy. He's a spoiled young man, for certain."

"Yes, he and his siblings got the best of everything growing up and now Bobby and his older brother run the company," Hugo said. "I thought he had red hair, though."

"Mmm, it's sort of reddish brown, actually." Ivan sat back in his chair and crossed his arms over his chest. "He's handsome as sin and is quite the playboy, so I hear. Rumor has it he dates a different lady every week."

"Definitely check him out," Hugo said as he put the paper on the table and tapped Bobby's name.

"There's one guy left," Reese said as she read the list. "Really, we forgot one?"

Hugo and Ivan looked at each other in confusion.

"Jack O'Casey."

"The computer nerd," they both said at the same time.

"I didn't believe that boy would ever even have sex with himself, let alone a pretty girl like Skylar," Ivan added. "He did marry someone a few years ago, though I find it amazing. His poor wife, having to deal with his attitude. He lives in his own little world, you know."

"Did we handle that wedding, Ivan?"

"No, unfortunately. It was lavish, from what I heard. It would have brought in big bucks."

"O'Casey is a computer programmer," Hugo said, rolling his eyes. "No social skills what-so-ever."

"He invented some sort of social media platform," Ivan added. "Stamp Champ or something like that."

"No, that's not what it's called," Hugo growled. "Whatever the name is, O'Casey's made kazillions and is literally rolling in the dough. Private jets, homes all over the world and enormous yachts—he's got them all. As a matter of fact, he does have dark hair and devilish good looks."

"I'll check him out, too," Reese said. "I appreciate all of your help. You've saved me tons of time."

The server appeared with a tray of food on her arm. She handed over Reese's salad, then set steaming plates in front of Hugo and Ivan.

"You should have ordered something besides rabbit food," Ivan said as he frowned at her order. "You'll starve."

"This is fine," Reese said, picking up her salad fork. "Besides, I keep myself on a diet and a salad is good for my waistline."

The server asked if they needed anything else. After promising to check on them later, she left. Everyone ate in silence.

"About that private investigator job of yours," Ivan piped up. "Tell me, how did you wind up in that line of work?"

Reese finished chewing a mouthful of lettuce and took a sip of wine. "Once upon a time," she said, "I used to work for the Denver Police Department. I started as an officer on the street and worked my way up to detective. I have the skills and training to be a decent private investigator, although I mostly conduct federal background investigations."

"Impressive," Ivan said. "Why'd you leave the police department? Or would you rather not say?"

"I got shot, and my partner got shot," Reese said, deciding to keep her explanation short and sweet. "That's when I decided to go solo and start my own agency."

"That is so courageous," Hugo said.

For the next half hour, Reese talked with the owners of Jackson's Black-Tie Events about the ups and downs of her career. She enjoyed the pleasant break from her work, however, she finally excused herself and headed back to her hotel.

TWENTY-EIGHT

REESE HAD WEIRD dreams again that night. They consisted of a disjointed mess of her adventuring across the world and performing amazing feats. They were so extraordinary that she tossed and turned.

Daisy made an appearance, once again pleading, "Find me."

"Enough is enough," Reese mumbled as she sat up in bed and wiped sleep out of her eyes. Although she yearned to stay asleep longer, she realized it was useless.

She showered, dressed and looked up Bobby Nation's address on her cell phone. It figured—he lived in Teton Village, where people owned multimillion-dollar homes and had stupendous views of the Teton Mountains.

No doubt the family mansion rivaled European castles located on windswept hills overlooking a waterscape. She imagined what it would be like to have that kind of money. She couldn't even come close to wrapping her mind around the concept of being fabulously wealthy.

After surfing the Internet more, she found miscellaneous information about Nation—who he currently dated and photos of the two of them out jet setting and mingling with the beautiful people. She perused shots of his home and his collection of exclusive sports cars.

"I need coffee," she muttered.

After running a brush through her hair and applying a touch of makeup, she left her motel room and climbed in Betty. She headed into Jackson where she easily located a Starbucks. She parked and entered the aromatic café where she ordered a mochaccino and a breakfast sandwich.

Sitting down at a table, she sipped the coffee and sighed with satisfaction as the flavorful warmth trailed down her throat. She'd missed this. Enjoying her cup of joe, she glanced around at the patrons—people reading the newspaper, staring at their cell phones, typing on laptops or reading books. Several others talked with acquaintances and friends at their tables, laughing and joking.

Since she didn't have Nation's phone number, she couldn't call to arrange a time to visit. It was best for her to simply show up and knock on his door. Hopefully he wouldn't be a million miles away, summering in the French Riviera or some other exotic location.

She glanced at her watch and frowned. It was 10 o'clock. Hopefully, Mr. Bobby wasn't a late sleeper. If she knew who invented the iPhone map, she'd thank them personally because it would help her find his house. Unfamiliar with the lay of the land, she feared she'd never have found it on her own.

Heading outside and blinking in the bright sunshine, she climbed in ol' Betty and fired her up. The Apple maps lady talked her through the navigation until she reached an area dotted with tall pines, winding roads and a maze of mansions—some nearly hidden from view by the shrubbery.

"Arrived," the Apple maps voice announced.

Surrounded by majestic green trees, Nation's expansive log mansion fronted the Snake River and included a matching log guest home. It had exquisite views of the Teton Range and the expanse unfolded like a slice of pure heaven. Winter, spring, summer or fall, this place would remain beautiful and inviting.

"Ah, the lives of the rich and famous," Reese whispered as she slowly drove toward the Nation home.

This place reminded Reese of the old movie, "Seven Brides for Seven Brothers," where an Oregon homesteader goes to town to bring home a wife to his rustic cabin in the woods. The Nation mansion was exceptionally rustic, but it wasn't small by any measure.

Split rail fences surrounded the property, but stopped at the driveway that curved toward a parking area full of cars. As she wondered what might be happening, she caught sight of a carved wooden "Nation" bar, about the size of a small vehicle, planted in the front yard. The chocolate confection that had made the Nations billionaires was on display for all to see.

After parking and climbing out of her truck, she headed past the lush lawn and flowering bushes, listening to birds singing in the trees. A breeze brushed her cheeks as she climbed stairs up onto a porch featuring a tall, arched entryway with a bank of windows at the top.

Three carved wooden bears greeted her—one held a fishing pole and a fish; one held a cluster of grapes and the other clutched a bee hive in its fat paws.

A huge doormat said, "Welcome," but Reese felt small compared to this opulent residence. She cleared her throat and looked around for a doorbell, but didn't see one anywhere. Of course, a simple doorbell would be passé with this crowd.

"Hello, may I help you," a male voice asked.

Reese about jumped out of her skin, wondering how she'd missed someone standing around, then she noticed an intercom unit on a wall. She relaxed.

"I'm here to see Bobby Nation."

"Are you one of Mr. Nation's pool party guests?"

"Ah, sure. Yes, that's right, I'm here for the pool party." She felt her face flush as she glanced down at her jeans, boots and T-shirt. Sure, she looked ready for a dip in the pool—not!

The carved wooden door opened and a huge, tree stump of a man, who looked as muscular as a professional weight lifter, appeared. Wearing all black, and practically bulging out of his clothing seams, he had brown hair and a graying Fu Manchu beard. He spoke into a headset, verifying one more party guest had arrived.

Reese inwardly shook her head. Wow, the movers and shakers of the world would of course have private security details. No simple maids for this gang of thieves.

He held up an iPad and asked, "Name?"

"Reese," she said, fidgeting.

"Last name?" he growled.

"Golden."

He frowned. "You're not on the guest list."

"Oh, I, ah recently divorced and took my maiden name back," she stammered. "Darn it anyway, I'm always forgetting—"

"Dayton?"

"Hmm?" She raised her brows in fake confusion, certain he must be tired of her stuttering and stumbling.

"Is it Dayton? Your maiden name, I mean. That's what's on the guest list. Reese Dayton."

"Dayton? Yes, that's it. I don't know why that catches me off guard all the time." She faked a few tears and sniffed. "See, it was a messy divorce and he, my ex, was a monster and—"

"Please, ma'am, take the double doors at the end of the hall," he instructed. "It will lead you to the pool area."

Most of the men she knew hated crying, emotional women. When the human stump glanced down at her attire and lifted a brow, she realized he'd taken notice of her not-for-the-pool clothing.

Reese smiled; aware he questioned her lack of a bathing suit. After brushing off a speck of invisible dust on her shoulder, she met his gaze.

"When I had to flee my home, I had to leave everything behind. All I had were the clothes on my back." She patted her jeans. "These clothes, and you see I—"

Scowling, his shaggy brows almost shading his eyes, he pointed one beefy arm toward the double doors.

Wiping away another fake tear, yet inside feeling proud of her performance, she sauntered toward her destination. With each step, she formulated questions to ask Bobby Nation, hoping the real Reese Dayton wouldn't show up and blow her cover.

TWENTY-NINE

THE SPARKLING RIVER and snow-capped mountains in the distance provided an amazing backdrop for Bobby Nation's extravagant pool. It wouldn't have surprised Reese to find out that he'd had the elaborate water feature imported from Disney World.

In order for it to be used in this four-season country, it was enclosed on three sides. The side facing the outdoor view had been constructed with a wall of windows. Inside, boulders and tropical plants complemented the décor. The lush greenery, in contrast to the turquoise pool water, provided a brilliant display.

Marble statues of dolphins, turtles and other aquatic animals added visual interest. A waterfall embedded in one mossy wall spilled with a gentle flow. The party guests appeared to be having a grand time, and wall-to-wall bodies splashed in the pool or stood nearby talking.

Along the patio area, people moved between banquet tables laden with food, fruit and other refreshment. Others sat at bistro tables, drinking and laughing. All wore appropriate pool attire, and once again, Reese frowned at her own jeans and boots, which were completely inappropriate.

No wonder people gave her odd stares. A fish out of water, yep, that would be her. She chose to ignore the stares. A server wearing a burgundy-colored dress and a white apron approached her. Her blue and purple hair was cut in a cropped style and she had a classy stud nose piercing. She carried a tray filled with flutes of champagne.

"Would you like one?" she asked in a cheerful tone.

"No, but can you tell me where Bobby Nation is?"

The server gave her a puzzled look.

Reese bit her lower lip. As an "invited" guest, she ought to know what her host looked like.

"I just left my optometrist appointment and I had my eyes dilated. Everything's fuzzy blurry. I can't find him." She blinked several times for emphasis.

Wow, little white lies roll off my tongue.

The server smiled and nodded toward a bamboo hut with a grass umbrella situated in a corner. "Over there, by the tiki bar. He's wearing the Hawaiian shirt with tan cargo shorts."

Reese looked in that direction, spotting Bobby right away. He was a shorter guy, appearing to be in his early thirties, with a head full of dark curly hair. In her mind, she could imagine him being callous enough to treat a young girl like Skylar with disrespect.

However, she realized it wasn't fair to judge him when she didn't know him. On the other hand, until she knew otherwise, he remained a suspect.

Bobby was talking to a couple of female guests and Reese could hear his booming laughter over the party noise.

"Thank you," she told the server.

The girl headed toward another cluster of guests to offer them champagne.

Making her way over to the tiki bar, Reese formulated what she would say to the chocolate bar heir. It wasn't easy. How should she introduce herself? She didn't think it would go over to well if she said, *Hey there, I crashed your pool party because I wanted to ask if you roofied my client Skylar Ellington and then kidnapped her little girl when you found out she's your daughter.*

Walking beneath colorful party lights, Reese approached Bobby, who was talking with two drop-dead gorgeous blond women. She listened to the polite banter about which Jackson restaurants served the best food and the best places to vacation.

Finally, Bobby noticed her and said, "Do I know you?"

"No."

The women made surprised noises.

"How did you make it in here past my security detail?"

She sighed, deciding in this situation, she needed to come clean so she could get to the point. "My name is Reese Golden and it's a long, boring story. Please don't blame the security guard you have posted at the door. Crying women make him nervous. Do they make you nervous? Because if they do, I can conjure up some tears."

"What?" Bobby said.

"Call the police," one of the bombshells said. "She's out of her mind."

"Yes, maybe she's got a gun! Maybe she's barged in here to take us all hostage and steal our money." She clutched the other woman's arm, her eyes wide.

"I just need to talk to you," Reese said to Bobby. "In private. This is a serious matter and a little girl's life depends on it."

He shook his head. "I'll have to ask you to leave. Or I will call the authorities."

"I'm a private investigator," Reese said as she handed him one of her business cards. She hoped the direct approach would be effective, along with pulling a few heartstrings. "I'm working on a case for a young lady named Skylar Ellington. Her family owns Wild Creek Ranch in Sage. I'm investigating the kidnapping of her daughter. Skylar would like to find her little girl or at least find some answers about what happened to her."

"Sounds like that's a job for the police," one of the women said with a sniff.

"They did as much as they could when it happened," Reese said. "I'm doing everything in my power to find out what happened to the girl and bring her home. I'm sure you ladies can understand how devastating it would be to have a child abducted. Especially from your own home."

The women made shocked sounds and Reese decided they looked so much alike; they could be twin sisters.

"Why, that's awful," one of them exclaimed.

"It's shocking, I'll agree," Reese said. "Someone had the audacity to cut the window screen and steal Skylar's four-year-old child from her bed while she was sleeping."

Bobby shifted uncomfortably and exchanged a glance with the ladies. A silent communication passed between them.

"I'll speak with you in my office where it's not so noisy," he said. "Follow me."

Reese nodded at the ladies and trotted behind the chocolate bar heir as he left the pool area. Entering the main house, he walked down a hallway and ushered her into an office appointed with mahogany furniture and towering bookshelves. Thick maroon carpeting covered the floor where an overstuffed leather couch and chair rested. The place was so pristine, Reese wondered if it was more for show than actual use.

Bobby pointed toward a chair in front of his desk and she sat down, while he plopped himself in a regal-looking office chair. He created an odd picture—a man in a wild floral print shirt and cargo shorts seated in an office fit for a king or a president.

He nodded toward a fish bowl filled with Nation chocolate bars. "Would you like one?"

"No, thank you," she said.

"What do I have to do with this woman and her daughter?" Bobby knitted his brow.

"That's what I'm here to find out," Reese said. "Hopefully, you'll answer my questions truthfully."

"Fire away," he said, swinging the chair from side to side. "I have nothing to hide."

"You look nervous," she said.

"Believe me, honey, with the amount of money I inherited, it's a rare day if I become nervous about anything."

Reese imagined he really didn't.

"You attended a fundraising party at Polly Ellington Beech's house about five years ago where she introduced her niece, Skylar, to everyone."

"Ah, ha! I wondered if your Skylar Ellington was related to Polly. That was a long time ago."

Reese nodded. "That summer Skylar was working in Jackson. She ran into one of Polly's guests at The Hideaway Bar a few weeks later. They left together and wound up at the Rawhide Motel outside of town."

"Okay."

"Skylar doesn't remember much from that night. However, nine months later, her daughter Daisy was born."

Bobby grabbed the arms of his chair, his knuckles white. "Are you saying I'm the child's father? That I perhaps took advantage of Skylar?"

"No. I'm asking if you know anything about it."

"Why would I risk my reputation and all that I have," he waved his hand around, "to be caught dead in a place like The Hideaway Bar or the Rawhide Motel? They're both dives. And I don't coerce young women into going to bed with me."

"What you do in your private life isn't my business," Reese said. "I only want to know if you were with Skylar that night."

"I'm a confirmed bachelor, lady. I prefer women who are hot to go to bed with me. I don't have to force any of them. If they don't love me, they love my money and social position. And that's fine, because I'm not in it for the long run. I don't believe in marriage and I refuse to have millstones of ex-wives, alimony and child support hanging around my neck."

"I'd like to believe you," Reese said. "You're convincing. But just so you know, in Wyoming, there's no statute of limitation on rape."

"Are you threatening me?" Bobby's face turned red.

"Do you have any skeletons in your past to be threatened with?"

He stood, glaring at Reese. "I don't know anything about Skylar Ellington and her kidnapped daughter. I want you to leave now."

"Not a problem," she said as she rose and walked toward the door. "I'll see myself out."

Reese nodded at the human tree trunk security guard as she left Nation's mansion. She headed out to her truck, started it and drove away. Bobby Nation was a rich playboy who enjoyed his power and influence over people. Take that away, and he'd be a weak little man afraid of his shadow.

Driving back to the heart of Jackson, she planned to pay a visit to The Hideaway Bar. If she was in luck, maybe she could find someone who had worked there around the time Skylar had lived in Jackson. Hopefully, someone who could verify whether or not Bobby Nation was a regular.

THIRTY

NATION WAS RIGHT—The Hideaway Bar was a dive, but it wasn't for her to judge where people got their jollies. It wasn't a tourist stop like Jackson's Million Dollar Cowboy Bar with saddles fashioned into bar stools. It had a couple of pool tables and a fairly large bar—enough to make it a decent watering hole.

This time of the day it was quiet. A radio blared in the background and a couple of people sat at one of the tables. Reese headed up to the counter and flashed a twenty-dollar bill.

A young lady with a mass of dark hair pinned atop her head looked up from her counter polishing. Behind her, a neon Crown Royal sign flashed as she approached Reese and asked, "What would you like?"

"Bud Light," she said.

When the girl returned with the beer and change, Reese gave her a two-dollar tip.

"How long have you worked here?" she asked, then took a sip.

"Almost a year," the young lady said as she tucked the money into a pocket of her red apron.

"Hmm, is there anyone here today who's been working at the bar for a while?"

"Ernie Farmer—he owns the place. Why?"

Reese slid one of her business cards across the bar. "I'd like to ask him a few questions about a case I'm working on."

The young lady read the card and nodded. "He's in his office but I'll see if he can come up here."

"Thanks," Reese said, sipping at her beer and pulling up one of the stools to sit on.

The young lady walked toward a door behind the bar and knocked. A few minutes later, a tall, thin man opened up and talked to her. He scratched his head, nodded and ambled toward Reese.

"You wanted to talk to me?" he asked, his eyes wide.

"I did. You've owned The Hideaway for a while?"

"Ten years now," he replied.

Reese pulled out her phone and searched the Internet for a picture of Bobby Nation. There were plenty, so it only took a second to find a good one.

"You recognize your regulars by now, right?"

He nodded. "That I do."

"What about this guy, has he ever been in here?" She showed him the photo.

"Bobby Nation? Ah, no." He laughed. "Ain't never seen him in here and I doubt he'd step foot inside my place. With his billions, he's more of the high class, upper echelon crowd."

She pulled up a picture of Jack O'Casey and showed it to Farmer.

He laughed again. "The social media king? What app was it he invented—ah, Swat Ass or something like that. Nah, I doubt he'd be seen in a place like this either. Not with his billions. My place mostly caters to the worker bees around town. The guys and gals who wait tables, clean motel rooms and groom ski runs."

"I see," Reese said, thinking she'd just wasted her time and his. "I appreciate you talking to me."

"Sure, no problem. I'm gonna head back to my office now. Got some bookwork to finish."

"I bet a place like this keeps you on your toes."

"That's for sure."

After he left, Reese put down her mostly full beer bottle, and headed outside into the daylight, which made her squint. In her truck, she looked up Jack O'Casey's address, which after some serious researching, she found in Jackson's Gros Ventre neighborhood.

She tapped his address on Huckleberry Drive into her phone. Seconds later, she was on her way, driving toward the social media mogul's home. A winding, twisting road through forest slopes took her there and she arrived at a two-story stone mansion beside a lake. Just like Nation's house, it was large and as grand as a European castle with trees and shrubbery fronting the property.

Minus the chocolate bar statue in the front yard.

Thinking she might have finally hit a dead end in this case, her optimism flagged. She hadn't ever followed up with the pedophile the Sage police had talked to, so maybe that would be her next move if the trip up here didn't prove fruitful.

She drove past O'Casey's home with a pit of dread in her stomach. Then she noticed a large number of cars parked in a lot alongside the mansion. There was even a horse trailer with the words, *Petting Zoo Parties* on the side, along with a phone number.

She slowed down, watching as adults and children carrying brightly wrapped gifts paraded toward a lawn filled with children's party paraphernalia. Under one awning sat white tables and chairs, along with a table laden with food and a gigantic birthday cake. A bouncy house sat further down on the lawn and laughing, screeching children ran in and out. In another penned area, children and parents pet small, furry animals. A clown in big, floppy shoes also drew a large crowd as he handed out balloons.

By far the biggest attraction, however, was the area where the little ones could enjoy pony rides. As she got closer, music and laughter filled the air. Reese's heart began to patter. Obviously, someone was having a birthday party.

Maybe a four-year-old girl?

THIRTY-ONE

REESE PULLED INTO the parking lot beside the horse trailer. Next to it sat a red Mercedes-Benz. Just like the one Skylar and Leyla had described when they told Reese about the young girl they'd seen in it—the one who looked like Daisy. Her mind raced as she decided how to handle this turn of good fortune.

"Time to crash another party," she murmured. Her stomach growled. It was underhanded, but there would be food. This way, she could scrounge another free meal. Kept her on budget.

Oh, the joys of mooching!

Spotting a forgotten gift wrapped in pink on the hood of someone's car, Reese picked it up. She walked toward the party, pasting a smile on her face as she ambled past a man and a woman wearing head sets—most likely more security guards.

She nodded at them and they nodded back. Good— she'd passed inspection.

Children wearing lopsided party hats ran back and forth on the lawn, balloons in hand, calling to each other. Their excited voices punctuated the fresh mountain air. Oh, to be young and not have a care in the world. It would be fabulous, Reese thought.

The sun shone down on a glorious, celebratory scene, with the jagged Tetons and a beautiful blue sky as backdrops.

If the child having a birthday was indeed Daisy Ellington, unfortunately, sinister intent peppered every air molecule. The little girl didn't belong here—she belonged back at Wild Creek Ranch with her mother, her uncle and her grandmother.

If her suspicions turned out to be correct, and Jack O'Casey had kidnapped his daughter, Vinny must have told him about her. The two could have cooked up a plot for Vinny to take the little girl. Vinny's dad and grandfather mentioned he'd come into a windfall of money, which could be from O'Casey as payment for a job well done.

Scanning the crowd, Reese tried to spot a child with dark hair and Skylar's distinct features. Everything moved so fast, flashing with a kaleidoscope of colors. She'd have to hang around until the cake was served and the birthday child was given a seat of honor to open birthday presents.

A table laden with gifts caught her eye, so she walked over to it and dropped off the one she'd nabbed. She made a beeline toward the food table where she filled a plate with couple of finger sandwiches, grapes and some plump pink shrimp.

Walking around, she munched the fare and tuned in her listening skills. People stood in clusters talking and laughing, so it wasn't difficult to glean information. Passing by the groups, she heard mom tips about potty training, carpooling, teething and proper infant swaddling. Good stuff to remember if she wanted to have a kid someday.

Overhearing someone discussing the finer points of nursery schools, she slowed down. Daisy would be about the right age for that. It didn't take her long to determine who was holding that particular conversation.

A tall woman with red hair was speaking animatedly

to an older couple. She gestured emphatically with her hands as she spoke. The three stood next to a wooden gazebo where an intricately decorated birthday cake sat on a pristine white tablecloth. Reese recalled Leyla mentioning an older couple in the car with the girl she'd believed could be Daisy.

Casually, she moved closer to the three, pretending to watch a cluster of children kicking a soccer ball. She zeroed in on the adults. All were dressed with impeccable style. The women wore print summer dresses form-fitted to their perfect shapes, and the man wore pressed trousers and a crisp white button-down shirt.

"It's called the Kinderreim School, Clara," the redhead said to the older woman who wore her white hair in a short bob. "It's European—German, actually. It's all the rage with the moms in town."

"Think about it, Nina, are you sure you don't want to send her to public school?" Clara asked. "That's where Stuart and I sent Jack. He turned out fine. Didn't he, dear?"

Where have I heard the name Nina before? Reese knew it had been recently, but she couldn't quite place it.

The man standing beside Clara had been staring at a young lady in a short skirt. When Clara spoke, he turned toward the women, a guilty expression on his face. With a long gray pony tail and wire-framed spectacles, he looked nothing short of being a decent individual, even if he did have an eye for the ladies.

Without missing a beat, he said, "Of course, Clara. Look at our boy, he's a computer genius!"

Stuart pointed to a dark-haired man, in his mid-thirties, wearing glasses. Dressed in tan khakis and a green polo shirt, he spoke to another man standing beside him wearing a gray suit and red tie.

Reese instantly recognized Jack O'Casey from the on-line photos she'd been perusing. He didn't appear preda-tory in any capacity, not that there was a certain look for someone like that.

Nevertheless, she found it difficult to imagine him lacing Skylar's drink with date rape drugs. He looked like a regular dad at his kid's birthday party, observing the fun. In fact, he looked like a complete nerd—just as Ivan and Hugo had described him.

Yet, Reese had run into plenty of innocent-looking people who had done terrible things. Behind the facade they put up for the general public lurked monstrous ten-dencies and skeletons rattling in their closets.

"True, it's amazing he excelled with only a simple public education," Nina said in a condescending tone. "I believe Dawna is even brighter than Jack, so think how far she'll go with Kinderreim's innovative curricu-lum. Jack and I visited with the staff last week and we believe it's the best place for her. She's advanced beyond her age, so we want her to attend a school where they can address her needs."

Reese listened closer, her heart skipping a beat. Skylar and Chance said Daisy was gifted and had exceptional intellect for her age. And could this elderly couple be the same one Leyla and Skylar had seen in the car during their Daisy sighting?

"I imagine it's expensive, isn't it?" Stuart folded his arms across his chest and frowned at Nina.

"Stop thinking like that, Stuart." Nina patted him on the forearm. "You know Jack and I can afford it. We only want the best for our little girl."

"I'm sure you two know what you're doing, dear," Clara said, her brow furrowed.

A little girl with sable-colored pigtails wearing a My

Little Pony T-shirt, sparkling purple capris and sandals, ran up and hugged Clara's legs. Clara affectionately patted the little girl's shoulders.

Reese sucked in a breath. It seemed unreal, but little Dawna resembled Daisy, in fact, Reese felt certain it was her. The weeks hadn't changed her much, except her hair appeared to have grown a bit longer.

"What are you guys talking about?" Dawna asked.

"Your new school," Nina said.

"I love school," the little girl said.

"I don't want those people to put undue pressure and expectations on my granddaughter," Clara said. "Right now, she's eager and excited to learn. If they make it into a chore and have strenuous expectations, they could ruin her enthusiasm."

"What people, Grammie?" Dawna looked up at Clara.

"Don't worry," Nina told the little girl, flashing Clara a firm look. "Everything's going to be fine. Remember when Daddy and I went to visit Kinderreim?"

Dawna nodded. "Uh, huh. You said they have a cool playground."

"They do." Nina smiled.

Dawna ran off to mingle with some other children, pigtails flying.

"Kinderreim is sending a teacher to our house next week to evaluate Dawna," Nina said. "That way they can individualize her learning program. In the fall, she'll begin attending."

"It sounds all settled," Clara said with a sigh, as though she realized she wouldn't change the course of events. "I can tell Dawna's excited to be at the school. She's practically bubbling with energy at the idea."

Clara and Nina began chattering about the Jackson Hole Golf Course's ladies league and an upcoming scramble they'd both signed up to play in. Meanwhile, Stuart's wandering eye once again focused on the young lady and her mesmerizing short skirt.

A sly smile curved Reese's lips as she pondered an idea. Perhaps Kinderreim would be able to evaluate Dawna sooner than next week. And just maybe, she could be the "teacher" sent to do it. This wasn't the first time she'd gone undercover to help a case.

Enthusiasm trailed up her spine. Had she managed to track down Skylar Ellington's little girl?

It was a distinct possibility, even though she didn't want to raise false hope.

When she returned to her hotel, she texted Jeremy to let him know about this new development. She also told him she planned to pose as a nursery school teacher who had been sent from Kinderreim to evaluate Dawna for entrance.

Jeremy texted her back, warning her not to go off half-cocked, but she promptly ignored him.

THIRTY-TWO

THE NEXT DAY, Reese put on the blue dress she'd worn to the dinner at Hayden's Post, her white espadrille sandals and her gold chandelier earrings. She decided adding the Navy-blue blazer, leather briefcase and reading glasses to the ensemble would give her the perfect "teacher" image.

She drove to the O'Caseys' house, practicing her spiel about why Kinderreim had been able to send her out to evaluate Dawna sooner than expected. She'd spent a long time going over Kinderreim's website and memorizing information about the school. Hopefully her homework session would prove valuable.

Mid-morning sun shone over the mountains with a golden glow, lending a warm atmosphere to the exclusive Gros Ventre neighborhood. The uber large stone and timber residences weren't the typical cookie cutter style found in city subdivisions. They were expansive and lavish, all with their own individual flair, as they sat in chunks of wilderness carved out for the owners.

Amenities in this area included docks that fronted the Snake River, private swimming pools and outbuildings that were probably chock full of toys like boats, ATVs, Jeeps and other four-wheel vehicles. Hiking trails and bicycle paths cut swaths across mountain slopes and velvety green backyards offered a bird's-eye view of the crisscross patterns.

People who lived here weren't simply rich. They were fabulously wealthy. Movie stars, sports figures and upper crust businesspeople called this place home. It was close enough to civilization to travel where they needed to go, yet they could maintain strict privacy.

Reese wheeled into the driveway of the O'Casey home and stepped out of her truck. She cleared her throat and straightened her blazer. Gripping the briefcase handle, she approached the front door and looked for a doorbell. Spotting the round button, she pressed.

Through the door, she could hear the muffled chime. An intercom buzzed on and a woman's voice said, "Yes?"

"I'm Kate Shaw from the Kinderreim School. I'm here to evaluate Dawna for our fall semester."

Reese inhaled sharply. Hopefully the O'Caseys wouldn't see past her ruse. Nervous, she waited a few seconds until Nina O'Casey opened the front door.

"We weren't expecting anyone today," she said. "The school's headmistress, Veronica Hansen, hasn't contacted us yet about when our daughter will be evaluated."

"We had some cancellations," Reese said, having rehearsed her cover story numerous times. "It freed up our schedule."

"I'm surprised someone didn't call ahead to let us know." Nina's eyes narrowed.

"Someone from the office was supposed to notify you," Reese said in a frustrated tone. "Would you like me to come back at a better time?"

Reese mentally crossed her fingers behind her back, hoping Nina wouldn't put her off.

"No, it's fine," Nina said. "I need to bring Dawna inside, though. She's playing out back on her swing set."

"Perfect," Reese said.

Nina pointed toward a large room where a wooden table surrounded by twelve chairs rested. Plush furnishings filled the area—a large China hutch, a large room-size carpet and gray velvet drapes on the windows.

"Please, have a seat," Nina said. "Will the dining room work for your evaluation?"

"We'll need privacy, so Dawna's not distracted," Reese said in her most authoritative voice.

"Of course," Nina said. "I'll close the double doors. It will be nice and quiet for the two of you."

"Excellent," Reese said.

She walked over to one of the chairs, pulled it out and sat down. She noticed a large framed photo hanging on the wall that depicted a beautiful lake surrounded by jutting, snow-capped peaks, which were reflected in the water's mirrored surface. A cozy-looking, A-frame cabin nestled in the nearby woods—nearly hidden by pines. A brass plate identified the place as, "Josephina Lake."

Nina continued to watch her, so she stopped ogling the photo and placed her briefcase on the table, withdrew some papers and shuffled them. She gave Nina an expectant smile and a nod.

Nina nodded back, then disappeared.

Reese sighed with relief. So far, so good.

A short time later, Nina returned holding the hand of a little girl wearing jeans shorts, a yellow T-shirt and tennis shoes. Her mussed dark hair and flushed face indicated she'd been enjoying the outdoors, and she clutched a worn, stuffed purple bunny.

Her big blue eyes looked just like Chance's.

"I'm sorry, Miss—"

"Shaw," Reese said.

"Miss Shaw," Nina said. "Dawna has been playing, so she's not in very tidy condition."

"We encourage our students to enjoy outdoor activities," Reese said with a smile. "It clears their minds and elevates their creativity levels."

Nina patted Dawna's back. "Dawna, this is Miss Shaw from the Kinderreim School. She wants to visit with you. Go sit by her at the table, okay?"

"Sure," Dawna said. She obediently walked over, pulled out a chair across from Reese and climbed into the seat.

"Be a good girl for your mama, now, and do what Miss Shaw tells you to do," Nina said, then added, "Dawna, would you like me to take Squiggles?"

"No," Dawna said, hugging the ragged purple bunny closer. She began chomping on her gum and blew a huge bubble, popping it with a finger.

Nina sighed and closed the double doors.

Dawna waited a few seconds, wrinkled her nose and stuck out her tongue at the closed wood panels.

Surprised, Reese asked, "Dawna, why did you do that?"

Turning her dirt-streaked face toward Reese, Dawna said, "Because she's an old meany. And she's not my mama."

THIRTY-THREE

REESE LIFTED AN EYEBROW. "Why do you say that?"

Dawna popped another bubble. "My real name is Daisy. Besides, my mama has light hair, like dandelion fluff. Not red."

"How did you come to live here?"

"I was asleep one night and this bad man came in my room and took me up to a cabin. I was really afraid, but he didn't hurt me. Then he drove me to this place where Nina was waiting. She told me my mommy didn't want me anymore and that she and Mr. Jack had adopted me. She said I was a really lucky girl because they could give me whatever I wanted."

"I see," Reese said as she withdrew her cell phone from her briefcase.

"I only call her Mama 'cause she makes me," Dawna added. "If I don't, she acts really mad. It scares me."

"I'm sorry about that," Reese said.

"I don't care what she and Mr. Jack can give me," Dawna continued. "I want my real mama. I want my real grandma and Uncle Chance. I don't believe they didn't want me anymore and that they gave me away."

Reese nodded, her mind clicking with ideas about how to handle this. She couldn't simply stroll out of the mansion hand in hand with Daisy. She had to do this carefully so Daisy wasn't traumatized further and so that the O'Caseys didn't call out their big guns. Otherwise, Daisy wouldn't get to go home, and neither would she.

"I need a photo of you for our new student display," Reese said. "Is that okay?"

"Sure," Dawna said.

"Smile!"

Dawna grinned and held up Squiggles. Reese took a close up shot of the girl that perfectly framed the little girl and her beloved bunny.

"Now, we're going to look at the alphabet, then some shapes and numbers," Reese said.

"At my other school, they asked my favorite color."

"That's very important," Reese said. "What is your favorite color?"

"Purple."

"Nice choice," Reese responded. "Do you have a favorite place, too?"

"The lady lake." Dawna pointed at the framed photograph Reese had admired earlier. "Sometimes Mr. Jack—Nina makes me call him daddy—takes us there to the cabin. When I'm in trouble, I like to hide in the bear home by the big rocks. Nina doesn't know where I go." Dawna took a deep breath. "Fairies live in the bear home, too. They help me feel better."

Reese smiled at Dawna, amazed by the girl's vivid imagination, which most likely had helped her cope these past weeks since she was taken. Obviously, Nina had a bad temper, considering the child felt the need to run from her at times.

"Are you ready to show me what you know?"

"Yep," Dawna said. "I learned lots at my other school. They told me I can't go there anymore 'cause I need one where I can learn new things. I miss my friend Karla. We had fun."

"Maybe Karla can come visit you," Reese said.

"I hope so," Dawna replied.

Reese pulled out a kid's workbook that she'd picked up at the local Big Lots store, and handed it to Dawna, along with a pencil.

"Dawna, I'd like to you complete all the pages you can," Reese told her. "If you don't understand something, just skip over it."

"Okay."

Reese observed as the girl wrote on the pages, her tongue tucked in the corner of her mouth. There wasn't a single page that she paused on or asked questions about, and it was a first-grade level workbook. She reminded herself this child was only four.

It wasn't long before Dawna handed it back to Reese.

"I'm done," she said. "Do you want me to do anything else?"

"No, this is fine."

"I'm bored," Dawna said. "Do you want to hear a new song I learned?"

"That sounds great," Reese said. "You sing while I look over your work."

As Dawna belted out the words in a clear, child's tone, Reese thumbed through the pages. Even though Reese knew Daisy was gifted, it surprised her that girl knew the alphabet by heart, she could count and wrote numbers flawlessly to 100 and she could read short sentences.

Dawna had also calculated all correct answers on a short addition and subtraction test. Even though she didn't have a lick of training in education, Reese could tell the child was advanced beyond her age.

When a half hour had gone by, which she judged to be about the adequate amount of time for an authentic educational evaluation, she decided the interview could end.

"Thank you for meeting with me today, Dawna."

Reese slid the workbook and Dawna's pencil into her briefcase and closed it.

"Good 'cause I want to go play outside again." The little girl pulled the gum from her mouth, strings of saliva attached, and stuck it under the table. Then she pressed her index finger over mouth and said, "Shh, don't tell Nina. She'll be grumpy."

Smiling, Reese stood.

"Bye, Miss Shaw," Dawna said as she ran to the double doors, opened them, and skipped from the room.

Reese was about to leave, when an idea occurred to her. Opening her purse, she pulled out an old grocery list. Over where Dawna had been sitting, she reached under the table and pulled the gum loose. Quickly, she folded it in the paper, dropped it in her bag, and walked out of the dining room.

Wondering if a lab could extract DNA from chewing gum, she walked over to Nina. The two women shook hands.

"She's really smart, isn't she, Miss Shaw?" Nina asked. "I've known it since, well, for a long time."

"We'll be in touch," Reese said as she walked toward the door.

Nina's cell phone rang and she answered it. When she shot Reese a funny look, Reese hurried from the mansion, ran toward her truck and climbed in. Tossing her briefcase in the passenger seat, she backed out. Nina stood at the front door, waving at her. Jack O'Casey appeared beside his wife, scowling.

Reese drove the Bronco down the driveway, turned at the corner and stepped on the gas. She suspected someone had called the Kinderreim School and now the O'Caseys knew they hadn't sent anyone out to evaluate Dawna today.

Busted.

She headed back to town at a breakneck pace. The trees and shrubbery alongside her windows whizzed by in a green blur. Eventually, she slowed down, thinking she'd managed to pull off her charade.

When a black SUV on a side road pulled out and began to follow her, her heart started doing the tango. She watched it, hoping it was only one of the residents going to town. She knew, with a sinking feeling that it wasn't, when the SUV got closer, pushing her to go faster.

Reese increased her speed, going around sharp curves way too fast. Unfortunately, the SUV continued to tail her. She moved to the side of the road, hoping the driver simply wanted to pass her.

The SUV moved in position beside her and began inching closer toward her Bronco, obviously trying to push her off onto the road's shoulder. Reese urged Betty to go faster. The SUV caught up and rode her bumper.

"Please, Lord, don't let any other vehicles show up!"

It would be a recipe for disaster. Sweat popped out on her forehead. She kept glancing in her rearview mirror. The SUV pushed forward, and she maintained a high speed to try and stay ahead.

"I know I'm not a praying person, Lord, and I haven't been terribly virtuous," Reese muttered. "But if you're up there, help me!"

Gravel sprayed across the road as both Betty and the SUV navigated a tight turn. She should reach Jackson soon. Once there, surely the SUV would back off.

The two vehicles slid around another hairpin turn, then Reese noticed a deep ravine. A little voice told her she'd wind up at the bottom if she didn't shake the jerk on her tail.

Reese made another attempt to outrun the SUV. Betty

made a valiant surge forward, then her engine stalled. The SUV rushed to take advantage, coming up beside the Bronco and slamming into it.

As though she was outside of her body watching, unable to do anything to stop what was happening, Reese watched through the windshield as Betty jumped over an embankment.

The ravine, full of dead wood and a tangle of forest shrubbery, swallowed Reese and her beloved Bronco into the deep green depths.

THIRTY-FOUR

Reese grabbed harder on the steering wheel and tensed.

As the Bronco rolled down the slope, it felt like a carnival ride that drops people from the top of a tower. A bolt of fear shot up Reese's spine as gravity pulled her and Betty downward.

The truck bumped its way over the rugged landscape, scraping the undercarriage, slamming against rocks. Loud cracking and drumming sounds tortured her ears. For some crazy reason, all she could think of was how hard she and her grandfather had worked to restore the Bronco. Now it was being torn to shreds.

Her entire body was being tortured, and she worried about the truck.

Fortunately, the ravine leveled out. The Bronco crashed its way through trees and brush. Somehow, it managed to miss big trees or boulders, jolting past them instead.

The motion threatened to rip Reese's hands from the steering wheel and at last the Bronco landed with a final thud. She must have hit her head at some point and blood dribbled down her forehead and onto her cheek. Mostly, however, she felt intact and felt thankful for that.

Meanwhile, the Bronco's condition remained a mystery and she hoped it could be repaired.

The ringing in her ears soon subsided and she looked around. It was hot in the truck, so she rolled down her window. Birds chirped and insects buzzed as the fresh air revived her. She inhaled deeply, thanking her lucky stars she wasn't in bad shape.

When she saw the man staring at her through the cracked Bronco windshield, she jumped. He had dark, cropped hair and when he grinned, she noted the piercings slashing through his lip. He had them along his brow, too. Small silver hoops and studs that made him look tough.

"Finally got you, didn't I, bitch?" He shouted. With a lighter, he lit the cigarette hanging from his mouth. "I warned you to leave, but you wouldn't. Now I'm going to let you to die down here. Serves you right for snooping around in things that ain't none of your business."

"Vinny?" She glared at him.

"You're damn right I'm Vinny. What about Skylar? She's mine. She just doesn't know it yet, but I'll wait for her till she's ready. And when that day comes, we don't need no kid hanging around. I got plenty of money in the bank for us to go wherever we want."

"You took Daisy," Reese said. "Why?"

"She don't belong to me, and that's a big problem. Besides, I hate kids, so I decided she should be with her dad and Nina. O'Casey's got plenty of money to treat her like a princess. The little brat ought to thank me for what I done."

"It's not your place to decide what happens to Daisy," Reese said. "It's not legal, moral or ethical. And it's not fair."

"It's not fair," he mimicked in a whiny tone. "It's not fair I grew up dirt poor and my dad beat the shit out of me every day of my life. At least he's been nice to me since I could buy him and Gramps a big screen TV and keep them in Twinkies."

"How did you..."

"How'd I find the money?" He snorted with derision. "Nina lined my pockets pretty good when I brought her the kid. The two of us both have a thing for Skylar. Nina hates her and I love her."

So, Nina had paid Vinny to kidnap Daisy.

Reese's theory had been all wrong. She thought Jack O'Casey had set it up. She bit her lower lip, trying to think. She couldn't recall where she'd heard the name Nina. It was driving her crazy.

Vinny held up a gun and said, "Buh, bye now."

Reese ducked down into the passenger seat. A loud shot rang out and the windshield shattered even more, spreading into tiny cracks with a spider-webbed design.

She huddled there, waiting and hoping Vinny would believe he'd shot her and had taken off. Finally, she peered over the dashboard, noting with relief he was indeed gone. He must have figured he'd finish her off with a shot to the head. Dimwit couldn't even aim straight, lucky for her.

In the distance, she heard an engine roar into life, and then fade. It would seem Vinny had taken off, believing he had shot her and left her here to die.

Relieved he'd gone, she reached for her briefcase and dug out her cell phone. It didn't have any reception, of course. She tried honking the Bronco's horn. It, too, was dead.

"Figures," she growled as she reached for her emergency bag in the back seat. When she'd first begun to drive at 16, her grandfather had assembled the black duffel bag full of first aid items and other necessities in case she had the misfortune of being caught during a snowstorm out on the road. Reese had used various items over the years, and she appreciated her grandfather's foresight.

Unfortunately, she'd never added emergency flares

as he'd suggested, and she cursed herself for not doing that. She could have used them right now.

She grabbed a bottle of water, sipped, then opened the truck door. Grabbing her keys, her cell phone and her purse, she jumped out of the vehicle. She noted the Bronco rested next to a trickle of moisture that at one point had probably been a creek or a stream. Shading her eyes from the sun, she looked up, noting how far down the slope the Bronco had traveled. Not all that far, she judged.

"I'm so sorry, Betty," she whispered, patting the dashboard. "I have to leave. But I promise I'll send somebody to come and get you. Then we'll hire a mechanic to fix you up."

Of course, no one was going to hear her if she tried calling out. People driving down the road would be in their closed, air-conditioned cars talking to other people or maybe playing the radio. Well, well, well, she'd gotten herself in a real predicament, but nothing she couldn't handle.

Jeremy had warned her not to go to the O'Caseys'. Had she listened? Nope. Stubborn and pigheaded, just like her mom had said, she wasn't used to taking orders from other people. She did things her way.

And, sure enough, she'd gotten herself in a jam. But she needed to get going and find some help. Daisy needed to get home to her real family. It was up to her to see that the little girl was returned safely.

THIRTY-FIVE

REESE BEGAN SCRAMBLING up the uneven ground of the ravine, her legs aching from exertion. Most certainly she didn't recommend hiking in white espadrille sandals, which would be destroyed by the time she reached the road. They were definitely more of a hindrance than a help.

About halfway up the slope, Reese decided someone needed to put a fork in her because she was done, done, done. She caught her breath, her body coated in perspiration. This literally sucked.

In her mind, she envisioned a steaming Starbucks Mocha Cappuccino. Once she made it up this hill and into town, she would treat herself to one. With that in mind, she continued her journey.

Summoning a fresh round of strength, she hiked further through the tall grass and wildflowers. She strained to hear cars on the road above her. A faint rushing noise drifted her way, and she smiled, encouraged by her progress.

"Almost there," she muttered, experiencing a surge of anticipation and a rush of energy.

Through the brush and weeds she moved, pausing every so often to catch her breath. Once she reached the asphalt roadway. She began walking, hoping to flag down a passing car as she trekked toward town.

When a sedan appeared, she waved her arms and called out, but the vehicle sped up and continued past her.

"Driver must think I'm a kook," Reese murmured. She couldn't blame people for not trusting a random person walking along the road. Shortly after that car passed her by, another one came around a curve. She waved her arms and called out, but this vehicle also zoomed past her.

Oh well, she thought as she continued walking. Maybe she'd run into a house where she could ask for help. Also, the closer she got to town; the better chance she'd have of finding help.

Mosquitoes kept flying in her face and she swatted them away. No wonder she felt so itchy—the critters had chewed on her mercilessly.

She drank from her water bottle, noting she didn't have much left as she tucked it into the pocket of her blazer.

One thing she learned right away—do not hike in espadrilles. She snorted, which sounded like a moose stuck in mud. The humor gave her another surge of energy and she continued to plod along, one foot after another. Concerned that Vinny might double back at any point, she kept her eyes peeled for his truck. Fortunately, he never appeared.

Clouds skimmed over the trees, darkening the skies, and the temperature dropped slightly. When rain began to patter, she recognized her good fortune. Though she felt like a drowned rat, and her hair soon became plastered on her head, she stuck out her tongue and enjoyed the cool moisture dribbling into her cottony mouth. It also felt good on her skin, reviving her.

Maybe the big guy upstairs knew what he was doing after all.

Taking a deep breath, she continued her slow progress. She focused on the surrounding area, hoping she might run into a house. Whether or not they'd open up their door to a stranger was another thing entirely.

To pass the time, she tried singing some of her favorite country western tunes—at least her version. She was terrible at memorizing. When she knew lost track of the words, she hummed.

Between snippets of songs, she continued to soak in the rain and drink what she could. Imagining what a hideous mess she must look like, she chuckled again. She'd been wanting to change her hair style and now nature had done it for her.

For free.

Wet dog coiffure.

A truck appeared and she waved at the driver.

"Hello," she called out, her voice sounding like gravel being poured into a wheelbarrow. Hot sun and exertion had begun to wear her down.

The driver swerved the truck to the other side of the road, giving her a wide swathe, but didn't stop. Reese frowned as it drove past her and on down the road.

She blew him a kiss.

THIRTY-SIX

RED AND BLUE flashing lights created impressionist art in the distance. Encouraged to see law enforcement coming her way, Reese waved at the police cruiser. God help her, she must look like a lunatic with her matted hair.

Maybe the driver of one of the vehicles that had passed her had called the cops. It's possible he or she had complained about a transient wandering alongside the road and the police had come to investigate.

Thank goodness for concerned citizens.

The squad car slowed to a stop alongside the road and a tall man in uniform stepped out. He placed his hand close to his gun belt and spoke in an authoritative voice.

"Ma'am, I need you to come over here where I can see you," he said.

"No problem," Reese said as she walked toward him. "I was talking to friends who live up here and I had an accident a ways back. A guy in a black SUV ran my truck off the road. It went over an embankment and it's stuck in a ravine."

"Are you new to town?"

"Just visiting." She gave him her name and why she was here and described where her truck had landed. "And I know the guy who ran me off the road. Vinny Warren, from Sage. I'm sure the cops down there would like to know his whereabouts."

"Did you see a license plate number or any other specific markings on the vehicle?"

"No," she said.

He spoke into the radio attached to his shoulder, reporting the specifics of her accident to dispatch, along with the fact that a black SUV had forced her over the embankment.

"Come with me and we'll get you taken care of," the officer said.

"Thank you," Reese said, relieved as she followed him to his squad car. "I can't tell you how glad I am that you drove by when you did."

RESTING ON AN exam table in the hospital emergency room, Reese waited to be seen by a doctor. A nurse had already been in to take her vitals and draw her blood for lab work. The woman had also attended to the cut on her head, dabbing away the blood and applying ointment.

She touched the bump on her noggin, which really wasn't much. It ached slightly, but the medicine made it feel better. Her bare legs also bore scratches from crawling around in the weeds. Those weren't really a big deal, either. Mainly, they just itched.

The accident hadn't caused her as much harm as her Bronco had suffered. That's what she was really worried about.

She and Betty had been through a lot together and it would break her heart to have to send the old truck to the junk yard. The very idea was so distasteful, she refused to even dwell on it for long.

She'd told Officer Nelson, the policeman who had given her a ride, that she was a private investigator hired by Skylar Ellington to find her kidnapped daughter. She added that she'd found the girl at Jack and Nina O'Casey's home and that he needed to inform the Jackson Police Department so they could follow up. Officer

Nelson promised he would, and expressed appreciation that she'd tracked down a missing child.

"I'm familiar with that case," Officer Nelson had said. "I'm sure Daisy's mother will be overjoyed to have her daughter home safe and sound."

Noticing a hangnail on her pinkie finger, Reese picked at it, impatient to get out of this place. She felt fine, but Nelson insisted she should be looked at, just in case she'd suffered any injuries during her accident.

Meanwhile, she was anxious to keep going on her investigation, although she appreciated the care she was being given. The point was, she would be fine, and she had no doubt about that. However, finding Daisy was huge, and she could hardly wait to make the next moves to get her back home.

She plugged in her cell phone to charge it so she could call Officer Savage to let him know about Daisy. Furrowing her brow, she mentally chastised herself for not thinking of recharging her phone as soon as she'd gotten in this room.

"Hey there," a deep voice rumbled.

She looked up, surprised to see him saunter in, decked out in his uniform and shiny black shoes.

"What are you doing here?" she asked, surprised. "I haven't had a chance to call you to let you know the latest update."

"I figured I better get up here when you left me that text message about going to O'Casey's house. You rush headlong into things, and that concerns me."

"Didn't think I could handle myself, huh?"

"I know you can, I'm just interested in what you found out."

"How did you know I was in the ER?"

"I checked with the Jackson PD. They said Officer Nelson picked you up after you had a car accident."

"Yeah, Vinny chased me down after I left the O'Caseys' and ran me off the road in his big black SUV. Obviously, after he killed Gayle, he came up here to hide out in Jackson. I imagine Nina O'Casey called him and told him to get rid of me and since he's her lap dog, he complied."

"Okay, back up the train," Jeremy said, folding his arms across his chest. "Start at the beginning. Give me the details."

"First off, I found Daisy. She's with the O'Caseys."

He frowned. "Is she okay?"

Reese nodded. "I got to talk with her when I pretended to be the Kinderreim teacher doing an interview. She's healthy, though not so happy because she'd like her real mama. And the O'Caseys call her Dawna."

"That is so great! What does Daisy remember about being kidnapped?"

"She said she was asleep one night and a bad man came in her room and took her up to a cabin. She said she was afraid, but she also said he didn't hurt her. He must have kept her there for a while, since we found evidence she'd been held there. At some point, Vinny drove her to meet up with Nina O'Casey."

"How does Nina O'Casey factor into all of this?"

"It's complicated," Reese said. "When Vinny ran me off the road, he stopped and climbed down into the ravine to see if I was dead. He bragged about Nina paying him big bucks to kidnap Daisy. He's obsessed with Skylar and figures with the girl out of the way, Skylar will pay him more attention."

"Poor Daisy, she must be so confused."

"She is, but she's hanging in there. It bothered her when Nina told her that Skylar didn't want her anymore and that she and Jack had adopted her. Nina tried to convince Daisy everything would be okay because they could give her whatever she wanted. That's not a replacement for her real mother, though."

"That little girl's been through a lot. But now we can intervene and get her home to her real family."

"She'll be thrilled," Reese said. "As will the entire Ellington family."

"People do such messed up things," Jeremy said. "What I don't understand, though, is why Nina paid Vinny to take Daisy Ellington. Why not some other child?"

"I know, it doesn't make any sense why she was targeted," Reese said. "I do have one possible theory."

"What's that?" Jeremy lifted his brows.

"I believe Jack O'Casey is Daisy's father."

Jeremy seemed to be mulling over the idea as he studied the ceiling.

"I suppose it's possible he was the guy Skylar hooked up with that summer she spent in Jackson," he finally said. "O'Casey's quite a fixture up there with his millions of dollars and his jet setting ways. But what makes you think he's the guy?"

"I checked out Skylar's aunt's guest list from a party where I believe Skylar met him. After narrowing down the names of the men she could have met at the bar with her friends, there's a strong possibility it was Jack O'Casey."

"I'm gonna go talk to the Jackson cops about this right now so we can get a search warrant," Jeremy said. "I think there's an arrest in the near future for the O'Caseys."

"Good," Reese said. "I also let Officer Nelson know

about Daisy being at the O'Caseys', and the process should already be underway."

"Excellent," Jeremy said. "What about you? Are you sure you are okay? You look like hell."

"Gosh, thanks. You really know how to compliment a girl."

"Sorry, that was putting it a bit harshly. How long were you in that ravine?"

"I hot footed it out of there once I was certain Vinny was gone," Reese said. "The Bronco rolled into a thicket where I knew no one would see me. It seemed like it took forever to climb up to the road."

"I'm glad you weren't hurt worse."

"A bump and some scratches aren't going to kill me," Reese admitted. "I'm just worried about my truck, though. It's a wreck."

"Vehicles can be replaced."

"Not my Betty. She's irreplaceable."

"Either way, finding a missing child and returning her to her family has got to be worth it."

"You're right on that account," Reese said. "Betty is important to me, but finding Daisy completes a bigger picture in the grand scheme of life."

"No kidding," Jeremy said. "I called the Sage Police Chief and he was eager to have me come up here and debrief you."

"I'm sure he was," she said.

"Plus, I worry about you," he added. "You are too hardheaded for your own good."

"That's the way I roll. No biggie."

The tension left Reese's body. For some reason, she wanted Jeremy's respect because he intrigued her—the mystery lawman locked away in Sage, tucked away from the world at large.

"This part you're not going to like." Jeremy frowned.

"What?" Tension rocketed through Reese's limbs again.

"The Chief wanted to arrest Skylar for false reporting. He's convinced she paid Vincent Warren to dispose of Daisy. He thinks she wanted her kid gone so she could resume the party life."

"No, he's got it all wrong!" Reese tried to get off of the exam table and Jeremy gently pressed her back down.

"You need to stay right where you are," he told her in a firm tone. "I convinced him to hold off on the arrest until I could talk to you. And now we know the truth, which I will inform him of right away."

"That puts my mind at ease," she said.

"By the way, the Jackson cops mentioned to me they located your truck and had it towed to Whitehall's Auto Repair downtown. The guys there are just waiting for you to claim it and let them know what to do with it."

"It's it in awful shape, I know." She grimaced.

"It isn't great, that's for sure. You can talk with the mechanic, but I bet it will cost an arm and a leg to repair. If it's even repairable."

"That truck is special," Reese said. "I'll pay whatever it takes."

Jeremy lifted a dark brow.

"My grandpa and I rebuilt it. The project consumed us, and we bonded during that time. I never knew my dad, but Gramps took care of me and counseled me like a father. He's gone now, but the truck keeps my memories of him alive. So, I'll go into hock if I have to get it repaired."

THIRTY-SEVEN

JEREMY BEGAN TO pace around the small room as he made some calls to the Jackson police, and his Sage Police Chief, sharing information about what he'd just learned from Reese. When he finished, he moved back over by the examining table.

"By the way, the Chief says the police lab found Vinny's fingerprints all over the knife used to kill Gayle."

"You found the murder weapon?" Reese asked.

Jeremy nodded. "Vinny tossed it in a hallway planter outside the room. I think you had it right—he thought you were in that hotel bed."

"When he followed me into that ravine, he admitted he's pissed about screwing up and not killing me at the hotel," Reese said. "He even tried to finish me off again by shooting at me through the windshield of my truck. I ducked, fortunately, and he missed his opportunity again."

Jeremy looked at her intently. "What else did he say?"

"That boy is a font of information," Reese said. "Vinny admitted he's been in love with Skylar since they were teenagers. He's been waiting for her to realize she should be with him."

"A crush?"

"More like he's obsessed. She was nice to him in high school and he's got it in his mind they should be a couple. He's desperate to have her. When I checked out the trailer where he's been living on his dad's property, I found the walls plastered with her photos."

"Wow," Jeremy said. "Obsession makes for bad business."

"Which is why he was more than willing to kidnap Daisy and bring her to Nina O'Casey," Reese said.

"I'm trying to think now, what's the name of that computer app Jack O'Casey invented—the one the kids are all addicted to? Is it called Blank Stamp?"

She smiled. "I don't think that's the name of it. I keep forgetting to research it. Whatever the name is, it's sure made him a lot of money. He is fabulously wealthy."

"It's hard to believe O'Casey is Daisy's father, but I think it's entirely possible," Jeremy said.

"When I talked with Skylar's friend Audra, she told me that Skylar met Daisy's father at one of her Aunt Polly's parties the summer she worked in Jackson. After I narrowed down the guest list, I figured out it had to be O'Casey. The two hooked up at a bar later that summer. Nine months later, Daisy was born."

"I'm still trying to figure out how Nina factors into this? Why would she want to have her husband's love child kidnapped? And how did she know Daisy belongs to him?"

"I've been trying to figure that out, too." Reese's brain flashed with a conversation she and Skylar had. "Oh my gosh, wait a minute, I remember Skylar mentioning one of the girlfriends who worked with her in Jackson was named Nina. It's got to be her! She and Vinny attended Sage High with Skylar, so they all know each other."

"What tangled webs we weave," Jeremy said, shaking his head.

"Nina went to the bar that night with Skylar and Audra, so she must have seen Skylar leave with O'Casey.

Supposedly Nina took off for college after that, but at some point, she obviously moved to Jackson and managed to convince O'Casey to marry her. Eventually she found out Skylar had a child, guessed that O'Casey was the father, and hatched a plot to pay Vinny to kidnap Daisy and bring her up to Jackson. Vinny was more than willing. He got big money and he also got Daisy out of the way so Skylar could focus on him. Or at least, that's what he hoped would happen."

"I don't understand why Nina would want to kidnap Daisy from Skylar," Jeremy asked. "Why not have her own child or adopt one?"

"I'm not sure," Reese said. "The jury is still out on that one."

"This is complex," Jeremy said. "But then, people are complex."

"It's mind boggling just talking about it. I guess drama like this is what keeps us employed. We become puzzle masters, fitting all the game pieces together."

"Skylar swore to the Sage police she didn't remember the guy she'd left with that night," Jeremy said. "Why would she lie to us?"

"I don't think she did," Reese said. "She honestly couldn't remember him because I believe someone slipped something into her drink. She wasn't conscious enough to know what was going on."

Jeremy's mouth dropped. "O'Casey roofied her? I can't believe he'd do that. He could have anyone he wanted with the money he has. No doubt women are falling at his feet."

"I promised Skylar I wouldn't tell anyone about the incident."

"This is huge," Jeremy said. "You've really done

your homework. You know, Skylar could also press rape charges against O'Casey."

"All these years later she can't really prove anything and she's embarrassed by the whole episode. She doesn't want her family to know, either."

"It's not her fault."

"I told her that, but she doesn't want to go public."

"What O'Casey did is criminal. He shouldn't be walking the streets."

"It's Skylar's call."

"Yeah, well. It's not right." He placed his hands on his hips. "You know, Vincent Warren has been in trouble with the Sage police most of his life. Petty theft, breaking and entering, assault, and more. What was he thinking when he kidnapped Skylar's child? Then when he killed poor Gayle? This will garner him some serious jail time. He'll be locked in the big house for the rest of his life."

Reese shook her head. "From what Skylar told me about Vinny, his mother left when he was little and his father whipped him mercilessly. I think all the beatings he took from his dad have warped his mind."

"That is so awful," Jeremy said. "His father ought to be jailed for doing that. But that's still no excuse for what Vinny's done."

"No, it isn't," Reese said. "But Vinny has developed such severe anger issues that he feels things differently than the rest of us. Skylar was nice to him back in high school, and he's become so obsessed he'd do anything to have her."

"Geez," Jeremy said.

"Again, in his own twisted version of life, Vinny figured Daisy would be treated like a princess living with Nina and Jack. He convinced himself he was doing a good deed."

Jeremy paced for a bit, then met Reese's gaze. "Well, all this craziness is going to come to a halt when we arrest O'Casey and his wife. There's already an APB out for Vinny. I let the Jackson cops know he's up here, so that ought to help them bring him in."

"It's going to make a huge stir around Jackson when you bring in Jack O'Casey and his wife," Reese said. "He's worth billions."

"Yeah, I know. The media will feast on this one. By the way, what else did Daisy say when you posed as the Kinderreim teacher at the O'Caseys'?"

"She's definitely a gifted child, just like Skylar told me. The poor kid says that Nina forces her to call her mama."

"Wait a minute," Jeremy said. "Skylar never mentioned to the Sage police that her daughter was gifted."

"Skylar was upset at the time," Reese said. "It's not surprising she missed some details."

"Yeah, but that would have been good to know."

"She's not a perfect person, but she's doing her best. Just like we all are. That doesn't make her guilty of anything but being human."

"The human factor becomes all too real at times."

Reese snapped her fingers. "I took pictures of Dawna, er, Daisy on my cell phone. Hopefully it's charged enough now to be able to text them to you."

She checked her phone which was still plugged it into a wall socket and sitting on the examination table next to her. It barely had any juice.

"Once this puppy is charged more, I'll send you the photo."

"I'll watch for it," Jeremy said.

Reese withdrew the crumpled grocery list from her purse. "Dawna was chewing gum when I talked to her.

When she spit it out, I grabbed it and wrapped it up in this. If the lab can extract DNA, you can see if it matches with Skylar's."

"I don't know, but it's worth a try." He narrowed his gaze at her. "Man, when you take on a case, you are like a dog with a bone."

"Well, thanks, I think."

Reese grinned, pleased she'd located Daisy, and pleased her search for the girl should end on a positive note. Her confidence in her abilities had begun to soar once again, and she thanked her lucky stars to be getting her life back on track.

And to be a big part of getting a little girl back to her home where she belonged. Now, it was just a matter of extricating the girl from the O'Casey home.

THIRTY-EIGHT

AFTER JEREMY LEFT, the nurse came in again to check on Reese. All about patient care, she looked over Reese's computer chart, and assured her a doctor would be coming soon.

Did medical staff ever find themselves bored of the same old routine? Probably not. For every tedious task there must be an intense hospital occurrence. As a patient, Reese was definitely bored and she wanted to be free.

How long had she been holed up in this examination room? She glanced at her watch, noting it had only been 20 minutes. The staff must be really busy, and since she hadn't suffered any serious wounds, she'd be low on the priority list.

She grabbed a remote control and flipped on a TV program about space aliens that held her interest for a couple of minutes, then she got tired of it. The four walls seemed to close in and her and she wanted to be on her way. The idea of hanging around this place much longer nearly gave her a case of the heebie-jeebies.

Hospitals were definitely not her thing.

A short time later, a doctor in a long white jacket entered her room. He was tall and wore black rimmed glasses. He reminded Reese of the college instructor she'd had in calculus. Professor Randall had been an old codger, stuffy and long-winded, but he knew his stuff.

"I'm Dr. Hill," he said as he studied the bump on her forehead. "I'm so sorry about the wait."

"Not a problem," Reese said.

"How are you feeling after your accident?"

"Fine," she said. "I wouldn't be here, except the police officer who helped me felt I should be looked at."

"It's always a good idea," the doctor said. He used a pin light to look at her eyes, then looked at her chart. "Better safe than sorry."

"True," she said.

"Your vitals all look normal," he said, lifting his bushy gray brows. "Are you experiencing any pain at all from that bump on your forehead?"

"Honestly, I feel fine," she said. "It was just a rough day at the office."

He chuckled. "What do you do for a living?"

"I'm a private investigator."

"I'd hate to have your job," he responded.

"I'm sure you would." She met his gaze. "Can I go now?"

He stepped over to read her computer chart. "You're a bit dehydrated, so try to drink plenty of fluids."

"Will do."

"It's good you're not in any pain, but if anything comes up, and you start feeling bad, don't hesitate to come back and let us check you out. Sometimes the residual effects of an incident can cause problems."

"Thank you, Dr. Hill," Reese said. "I appreciate it. So, I can go now?"

"You sure can."

When he bid her goodbye and left, she picked up her cell, now charged a bit more, and texted Dawna's picture to Jeremy. Tucking her phone and charger into her purse, she left the room and walked out of the double doors past the nurse's station. She nodded at the staff and thanked them, and they all wished her well.

She pushed through the ER doors and made her way outside. After calling a Lyft and registering her credit card, she waited in front of the two-story, tan stucco hospital. Warmth washed over her as the glowing summer sun showered her skin. The antiseptic smell of hospitals bothered her, so she welcomed the reviving fresh air.

The mountains and the arching blue sky reassured her that even though her world had been on hold for a time while she waited in the emergency room, the earth had continued spinning.

When the driver arrived in a dark blue sedan, she slid into the back seat and shut the door, smelling a pine-scented air freshener.

"Where to?" he asked, a curious expression on his face as he perused her dirty clothing and wild hair. She figured the lump on her forehead added to her unusual appearance.

"Somewhere I can rent a car," she said, pulling a brush from her purse and doing her best to straighten her fly-away tresses.

"That would be the airport." He wheeled through the drop off loop, passed by the Emergency Room entrance, and headed downtown.

A young guy, the driver continued glancing at her in his rearview mirror. Uncomfortable with his perusal, Reese stared out of the window at the colorful cityscape imprinted with western flair.

"I know I look like death warmed over," she finally said. "I had a little car accident and had to hike a distance to find help."

"I'm sorry to hear that happened," he said. "Are you sure you're all right?"

"I'm really fine," she said.

He continued to keep an eye on her as he drove through Jackson. Reese decided he was worried she'd keel over any minute and he'd be stuck with her. But honestly, except for her forehead being a bit sore, she was none the worse for wear. The idea of her beat up truck sitting at the shop didn't sit well with her. However, that was another story.

Eventually the driver pulled in front of the one-level airport constructed of timber beams and huge glass windows. The jagged Teton Mountains provided a colorful, breathtaking backdrop.

"You'll find all the typical car rental places in here," he said, relief evident in his voice. "Enterprise, Hertz, and more."

"Thanks for the ride," she said, reaching up to hand him a tip.

"Appreciate it," His eyes widened when he saw the bill denomination. "Have a good day, ma'am."

She got out of the car, closed the door and headed inside the airport. After she got some wheels, she intended to head back to her hotel. A hot shower literally called to her, and she knew it would revive her. Then she'd put on clean clothes and head to the auto body shop to talk to one of their mechanics about fixing up Betty.

THIRTY-NINE

STANDING AT WHITEHALL'S AUTO REPAIR beside a grease-smudged mechanic named Max, Reese's heart plummeted. She stared at Betty's beat-up frame and dented exterior, knowing the poor old gal needed major work done to bring her up to speed.

And it wouldn't be cheap.

As Max listed everything that needed to be repaired on the Bronco, Reese's gut twisted. It felt like someone had punched her with a meaty fist.

"You sure you want to fix 'er up?" he asked.

Reese strained to hear over the explosion of noise in the shop. A couple of mechanics were busy working on other vehicles, the roaring and clacking equipment hammering in her hears.

"Definitely," she said in a loud voice.

"Come with me." Max ushered her into the store area. She glanced at the shelves full of air filters, cans of oil, tire displays and other automobile paraphernalia, not really seeing them.

She was too concerned about her truck.

"There may be even more things that need to be fixed," Max added, shaking his head. "I won't know for sure until I look 'er over. My suggestion is you scrap the truck. The junk yard might pay couple hundred dollars for the scrap metal."

"No," she insisted. "I'd like you to fix my truck."

"We're talking a couple thousand. Maybe more," he

said, wiping his hands on a dirty rag. "That's a lot of dough. You could purchase another good, used vehicle for that."

"I don't care, Max," she said, stubbornly refusing to part with Betty.

When her cell phone chimed, she reached into her purse and silenced the ringer. Advocating for Betty's future was too critical right now. Later, she'd find out who had called and check back with them.

Reese jotted her cell phone number on a yellow sticky note and handed it to Max.

"Call me with when you have an estimate," she said. "That way I'll have a good idea of how much it will take for my Bronco to be roadworthy again."

"You're the boss," he said. "Just so you know, the truck will be out of commission for a while. But you've come to the right place. My specialty is fixing up old junkers."

Reese winced—she hated hearing Max refer to her baby as an "old junker." Nevertheless, she appreciated that he felt confident to perform the needed repairs that would bring Betty back to life.

"That's fine," she told him. "Take whatever time you need. I'll talk to you later."

He held up a hand in farewell and disappeared back into the shop.

Reese walked outside into the sunshine; feeling deflated at the idea of her truck being in such bad condition. The afternoon sun blazed over Jackson like a giant heating element. As she walked to her rental car, a Subaru Forester, she dug into her briefcase and withdrew her cell phone.

"Jeremy," she murmured when she recognized his

number on her missed calls. She punched his number and waited until he answered.

"Hey, Reese," he said.

"Hey yourself," she returned. "What's up?"

"A judge signed off on that arrest warrant for the O'Caseys. Me and a couple of Jackson cops are almost at their house."

"Hallelujah," Reese said. "I'll head up there right now."

"Reese, stay put," he growled. "Things up here are… complicated."

"What does that mean?"

"It means you need to stay where you are."

She laughed. "I've been out for a couple of hours now. I got a rental car and I've just finished checking on my truck."

"You should go back to your hotel room and rest, then."

"I've got too much going on to roll around in bed like a hot dog on a rotisserie," Reese insisted.

"You don't need to come up to the O'Caseys', Reese. It's a police matter, anyway."

"I won't interfere. I just want to see justice served. Besides, Dawna will be frightened and she knows me. By a different name, of course. But it might help her."

"Seriously, stay put," Jeremy insisted.

"Buh, bye now."

"Reese!"

She hung up, jumped in the Forester, and wheeled out of Whitehall's parking lot. Determination coursed through her blood as she drove toward the Gros Ventre neighborhood where the O'Caseys lived.

Was Dawna O'Casey actually Daisy Ellington? She felt certain of it. DNA results would tell the full truth, but

Reese believed they would prove her theory. After all, the kid knew her name was Daisy and she had talked about her mother, her grandmother, and her Uncle Chance.

Reese couldn't wait to tell Skylar that her instincts had been right all along.

Her daughter was alive.

FORTY

THE BREATHTAKING VIEWS along the drive to the O'Caseys' mansion dazzled Reese, just as they had during the first trip she'd made up here. The lofty green mountains, the thick, fringed patches of forest, the arching blue sky— the combination of nature at its finest. If she had been asked to caption a photograph of the place, she would call it "Heaven on Earth."

Cliché, but true.

She passed by the area where Vinny had used his SUV to push her Bronco over the steep incline. A breath caught in her throat. That lunatic had been crafty enough to make sure he made the final shove to her truck right before a guard rail would have provided safety. No wonder she'd lost control and Betty had crashed down the steep incline, ending up in a tangle of trees and undergrowth.

A shiver rocketed up her spine. She forced herself to look away and focused on the winding, curvy road. It didn't do any good to obsess over what had happened. If that creep thought she was that easy to shake off, he was a fool.

Turning off onto Huckleberry Drive, she drove toward the O'Caseys' two-story stone mansion that fronted a beautiful, glassy blue lake. Just as before, the place looked pristine and gorgeous.

Too fancy for her taste.

However, the expansive estate was surrounded by police cars with flashing lights. A white van, marked with block lettering that spelled out COUNTY CORONER, sat in the parking area, setting Reese's mind abuzz.

This should be a simple arrest, so why bring in the coroner?

There are complications, Reese recalled Jeremy telling her. Why hadn't he explained what that meant?

A sense of foreboding washed over her as she parked the Forester and scrambled out from behind the steering wheel. Shutting the driver's door, she began walking toward the hive of activity.

She desperately wanted to catch a glance of the O'Caseys being hauled to the tank. Deep down, she had a sense of foreboding and knew that would most likely not happen.

The sound of squawking police radios bounced through the air, along with the serious voices of law enforcement types in uniform. A couple of the officers gave her firm glances as she walked up to them, and she knew they would bark at her to leave.

Jeremy came up behind her, took her arm and whispered harshly. "You sure don't listen, do you?"

"Nope." She nodded toward the house, where cops trotted in and out. One had begun stringing up yellow crime scene tape. "What's the story?"

"I'm not at liberty to discuss this," Jeremy said. "You should go back to your hotel. I'll call you later."

Reese shoved her hands on her hips and glared at him. "Cut the crap, Jeremy. I'm Detective Reese Golden, formerly of the Denver Police Department."

"Emphasis on the formerly," Jeremy said.

"I outrank you, buddy. And this is definitely not my first rodeo. Believe me, I've seen it all."

"This doesn't involve you, Reese."

"The hell it doesn't! I'm working on a case, too. I'm trying to find Daisy Ellington, and the O'Caseys are an important lead."

"You're lucky I like you," Jeremy said, his nostrils flaring. "It's against my better judgment, but I'll read you in on this. Shit, I'll show you since you insist on knowing every detail."

"What will you tell them?" Reese glanced at the cops guarding the entrance.

"I'll make up something," he growled.

Irritated by Jeremy's behavior, albeit happy he'd relented, she followed him to the front door. The uniforms shot them stern looks.

"Officer Jeremy Savage of the Sage Police Department," Jeremy told them, whipping out his badge. "And this is Reese Golden, a professional consultant I've called in. Let us pass."

The uniforms stood aside.

Reese followed Jeremy into the O'Caseys' abode, once again overwhelmed by the lavish décor and tall windows that allowed panoramic views of the surrounding mountain wilderness. Having been raised in humble environments, where money was carefully budgeted, she found it difficult to imagine what it would be like to be so wealthy.

She walked beside Jeremy and entered the home's grand dining room where she'd sat with Dawna for her Kinderreim School "interview."

Her nostrils twitched as the distinctive scent of death assailed her and she quelled her gag reflex—something she'd always had difficulty accomplishing, despite her years of crime scene investigation.

Then she saw the deceased. Two people had collapsed

beside the table, gripping their throats, their complexions set with a gray pallor.

Forks rested on the polished wooden floorboards next to each body. On the table sat three place settings, but only two China plates held food. The other shiny round surface bore not a single morsel.

As she and Jeremy walked closer, Reese recognized the victims—Vinny Warren and Jack O'Casey. Her mind flashed with theory after theory about who had done them in and why. She had so many thoughts running through her head, she couldn't utter a word.

Murder, most foul, had been accomplished in one of the most beautiful homes Reese had seen in her life. It demonstrated that homicide holds no class barriers.

CSI processors worked the area, testing items and dropping things in evidence bags. A woman in a dark brown jacket with the words "Teton County Coroner" examined the corpses while talking with another individual in an identical jacket.

"Son of a…banana," Reese finally said, her respect for the recently deceased preventing her from speaking the word she honestly had intended. "It looks like those two were poisoned. What's the COD or do they know yet?"

"From her initial examination, Eve Billings, the coroner, agrees with you that it looks like poison." Jeremy rubbed the back of his neck. "She estimates these two have been dead for a couple of hours or so. She won't know for certain until she examines them closer in her morgue."

Reese frowned. "Where are Nina and Dawna?"

"We haven't located them anywhere," Jeremy said.

"Maybe O'Casey had enemies and that's who did this," Reese said. "It's possible Nina and Dawna weren't here or they got away and are running scared."

"There's any number of things that could have happened," Jeremy said.

"Or Nina might have poisoned these guys," Reese said, shocked by the woman's potential cunning. "Which would be strange—I figured Jack O'Casey had helped orchestrate Daisy's kidnapping."

"It's hard to say right now," Jeremy said, folding his arms across his chest. He shot her a look that suggested he didn't want to speculate further.

Reese's mind always worked overtime when she handled homicides. She'd spent many sleepless nights trying to string together evidence and come up with plausible theories.

Jeremy sighed. "I know what you're thinking."

"Really?"

"Let's go outside for some fresh air."

"Sounds like a top-notch idea to me," she said, more than agreeable to comply.

Reese walked with Jeremy past the cops and CSI workers, out into the bright sunshine. They stopped beside a bristling blue spruce tree standing in a rock garden speckled with colorful wildflowers and tall, ornamental grass.

"What's on your mind?" Reese asked Jeremy.

"I saw some gossip on the Internet a while ago that O'Casey had some beefs with a competitor who said he'd stolen his social media idea," he said. "I think his enemies ordered a hit. I don't think they took Nina and the girl because there's no signs of a scuffle. I bet they are running scared, just like you suggested."

"Where would they be?"

"I've done some background investigation on Nina. I think she took Dawna and flew with her to Hawaii, which is where her parents retired. Nina probably hopes the goons won't find them there."

"What about Vinny Warren? Why would he be killed, too?"

"Collateral damage."

Reese shook her head. "If O'Casey had made an enemy by stealing intellectual property, a pissed off competitor would have ordered him shot dead in the street or run over and smooshed like a pancake."

Jeremy knitted his brows. "That's probably more likely, now that you mention it."

"It sends a message to others in the biz not to steal, otherwise they'll wind up being someone's hood ornament."

"Yeah, I'll bet," he said.

"The scene is pretty clean, as in someone didn't want to make a mess. Someone tricked those guys into eating food that had been poisoned. Someone they trusted. Females overwhelmingly choose poison as a preferred method for murder."

"Complicated, but entirely plausible."

"I don't see it as complicated," Reese said. "Vinny and Nina were working together—that much I know. She realized we were closing in on the truth. Everyone associated with Dawna, er, Daisy's kidnapping needed to go."

"She's got plenty of money to high tail it out of the country," Jeremy said. "She's made it all the way to Timbuktu by now in that case."

"It might be difficult to find her," Reese said, a pit of disappointment forming in her gut.

She decided if her theory about Nina was correct, she could hardly believe the woman's depravity. She'd orchestrated the kidnapping of an innocent child and killed two people! It was amazing the lengths Nina would go to have her way.

What had driven her to such desperation?

"There's not much to be done now," Jeremy said. "At least until CSI's collected their evidence and detectives comb through it. Then maybe they'll be able to come up with some ideas."

"Meanwhile, a little girl has been taken away from her rightful family," Reese postulated. "Technically, she's being held hostage. Hopefully Nina's taking care of her."

"She hasn't hurt her all this time," Jeremy said.

"Dawna claims she can get mean."

"How can anybody be mean to a kid?" Jeremy snarled. "It's disturbing."

"I'm not willing to wait around for the local cops to come up with a theory about what happened here," Reese said. "It could take weeks."

"Hold on there, lady. I don't like the sound of that. And the tone in your voice, well, I've heard it before. You're gonna go and do something stupid."

"You know me too well, Jeremy." Reese grinned.

"It's not funny," Jeremy shot back. "Last time you did something on a whim you wound up in a ditch."

"Hazards of the job," she returned.

"I'm warning you, let the police handle this."

"You know I'm not going to. That's one of the reasons I left the DPD. I got tired of being told to stand down, when I knew better."

"You went rogue," he said.

"Not rogue. I just wanted to handle things using my own set of rules. And a big part of those rules is to follow my gut instinct."

Jeremy rubbed his chin. "You've got that gleam in your eye. And it's not good."

"I'm not asking you to do anything," Reese said, then paused and added, "Except help me find a way into the O'Caseys' house again. I want a closer look."

"No way."

"Please?"

He glared at her.

"I want to try and find something that would hint about where Nina went," Reese said as she studied him. "It's long shot, but I'm not willing to give up yet, when we were so close to rescuing Daisy."

"You don't even know Nina's on the run," he growled. "She could have taken the kid and gone to a friend's wedding or something like that."

"We're wasting time," Reese said. "I know more about what's been going with this family than the cops do. If I'm wrong, I'm wrong. But I'm willing to take that chance. Skylar hired me to find answers."

He groaned. "If someone sees you—"

"I'll say I got lost trying to find a bathroom. You've already vouched for me by telling the Jackson uniforms I'm a special consultant."

Several emotions crossed Jeremy's face, and she knew he felt conflicted. She always found it difficult to explain to people how she relied on her best judgement. They never understood, and in all truth, neither did she. Nevertheless, she'd learned from experience not to ignore her hunches.

Especially with this case, considering little Daisy's future was hanging in the balance, she insisted on sticking to her guns. The girl knew who she was and she wanted to go home. Reese couldn't ignore that.

"Obviously, there's no stopping you when you're on the prowl." Jeremy held up his hands in frustration. "As I said before, you're like a dog—"

"With a bone," Reese finished. "Yeah, yeah, I know. Think of the possible end result. Think how wonderful it will be to reunite Skylar Ellington with her daughter."

"Far be it from me to put a kink in your plans," he told Reese as he began walking toward the mansion. "You didn't manage to pull off your last acting gig as a teacher very well."

"I'll do better this time," Reese assured him as she kept pace with his long strides.

FORTY-ONE

WHEN REESE AND Jeremy re-entered the O'Casey mansion, the police guards stopped them.

Jeremy flashed his badge and nodded at Reese.

"Remember, Officers, she's the special consultant I told you about."

"Roger that," one of the officers said.

Reese nodded at the guards, then followed Jeremy into the dining room. The same cops continued to mill around, along with the coroner. The harsh odors assailed her again. The room looked the same as when she'd been in here a short time ago, when she'd been focusing on the crime scene.

Now she noted a missing object.

"I didn't see before, but it's gone," she told Jeremy, putting a hand on his arm.

He frowned. "What's gone?"

"When I met with Dawna, there was a framed photograph of Josephina Lake hanging over there by that big China hutch."

Jeremy looked at the empty spot. "Maybe the O'Caseys were in the middle of redecorating."

"I think somebody took it."

"Who?"

"I don't know, yet."

"Okay, but I don't understand where you're going with this."

"The O'Caseys own a cabin up there. It's mostly hidden by trees and foliage. Dawna told me that's her favorite place. She calls it the Lady Lake."

"I'm not following." Jeremy looked irritated.

"It's a perfect place to hide. Remote and difficult to find."

"You think Nina took the kid up there?"

She nodded.

"Nah, with all the money she's got, if she killed those guys, more than likely she's hot-footed it out of the country." He nodded toward the bodies. "She doesn't want to be caught."

"Nina's not Dawna's real mother, so she wouldn't have a birth certificate for her, which means she couldn't order a passport. That would make international travel impossible. I think it's more likely she'd hide out at the lake."

Jeremy shook his head. "She could have claimed she had Dawna during a home birth and requested a birth certificate from the county. But I'm betting that if she's on the run, she'd take the kid to Hawaii."

"That's the first place the cops will look for her," Reese said. "Nina may not be a hardened criminal, but she's no dummy."

Jeremy crossed his arms over his chest. "I'm not buying it. Especially since we don't even know for sure who murdered these guys."

"Like I said, I've got a hunch," Reese said. Pressing an index finger against her mouth to keep him from saying anything, she slipped from the room and went down a hall. Breathing softly, she leaned against a wooden panel, hoping not to be noticed.

No one called out, telling her to halt. Encouraged she'd made good her escape, she glanced around. From her viewpoint, she could see into the kitchen where investigators wearing blue latex gloves processed the area.

Hurrying across the foyer, careful to step softly so her boots didn't make noise, Reese headed up the staircase. She checked in several bedrooms, once again, lavishly decorated, but with no signs of activity.

She found the master, which featured a large bathroom complete with a jet tub, double shower and a room size walk-in closet. Clothes had been tossed haphazardly across beds, dressers and the floor. It appeared someone had packed in a big hurry.

In the next bedroom Reese entered, she found it decorated in soft shades of pink, yellow and green. It contained a juvenile bed, small scale furniture and girly decorations that left no doubt in her mind she'd found Dawna's room.

The child's clothing had been thrown around, just like in the master bedroom. Once again, there were signs someone had packed in a hurry. Absent from the row of stuffed animals on top of the dresser was Squiggles, Dawna's favorite purple bunny that she'd clung to during Reese's interview with her.

Wedged between the mass of furry bodies, where Squiggles had been, sat the missing photograph of Josephina Lake.

"Bingo," Reese murmured, a sense of urgency rushing through her mind.

The photograph wouldn't ring a bell for the police. They wouldn't understand the significance.

However, since Reese had talked with Dawna about the O'Casey family's visits up there, she had a good idea where Nina had taken the girl.

Clever and precocious, Dawna, really Daisy, had sensed danger when Nina began packing to leave. The little girl must have been very frightened, especially if she'd seen the bodies in the dining room, so she'd managed to leave the best clue.

FORTY-TWO

REESE LEFT DAWNA'S room and headed back down the stairs. She stopped by the dining room, where the CSI activity continued to hum as staff members finished their investigation.

Reese nudged Jeremy with her elbow. "I'm headed out," she told him.

"You going back to your hotel?"

"No. I'm going up to Josephina Lake."

Jeremy's brows arched. "Reese, that's in the middle of nowhere."

Fishing her phone from her purse, Reese punched Josephina Lake into her iPhone map. "Yep, you're right."

She held up the illustration on her device.

Jeremy frowned. "You and your wild ideas. How'd you even come up with that?"

"Remember the framed photograph that I noticed had gone missing?"

He glanced at the empty spot by the China hutch. "Sure."

"I found it in Dawna's room. I think she climbed on a chair, hauled it down, and left it as a clue."

"You watch too many police shows on TV."

"I could consult on TV cop shows," Reese returned.

"I think you're pushing the envelope on this."

"It's my time and my gas, so I'm taking a road trip."

"Another wild goose chase," Jeremy said.

"Or not," Reese said.

"I'd go with you but I'm needed back in Sage." Jeremy's expression lined with concern. "The Chief gave me direct orders to return this afternoon."

"I can handle this."

"Somebody's got to keep you out of trouble."

"It's cool. If Nina and Dawna aren't there, I'll head back to Jackson. If they are…"

"That's right, if they are, what are you going to do?"

"I'll figure something out."

"No, you shouldn't. You ought to head back down to Jackson and let the cops know."

Reese nodded. "Maybe."

"Maybe what?"

"Maybe I'll think about it," she answered. "It depends on what I find."

"You absolutely should not chase after them."

"I absolutely should," she said. "My client is counting on me."

"Don't try to be a hero," Jeremy said. "You aren't a cop anymore. You won't have backup. And you don't have a gun."

Reese tapped her sore forehead. "I've got my wits."

"Which got knocked around when your truck wound up in the ravine." He frowned. "Next time somebody comes after you, you might not be so lucky."

"I'm not leaving that kid up there with Nina, if that's where they are. That woman's not in her right mind. Who knows what she'll do?"

"True, but you're not a one person police force, either."

Reese understood some of what Jeremy was worried about—he'd never seen her in action when she'd been on active duty. He didn't know how she'd handled herself as a cop while working the streets, and he wasn't familiar with the tough cases she'd solved as a detective.

She wouldn't allow him to prevent her from doing her job, no matter what reservations he had. She liked him, but she wasn't going to let him sway her confidence.

The confidence she'd managed to restore from the ashes. The confidence that now surged through her veins and pushed her forward.

"Give me some credit, will you? I've been in tight spots before." She turned around and began walking out the door.

"Wait," Jeremy growled.

She looked over her shoulder at him, pressing her lips into a firm line.

"At least call and let me know when you arrive," he said. "Or text. Either way, stay in touch."

She lifted a brow.

"Please," he added.

"I will," she said, then left the room and walked from the O'Casey mansion.

"Hang on, Daisy," she whispered as she headed toward the Forester. "I got your message loud and clear."

FORTY-THREE

REESE SETTLED IN for the long drive up to Josephina Lake. Just as when she'd traveled up to Sage, the radio stations soon faded into static.

Without Betty and her favorite cassette tapes, she needed to summon some creativity to survive nail-biting boredom. To bide her time, she began singing, making up words when she didn't remember them.

After an hour of driving through forested landscape and grassy meadows on a two-lane asphalt road, her iPhone map directed her to turn onto a dirt road, which appeared to have been built long ago. A brown sign outlined in white called it, "Wilderness River Road. OPEN."

"That's a relief," Reese muttered to herself, glad there hadn't been bad weather that would have prevented her passage. Although if that had been the case, Nina wouldn't have been able to travel up to the cabin, either.

Maybe only 14 feet wide, the road barely presented enough room for one vehicle travel, let alone two. The rugged dirt pathway began to climb up higher and higher, offering a rocky incline to her right and grassy hill on her left. In the distance, a mountain pass covered in evergreens offered a breathtaking view.

A clear blue sky adorned with wispy white cirrus clouds arched overhead, lending the scene a surreal aspect. A thrill of excitement shot through Reese—it felt like she'd climbed to the top of the world.

Then she thought of poor Daisy trapped with crazy Nina,

and she sobered. The woman was highly dangerous—she'd killed two people without reservation.

Her husband and her friend.

Reese slowed down to about 15 miles per hour in order to safely handle the frequent hairpin turns. The steeper the road went, the more rugged the rocky landscape became. It looked like giants had hacked out the brown and gray boulders and stacked them in odd formations.

At last the terrain leveled out, offering a wide vista of grassy mountaintops. Although it was August, dirty brown snow remained crusted along ridges and filled crevasses.

The tree-lined road led her down an incline a short distance, then a valley opened up to reveal a blue lake with a mirrored surface reflecting the flora and fauna. Pine- and spruce-covered mountains ringed the watery feature like towering sentinels assigned to guard the pristine beauty.

Reese decided the real lake displayed more exquisite character than the framed photograph Daisy had hidden in her room. But of course, that made sense. Everything was better in person. No wonder Daisy loved it here.

Not right now, Reese guessed. Not under the current circumstances.

Lord only knew how unbalanced Nina was behaving right now, considering her recent erratic behavior. With the police closing in on the truth about Daisy's kidnapping, Nina had become so desperate, she'd silenced her husband by poisoning him, and clueless Vinny had received the same death sentence.

Nina wanted Dawna/Daisy all to herself. The question Reese wanted answered was why? What made the little girl so special that Nina would commit murder and risk everything to have her?

Reese noticed a few other vacation homes nestled in the mountain landscape. Then she finally spotted the O'Caseys' cabin near the lake's edge, nearly hidden by trees, bushes and fallen logs. Because of the concealing undergrowth, she couldn't see a vehicle anywhere.

Was Nina really here?

Refusing to allow doubts to weaken her resolve, Reese pushed them from her mind.

A pullout along the road came into view, and she edged the Forester onto the gravel spot and parked. Fortunately, an outcropping hid her vehicle from prying eyes, mainly those of Nina O'Casey, so no one would be able to spot it.

She got out of the car and closed the door. Peering around a boulder, she studied the visible parts of the O'Casey cabin. She couldn't simply drive up to the place. The motor would alert Nina to her presence and destroy the element of surprise. And she couldn't walk up and knock on the door like a neighbor wanting to borrow a cup of sugar.

She needed to take stock of the cabin's layout and see what advantages she may be able to use against Nina. It was also important she find out where Dawna was. Above all, Reese prioritized keeping the little girl safe.

Recalling she'd promised to keep Jeremy apprised of her activity, she removed her cell phone from her back pocket and texted him.

"I'm at the lake," she texted him.

"Be careful," he responded. "Let cops do the dirty work. You're only on a scouting mission."

Ignoring Jeremy's request, Reese entered the forest and began hiking down the slope toward the O'Casey cabin. Birds called to each other and insects buzzed as all of nature followed its well-ordered day. When the cool, camouflaging depths swallowed Reese, she realized that she, too, was following her own well-ordered day.

The next item on her agenda: finding a kidnapped child and dealing with a murderer.

FORTY-FOUR

REESE WADED THROUGH a shallow creek, careful not to slip on the wet stones. Arriving on the other side, she pushed aside leafy branches. She stepped forward, doing her best to keep her boots from crunching too loudly on fallen forest debris.

She stopped beside a cluster of bushes, then realized it was actually camouflage netting. Lifting up the cover, she recognized the black SUV Vinny had used to force Betty off the road. Scratches raked across the paint on the side where he'd pushed her vehicle. Apparently, Vinny must have borrowed the vehicle from Nina.

He'd trusted Nina, but he shouldn't have, because he was dead now. Vinny's obsession with Skylar had made him vulnerable and he'd taken chances with Nina, his friend from high school, and that had gotten him killed.

All because he'd been obsessed with Skylar.

Reese continued moving slowly toward the cabin. She kept her gaze attuned to her surroundings, checking for signs of life as she parted the underbrush.

Halting behind a bush, she stared at a small A-Frame cabin that jutted from a clearing—an island buried in deep green undergrowth. The porch held a stack of firewood. Stumps, obviously used as seating, circled an outdoor firepit. Used paper plates, cups and plastic utensils littered the top of a metal table.

She glanced up at the sky, noting the orange and pink clouds on the western horizon. Twilight shadows gathered, and she realized the light would soon fade. Pushing aside branches, she made her way through the woods. Then she stepped over beside a large propane tank to peer through a cabin window.

A charcoal-colored couch dominated one corner, with a large, matching footstool resting in front of it. A nubby blue rug covered the floor. On the other side of the room, a basic kitchen appeared behind a tall counter featuring three bar stools. Two lit kerosene lamps flickered on a log hewn table in front of a black coal stove.

When Nina appeared holding a box, Reese scooted behind a tall shrub. She dared to peek again, noting Nina had put the box on the floor and now assembled a small, artificial Christmas tree. She pulled sparkly silver tinsel garland from the box and draped it across the fluffy branches.

What the heck?

The calendar said it was August, not December. But it appeared Nina planned to decorate for the winter holiday. After committing murder and going on the run, she'd obviously lost her mind.

Reese narrowed her gaze, noting Nina wore a pink dress, heels and a white apron decorated with red rick rack and dancing gingerbread men. An image of Betty Crocker, like the one on her grandmother's old cookbook, popped into Reese's mind.

What in the world was going on with Nina?

Reese tensed—the woman must be having a mental breakdown. This was crazy. As a police officer, she'd seen people lose their minds plenty of times when they became desperate. Most important, Reese needed to handle this in a sensitive manner, otherwise Nina might panic and hurt Daisy.

"Come out of your bedroom, Dawna," Nina called.

"It's your job to hang the ornaments. You know Daddy expects you to help me."

Dawna said something Reese couldn't hear well through the glass window panes.

"What dear?" Nina asked.

"It's not Christmas," Daisy shouted. "And I don't want to hang ornaments on your stupid tree."

"Come now, Dawna, you shouldn't talk back to me like that. When your father arrives to have dinner with us, he'll be disappointed that you aren't cooperating." Nina continued looping the garland, a lopsided grin on her face. "Come on now. You need to do your job or I'll have to punish you."

Oh, Lord. Poor Daisy.

With a sober expression, Daisy, who wore a My Little Pony nightgown, plodded barefoot into the living area. One by one, she dragged sparkling baubles from green tissue paper. Standing on tip toe, she lifted them as high as she could reach, hooking them on branches.

"That's a good girl," Nina said in an encouraging tone. She pulled an angel from the box and handed the blue and gold item to Dawna. Then she lifted the little girl up so she could place it atop the tree. Returning Dawna to the floor, Nina clapped.

Reese's gut churned, and she looked away from the bizarre show. At first glance, the scene in the O'Caseys' cabin appeared to be that of a mother and child putting up a Christmas tree.

Except the holidays were several months away. It looked like a scene from the Twilight Zone.

FORTY-FIVE

WHEN NINA WALKED from the room, stating she needed to get more decorations from the closet, Daisy started crying. She plopped down in a rocking chair and wiped her eyes with her balled fists. Her thin shoulders shook with each sob.

Reese gritted her teeth, outraged that this innocent young child should have to suffer the consequences of Nina O'Casey's mental breakdown. She'd been kidnapped from her bed, brought all the way up to Jackson and forced to live a lie for weeks. Enough was enough.

I've got to get the kid out of there.

Daisy must be so confused. That broke Reese's heart. Her mind began humming with ideas of how to handle Nina. She was no psychologist, but she knew she'd need to be very careful not to set off the deranged woman so that she would lose it completely.

The sound of a branch breaking alerted her, and she spun around.

Nina stood in front of Reese; a pistol pointed directly at her chest. Slowly, Reese raised her hands.

"Nina, I'm not here to hurt you," Reese said, cursing herself silently for not being more alert. "I'm only asking you to think about what you're doing."

"Well, well, well." Nina gave a wicked laugh. "Will you be joining us for Christmas dinner?"

"Depends what's on the menu," Reese said, then swallowed hard. All the moisture had drained from her mouth. It felt like someone had shoved a wad of cotton on top of her tongue.

"I'm afraid we're not cooking anything fancy this year," Nina drawled. "How does dead preschool teacher sound to you?"

Reese stared at the crazed woman, unable to speak. One concern rattled in her brain.

Am I ready to meet my maker?

"You lied to me," Nina snapped.

Reese's thoughts played with the idea of what it would be like to die, but she did her best to listen to Nina's words. Staring at the gun, she decided she did not want to get shot again. Once was enough.

"Why do you think that?" Honestly, Reese couldn't recall at the moment what she'd done to deserve that comment.

"You aren't from the Kinderreim School."

"Oh, r-right. I'm not. I'm sorry about that." Reese cleared her throat and decided the best course of action was to tell the truth and try to make friends with Nina, perhaps gaining her trust. "I'm a private investigator. Skylar Ellington hired me to find her daughter."

"When you left my house after Dawna's interview, Vinny told me who you were and what you were doing. He came to hide out at my house after he killed that hotel maid. Too bad he couldn't manage to kill you, but he bungled all his attempts." Nina rolled her eyes. "I can't stand fools."

"Is that why you felt like you needed to poison him?" Reese asked. "And your husband? Their being alive threatened everything you'd worked hard to accomplish, didn't it?"

"Of course, and maybe you understand why I only did what I had to do," Nina said. "Unfortunately for Vinny and Jack, I considered them only useful idiots. Jack even bought my story that we'd gotten Dawna through a private adoption. He was so busy with his company that he didn't concern himself with minor details. He simply scribbled his name on the adoption paperwork I'd drafted in our home office. The dolt never even realized Dawna is his real daughter. He played right into my plan."

"What do you mean?"

"Jack married me and gave me the lifestyle I deserved." Nina's nostrils flared. "And Vinny, well, he kept an eye on Skylar and let me know what she was up to. He told me about Dawna and I finally convinced him to take her away from Skylar so I could give her the best of everything."

"Dawna isn't your daughter," Reese said. "She doesn't belong to you."

"Yes, she does." Nina stood taller.

"How do you figure?"

"It goes way back, you see. From the time she was born, Skylar got whatever she ever wanted. She was her daddy's pampered princess. She had the best toys, the best clothes, the best birthday parties and anything else she whined about. Growing up, she learned to ride horses and became a barrel jumper. She modeled, she traveled to Paris and England on high school trips. As valedictorian of our class, she got special attention. It wasn't fair."

"I never had any special advantages growing up," Reese said. "Not all of us do. It's just how life works out sometimes."

"You don't understand. She got the life I deserved to have. Then after graduation, when we went up to Jackson to work for the summer, she even got Jack's attention. He was rich and had everything. He should have picked me."

"He was terrible to Skylar. He roofied her, then dumped her in a motel to wake up alone."

Nina roared with laughter. "I put the drugs in Skylar's drink when Jack wasn't looking. He was too stupid to think of doing that. He'd have never gotten past first base on his own, but I dared him to have sex with her. When she didn't protest, he managed just fine."

Reese's mouth dropped open, shocked Nina would do such a thing to her friend. News flash, she had only posed as a friend. It was disgusting, the way people behaved when they were jealous or envious. She'd seen it all too often in her line of work.

One thing continued to confuse her.

"You've known all along Jack is Daisy, er Dawna's father, then."

"Yep," Nina said.

"Why didn't you have your own baby with him? Why kidnap Skylar's child?"

"She doesn't deserve to have Dawna. She couldn't offer her the lifestyle Jack and I have been able to."

"But you could have—"

"I can't have children," she snarled. "if that's what you're going to say. I've got a kidney disorder. The doctor said it would kill me to get pregnant."

"I see," Reese murmured. "I'm so sorry, Nina. I truly am."

Tears rolled down Nina's cheeks. "Once again, Skylar wins the prize. But I'm always damaged goods."

Reese's arms were starting to ache. She wanted desperately to put them down, but she didn't dare move for fear Nina would shoot. Maybe if she sympathized with Nina, the woman would stand down. Psychology wasn't one of her strong suits, but it was worth a try.

"You've really had difficulties," Reese said. "That's

obvious. But resenting Skylar is eating away at you. It's making you ill. Why don't you let it go?"

"Because she's my sister," Nina spat. "Everyone thought Matthew Ellington was the best person, but he was depraved. My mom waited tables at the Sage Diner and he got her pregnant with me, then brushed her aside like a dirty rag. Mom said he never even came to see me when I was born. I didn't exist for him. He lavished all his love and attention on Skylar and her brother."

"That was wrong," Reese said, shocked to find out Skylar's father had a secret love child. "I can see why that upset you. An honest man would have helped you and your mother."

"Right? That's what I've always believed." Nina sniffed and wiped her nose on her sleeve.

"I'd like to be your friend, Nina," Reese said softly. "I want to help you."

"No, you don't," Nina shouted, the gun shaking in her hands. "You'll tell the cops where I am. They'll come to arrest me and take Dawna away. They'll put me in jail."

"Please, Nina," Reese said.

"I have to kill you. That's the only way."

"Mama, why are pointing a gun at Miss Shaw?"

Both Reese and Nina turned to see Dawna approach, her face pale, her expression lined with confusion.

"Dawna! I told you to stay in the cabin," Nina scolded.

"But I heard you guys fighting. I'm scared." Dawna pouted, and huge tears glimmered in her eyes. "I don't like this."

"Baby, go back inside."

Dawna stomped her foot. "No. I don't want to."

"I have to take care of something," Nina insisted. "Then I'll come inside with you. We can make Christmas cookies."

"I won't go." Dawna jutted her small chin, defiance radiating from her small face.

Rage glimmered in Nina's eyes and her face got red. "Dawna Shae O'Casey, go inside the cabin this instant, otherwise I'll be forced to punish you."

Dawna stared at Nina, but wouldn't budge.

"Nina," Reese said, amazed by the four-year-old's bravery. "You've been taking such good care of your daughter. She's beautiful, she's smart. But you're scaring her. You don't want to do that, do you?"

Nina blinked at Reese; her cheeks covered in tears. "You really think I've done a good job taking care of Dawna?"

"I do. Anyone can see that. And Dawna appreciates all you've done for her."

Reese and Dawna exchanged glances.

"Dawna, honey, I've been good to you, haven't I?" Nina met the little girl's gaze, a pleading expression on her face.

Reese tensed. She knew what Dawna most likely wanted to say, but she prayed the kid would lie. Though advanced for her age, could she understand the levity of the situation?

Dawna slowly nodded, and Reese breathed a sigh of relief.

Nina's tears stopped. "Do you love Mommy?"

Reese prayed once more, hoping the kid would continue to lie.

"Uh, huh," Dawna said. "Let's go make Christmas cookies now. I want my teacher to come with us."

"If that's what makes you happy," Nina said. She grabbed Reese's arm and pressed the gun in her ribs, shoving her forward.

As Dawna headed toward the cabin entrance, she kept glancing back at Nina, who continued pushing Reese.

Nina whispered in Reese's ear, "I'll deal with you later, *Miss Shaw.*"

FORTY-SIX

"Sɪᴛ," Nɪɴᴀ ʙᴀʀᴋᴇᴅ when they entered the cabin. She shoved Reese toward a ladder-back chair.

Reese plopped down.

Nina reached into a trunk and pulled out some long white cord. She tied Reese's wrists behind the chair back. Using another piece, she tied Reese's booted ankles. Finally, she looped the cord around Reese's shoulders, pinning her to the chair.

"You're pretty darn good with those knots." Reese grinned. "Did you and your hubby like it kinky once in a while?"

"Ha, ha," Nina sneered.

Dawna innocently asked, "What does kinky mean?"

"Never mind, sweetheart." Nina glared at Reese, then walked over to Dawna and placed her hands on the girl's shoulders. "What kind of cookies do you want to make?"

"I guess the cutout kind with all the shapes," Dawna said halfheartedly.

"That'll take a really long time," Nina warned.

"That's what I want." Dawna watched as Nina tapped her foot. Then she plastered a grin on her face. "Please, Mama?"

Nina glanced at Reese; her impatience evident. The so-called good mother didn't want to grant her so-called daughter's wish. Imagine that.

Nevertheless, Nina turned to Dawna and said, "I'll gather everything we need."

As Nina collected items from the cupboards and the refrigerator, Reese twisted and turned, trying to loosen the cords. She swore under her breath. At this rate, she'd saw her body in half before she made any progress.

As Dawna stacked ingredients on the counter, she darted glances at Reese. "Mama, I don't think you should have tied up Miss Shaw."

"What, why?" Nina stopped pawing through cupboards and turned to Dawna.

"It's not nice," the little girl said.

"Um, Miss Shaw wanted me to do that," Nina lied.

"Huh?" Dawna looked at her wide eyed.

"She's got back problems," Nina lied again. "This will help her."

"How?"

"Don't worry about it. Let's begin making the cookies."

Reese watched Nina help Dawna combine ingredients in a large yellow mixing bowl. Nina demonstrated how to roll out the dough so the little girl could use cookie cutters to create stars, trees and snowmen, which she placed carefully on a metal sheet.

After putting the shapes in the oven to bake, Nina washed her floury hands.

Dawna licked her lips. "Are we eating cookies for dinner? Cuz' I'm hungry."

"Oh, shi—I mean shoot," Nina said. "How about a tuna sandwich and tomato soup?"

"Okay," Dawna said, and Nina busied herself preparing dinner. "You're making one for Miss Shaw, aren't you? I bet she's hungry."

Reese's stomach growled loud enough for everyone to hear.

Nina glared at Reese.

"It wouldn't be polite to eat in front of her," Dawna pointed out.

After pulling out the cookie sheet from the oven and placing it on a thick wooden cutting board, Nina said, "Don't worry, honey. I'll make her a sandwich, too."

Dawna sucked in her lower lip. She looked worried as she glanced at Reese, then at Nina. Poor kid, Reese thought. She'd been through so much, but she was handling this irrational turn of events like a trooper.

Had she seen Jack and Vinny's bodies before Nina dragged her from the mansion? Reese hoped not. She'd suffered more than enough traumatic events for someone so young.

Once Nina had prepared the meal, she placed the sandwich and soup in front of Dawna at the counter. The little girl ate, then she lifted another sandwich from a plate. She crawled off of her stool, walked over to Reese, and held it to her mouth.

"Here's your dinner, Miss Shaw. I hope your back is feeling better."

"Thank you, Dawna."

Reese munched on the sandwich, appreciating the sustenance. When she finished eating it, Dawna grinned at her and went back to the counter. After crawling up on her stool, she drank the glass of milk by her plate.

Nina shot Reese another dirty look.

Reese smiled back, hoping it would unnerve her. She was out of her mind and the best Reese could hope for was that she would lose her train of thought and waffle. Maybe at a certain point, when Nina was preoccupied, Reese could manage to get free.

Holy crap, she'd gotten herself in a bind. She wanted to kick her own butt for letting Nina get the upper hand.

And to top it off, her muscles were screaming. She wasn't in any shape to be sitting in a cramped position like this.

After dinner, Nina helped Dawna mix colored frosting. The little girl slathered it on the cookies, licking her fingers. Nina let her eat one, and as she chewed, an expression of pure joy covered her face, then apprehension replaced it when she must have remembered Nina was off her rocker.

"Time for bed now so Santa can bring your presents," Nina said as she put a plate of decorated cookies by the fireplace.

"Are you sure he can find me way out here?" Dawna frowned. "There's no snow. It's not even cold. It's not really Christmas, is it?"

"Of course it is," Nina snapped.

Ho, ho, ho, Reese thought dismally.

Dawna kicked her toe on the floor. "Okay, if you say so."

"Hurry up now. It's time for you to be in bed."

"It's light outside." Dawna's eyes filled with tears as she started sobbing. "I don't have to go to bed yet, do I?"

"Yes, you do." Nina grabbed Dawna's arm and marched her down the hall.

The child's cries tore through Reese. Twisting and turning all over again, she worked at trying to free herself free from the cords. All her struggles slightly loosened her binds, but not enough for her to escape. Hope trickled from her.

"Shit," she whispered, gathering her strength to start wriggling and fighting against the cords again. "I've got to do this!"

Even though she felt helpless and angry at herself for being in this predicament, she knew was running out of time. Nina had experienced a break with reality. She was dangerous.

It was only a matter of time before she completely snapped.

FORTY-SEVEN

"You have to read me a story," Dawna insisted as she crawled into bed. "Mr. Jack, I mean, Daddy, always reads one to me at bedtime."

Nina stood in the hallway, hands fisted at her sides, her face red. "Go to sleep, Dawna!"

"No!"

"Puh-leese!"

"Read to the kid, Nina. It won't hurt you," Reese said as she watched from her position in the chair. She'd give anything if she could break free from these cords, run down the hall and kick Nina's butt.

"I'm gonna kill the brat if she doesn't go to sleep," Nina called out to her.

Dawna drew her knees up to her chin, buried her face in them and began to bawl. Her sobs tore at Reese.

Reese tensed. "Nina, you love Dawna, remember? You've worked hard to bring her into your life. You only want what's best for her, right?"

Nina pointed a finger at Reese. "Shut up! I've heard enough out of you."

"It's not that difficult to handle a child, Nina," Reese persisted in what she hoped was a soothing tone. "Surely you can do it. She needs you to reassure her everything will be fine."

"Jack usually takes care of her," Nina growled. "This is harder than I imagined it would be."

"You're doing fine," Reese insisted. "Calm down, get a hold of yourself and be patient. That will help."

"What do you know about raising kids?" Nina barked.

"I had a little brother. His name was Jesse. I used to rock him when he was a baby and read stories to him. I miss him a lot."

Nina tilted her head. "Did he get whiny, too?"

"Sometimes, but I tried hard to make him happy. Mostly, when he got like that, he just needed attention and love. It takes time, but it's important to listen to kids and reassure them. Dawna needs you now and you need to be there for her."

Various emotions flickered over Nina's face. She stopped stewing and listened to Dawna's cries. Finally, she spun around and stomped back into the little girl's bedroom.

"Fine," she told Dawna. "Scoot your butt over and let me slide in beside you. What frickin' story do you want first?"

Dawna stopped sniffling and said, "Little Red Riding Hood 'cause she is in the woods like us."

As Nina began reading, Reese resumed struggling. After what she assumed was around twenty minutes, the cords on her wrists loosened. Finally, she gave up, stewing inwardly about her inability to break loose. She'd become so worn out attempting to do it, that she needed a rest before starting in again.

She listened as Nina read the same story to Dawna for the third time, then her voice trailed off. A few seconds later, loud snores drifted from the bedroom. It sounded like Nina had read both herself and Dawna to sleep.

Reese resumed trying to loosen the cords that held her captive. Finally, angry at herself for not being more successful at freeing herself, she dozed off into a fitful nap.

HOURS LATER, a scream awakened her.

Reese blinked and looked around. Dawn cast the windows in a pale purple haze, with bright sun showering rays of light across the room.

She smacked her lips, angry that she'd passed out.

Nina flew out of the bedroom, her red hair mussed and sticking out at odd angles. Small pink, yellow and blue barrettes also decorated her hair, along with bows and hair ties. It looked like Dawna had decided to decorate Nina's hair while she was asleep. Dark circles spread under her eyes, making her look like a clownish raccoon.

Reese forced back a grin. "What's wrong?"

"Dawna's missing."

Concern poured over Reese and she realized that in Nina's emotional state, she could have done something to the girl.

"She's not in bed?"

Nina shook her head. "Both she and Squiggles are gone."

"Nina, think hard. You didn't hurt her, did you?"

She stomped on the floorboards. "What kind of monster do you think I am? Besides, the brat has done this before. She likes to hide from me when we come up here."

"You need my help," Reese quickly replied, remembering when she interviewed Dawna, the girl had revealed her favorite hiding place. Sensing an opportunity to break down Nina's resolve, her heart beat with eagerness.

"Untie me," Reese insisted. "I can help you look."

"You'll try to trick me."

"I'm worried about Dawna, too," Reese added. "She told me she loves coming up here and where she likes to explore."

"You're lying."

"I'm not. I won't tell you where to look unless you untie me."

"You want to take Dawna from me."

"Now I'm trying to help you find her. Besides, I need to use the bathroom."

Nina frowned.

"Hey, I can pee all over this expensive looking room carpet if you want," Reese said. "It can't be that difficult to clean, right?"

"Damn it," Nina growled.

She grabbed the handgun she'd left on the counter and held it on Reese. Then she pulled a pair of shears from a kitchen drawer and cut the bindings off of Reese's hands and feet.

Reese brushed the cords aside and hurried down the hall. She didn't notice Dawna in either bedroom. Spotting a bathroom, she went inside, disappointed there was no window. After shutting the door, she took care of necessities.

She turned on a faucet, splashed water on her face, filled a cup and drank. The icy cold liquid revived her parched throat and her spirits. She rubbed her hands and arms, doing her best to bring circulation back into them.

"Hurry up," Nina said as she hammered and kicked on the door.

Reese opened it. "Let's go."

"You first," Nina said. "I'm keeping a close eye on you. Remember, no funny business."

Reese strode from the cabin and stepped outside into the bright sunlit forest clearing. She blinked several times as her eyes adjusted.

"Where did she go?" Nina asked in a near frantic tone.

"Dawna said she likes to hide in the bear home by

the big rocks," Reese said. "Where do you think that might be?"

Nina began pacing, her gaze focused on the ground. Reese tensed, ready to jump her and try to seize the weapon. She was about ready to spring into action when Nina stopped moving and met her gaze.

"I bet Dawna's over by the waterfall. She loves that place and it's surrounded by boulders. Go down that path."

Nina pointed toward a narrow dirt trail and Reese began following it. She looked over her shoulder, noting Nina was right behind her, gun pointed at her back. Telling herself to watch for the next opportunity to get the drop on Nina, she studied the rocky landscape. There had to be another way to catch Nina off guard, and she was determined to do it.

FORTY-EIGHT

DEEP FOREST DEPTHS enclosed the trail, blotting out the morning sun. Goosebumps peppered the skin on Reese's arms and she rubbed them, trying to generate warmth. Tromping along the muddy path, her ears perked up at the sound of rushing water echoing through the trees. She shivered as a fine mist sprinkled the air, and the cool glade refreshed her.

The trees gave way to low lying bushes and shrubs. A wooden bridge appeared in the distance, arched over frothy white water tumbling through a network of rocks. The lacy effect reminded Reese of a bride's veil. Below, a pool of turquoise water stretched into the leafy forest.

"I bet Dawna's hiding in that cave over there," Nina said loud enough to hear over the roaring waterfall. She pointed toward a dark, hollow entrance in the side of a hill.

"Dawna," Nina called out. "Come out of there right now, young lady!"

Reese cupped her hands around her mouth and shouted, "Dawna, please stop hiding. Come out!"

Only nature's sounds of birds and water resounded throughout the clearing.

"She's such a little shit," Nina growled. "We'll have to go up there and drag her out."

Reese stepped over fallen logs and began climbing toward the cave entrance. The slope was steeper than she'd expected. Her boot soles didn't grip the wet ground very well, and she slid backward into Nina.

"Klutz," she screamed as she shoved Reese away.

Reese fell to her knees, watching as Nina fumbled with the gun. She sprang to her feet, prepared to pounce on her.

Nina was too quick. She finally got a steady grip on the weapon and shook it at Reese.

"Move it! This time watch your step."

Reese began climbing up to the cave again, noting Dawna's small foot prints dotted the muddy slope.

Dawna appeared at the cave entrance wearing her PJs, but now she'd added fuzzy pink slippers, which were covered in brown goo. She gripped a yellow striped blanket and Squiggles, her stuffed purple bunny.

"Go away, go away," she screamed, tears running down her face.

"Dawna, get your little butt down here," Nina shouted.

"No," the girl cried. "This is my secret spot. Go away or you'll scare the fairies."

"Damn it, Dawna!" Nina swore.

"You can't come in here," Dawna shouted, then disappeared inside the cave.

"Nina, you're scaring her," Reese said. "We need to reason with her."

"I'm tired of treating her with kid gloves like Jack did," Nina said breathlessly. "I'm in charge now. And I'm going to raise her with stern discipline. The way my mother raised me. I wasn't allowed to have hissy fits or tantrums."

Reese stepped over to the rocky ledge and entered the cave. Nina followed close behind her. Sunshine lit the area with an amber glow, illuminating nooks and crannies. Shivering and crying, Dawna sat on a braided rug, her knees drawn up under her chin.

Surrounded by blankets, pillows, dolls, and a couple of camping lanterns, it appeared that over several visits, she'd created a small hideout. She'd even hauled up a basket brimming with picture books, crayons and coloring books.

"You'll scare m-my fairies," she cried. "They're my friends. M-my only friends."

Reese forced back tears. The entire scenario was so touching and sad. Meanwhile, she watched and waited for an opportune moment to spring into action and take down Nina. It was tricky, however, because Nina had a gun and Reese didn't want anyone to get hurt.

"Dawna, if you don't come this instant and stop bawling, I'm really going to give you something to cry about." Nina shoved her hands on her hips.

The little girl hugged her knees even tighter and buried her head in them.

"Let me talk to her, Nina," Reese said in a low voice.

"What makes you think you can reason with this little shit?" Nina glared at her.

"Remember, I had a younger brother. I've dealt with this type of behavior before."

Nina snorted with derision. "You try then."

Reese slowly approached the frightened girl. "Dawna, come with me. Please."

Dawna raised her tear-streaked face. "I hate you. You told where my secret spot is. Nobody is s'posed to know."

"I'm sorry," Reese said. "But we were worried about you. You can understand that, right?"

Dawna nodded slowly.

"Will you come now?" Reese held out her hand. "Nobody's going to hurt you. Remember, I only want to help you."

Dawna clutched her purple rabbit and stood. She scowled at Nina. "She's going to yell and scream at me. And she's probably going to spank me really hard. I don't like that."

"Nobody likes that," Reese said, giving Nina a pointed look.

"I won't yell and scream," Nina said. "I promise. And no spanking this time."

"That's what you always say." Dawna sniffed and took Reese's hand. The two walked to the cave entrance.

"Let's go back to the cabin," Nina said.

"I hate that gun," Dawna said. "It's ugly."

"I'm keeping it, young lady," Nina said. "It's for your protection."

"I don't like it," Dawna said.

They left the cave and descended the slope. Reese hoped Nina would slip and fall, giving her a chance to try and grab the gun. Unfortunately, the woman remained careful and sure-footed. Like a mountain goat.

As they got closer to the cascading water, the roaring sounds increased. Gripping Dawna's small hand, Reese started walking with her down the trail.

"Stop," Nina hollered.

Both Reese and Dawna turned to look at her.

"Reese, go stand over there." Nina pointed toward a scraggly pine at the edge of the waterfall.

"Why?" Reese's heart drummed in her ears.

"Just do it," Nina demanded, her tone ominous.

Swallowing hard, Reese let go of Dawna's hand. "It's going to be all right," she tried to assure the girl.

Tears rolled from Dawna's eyes and down her cheeks.

Her glance at Reese seemed to plead with her to make things all right.

Anxiety stole Reese's breath, and she did her best to inhale and exhale deeply to keep her knees from knocking together. Her mind seemed ready to split in two—she had to do something, now.

"Don't leave me alone with her," Dawna whimpered, her expression beseeching, her little body shaking.

"I'm sorry, but I have to do what she says."

"No, no, no," Dawna cried, burying her face in Squiggles' purple fur.

Reese moved over and stood beside the tree, the crashing sounds of the waterfall roaring in her ears. She glanced around, trying desperately to find something that she could use to stop Nina.

Nina clicked off the safety and aimed her gun at Reese.

Finally, Reese closed her eyes. This was it. She'd worked so hard to find Daisy, and she'd done a good job. Skylar's daughter was right here, safe and sound, albeit scared. Her hunches had proved correct. Unfortunately, Reese had managed to blow the entire operation.

Now she would die, and Daisy would be stuck with crazy Nina.

A thump resounded in Reese's ears.

"Arrrgh!" Nina cried, and a gunshot rang out.

Reese tensed and gritted her teeth. When she didn't feel a bullet ripping through her flesh, she opened her eyes.

Nina sprawled face-down on the ground with Dawna and Squiggles sitting on her back. Her forehead bled profusely where it had split open on a rock. She'd dropped the gun, and it lay a short distance from her bent and twisted hand.

Reese dove for the weapon, blood pumping heatedly through her veins. She felt triumphant when she jumped up and pointed the pistol at Nina. Thank God the tables had been turned.

Dawna's bravery had saved the day.

Reese walked over to Nina, who breathed heavily as she rose, sending the little girl sprawling onto the ground. Reaching out, Reese took Dawna's hand. Clutching her bunny, the little girl, streaked with brown grime, stood up.

Nina whimpered as she cradled an injured hand that looked bent and misshapen. She looked down at her pristine white and tan clothing, covered in mud and grass stains. Her face crumpled and her shoulders slumped.

"What have you done, Dawna! This is all wrong! Reese needs to die."

"She can't hurt us anymore, can she?" Dawna looked up at Reese, her face pale and streaked with tears.

"She'll never hurt anyone again," Reese assured her.

"This is bullshit," Nina growled at Dawna. "I thought I deserved you more than your mama, but it turns out you're a spoiled brat. I don't want a kid like you."

"You're not nice at all," Dawna shouted at Nina. "I sure don't want a mama like you!"

"Nina's confused," Reese told Dawna. "Don't listen."

"She's confused," Nina mimicked, then laughed like a banshee at high midnight. "On the contrary, I know exactly what I'm doing. And I will not be going to prison or a looney bin."

A determined expression on her face, she shot past Reese and Dawna and headed toward the cliff.

"Stop!" Reese shouted. She let go of Dawna's hand and tried to reach Nina, but she couldn't catch her in time.

The woman jumped, screaming as she fell over the ledge.

Dawna screamed, and Reese hurried back to the little girl. Setting aside the gun, she hunkered down and hugged her. What a terrible thing for a child to see, she thought. The kid would definitely need some professional counseling after this nightmare.

"Shhh, Dawna," Reese told her in comforting tones, patting her back. "I know this has been terrible for you, but it's going to be all right now. I promise."

"My name is Daisy," she sobbed, her entire body wracked with trembling. "And I w-want to go h-home."

"That's exactly where you'll be going," Reese said. "Back home to your real family."

FORTY-NINE

WARM SUN BATHED Reese's skin as she jogged through the Meadowlark Valley City Park—her favorite physical activity aside from chowing down hamburgers, which she hated admitting. Her friend Kiki ran at her side, her long afro hairstyle coiled into a beautiful high bun.

"I love this," she told Kiki. "Mornings are awesome here."

"And the place is nearly deserted," Kiki added. "Ni-i-i-ce."

Reese scanned the surrounding area, noting the elderly gentleman seated on the wooden pier fishing, and a young woman pushing a baby carriage, a large dog trotting alongside her. Other than the birds perched in the trees and a few insects buzzing past her face, she didn't see anyone else.

As they jogged past a Victorian gazebo perched beside the rippling blue lake, Reese checked her Fitbit.

"We're done," she announced breathlessly, satisfied they'd finished a twenty-minute run.

She slowed down and jogged in place. Breathing regularly in and out, she allowed her heart rate to lower.

At her side, Kiki did the same, then leaned over to grip her knees. "Girl, I thought I was going to lose it toward the end," she said. "I'm wiped out."

"Want to come to my house for a breakfast smoothie before you head home? I've got some fresh raspberries and bananas," Reese suggested.

"Sounds good," Kiki said.

Walking side by side, Reese and Kiki left the park and headed down the sidewalk. Though it was early and the day hadn't reached its peak temperature, warmth rose from the concrete.

Reese thought of the cool shower she'd take after breakfast, which would revive her. She needed to be ready to organize the pile of files and paperwork stacked on her home office desk. After putting it off for a while, she knew she needed to attack it before it attacked her.

As they approached Reese's small brick bungalow, she spotted movement on the porch.

"Who's that?" Kiki asked, narrowing her gaze.

"I'm not sure. Maybe it's a potential client..." She stopped talking when she spotted her Bronco parked beside the curb, the truck's dents and dings all repaired and the paint shining. Walking up to the truck, she smoothed her hand over the bumper, amazed at how good it looked.

"What's Betty doing home?" Kiki asked as she came up beside Reese. "I thought she was still in the shop."

Officer Savage walked down the porch steps and approached them. "Good morning, ladies," he said. "I've got the day off, so I decided to drive down your truck, Reese."

"Thank you," she said. "I realize coming to Meadowlark Valley was out of your way, but I sure appreciate it."

"I don't mind doing a good turn for you. You helped solve a big case, after all." He folded his arms over his chest. "There's nothing better than recovering a kidnapped child, especially finding her alive and in good condition. Although, frightened and confused."

Instead of his typical police uniform, which Reese had become accustomed to seeing him in, he wore jeans and a gray T-shirt. It seemed odd to see him dressed that way, but even law enforcement deserved a day off. Back when she'd been on the force, she had sure appreciated down time.

"How are things going in Sage?" she asked, overjoyed to have Betty home and already making plans to return her rental car. She'd sure missed having the old vehicle living under her carport.

"Things are good, we're just busy in the cop shop. The buzz after Gayle's murder has fortunately died down, especially since the culprit is out of the picture. People feel safe again."

"That's good," Reese said.

"Ahem," Kiki said, looking back and forth between the two of them, her gaze questioning.

"I'm so sorry," Reese said. "Kiki, this is Officer Jeremy Savage from Sage. Jeremy, this is my friend Kiki Morningstar."

The two shook hands and exchanged pleasantries.

"I need to return to my store," Kiki said, shooting Reese a hurried look. "Call me later, Reese, okay?"

"You bet," Reese said.

After Kiki jogged off, Reese turned to Jeremy. "It's nice you finally got a break."

"Yeah, it is. The truck's been finished a couple of days, but I couldn't get away," he said with a frown. "When you work for a small police department, you're almost needed 24/7. We've been busier than busy."

Reese nodded. "I totally understand.

"Again, thanks for bringing back Betty. I can't thank you enough for that."

His brows arched. "Sure."

"And for seeing that Daisy was reunited with her family. I didn't feel that I could contribute much with all the red tape that was involved. That's for the social workers and Child Protective Services to handle."

"They do have a thorough process," he admitted. "But they did a good job. The family seems to have adjusted well and they are thrilled to have Daisy back home. Of course, she's thrilled, too."

Reese pointed to the porch where she'd arranged two wicker chairs facing a matching table. "Let's sit in the shade. My house doesn't have air conditioning and it's stuffy."

They both climbed onto the porch and sat down.

"How are you doing?" Jeremy asked. "Tell me honestly. You took some serious risks rescuing Daisy from Nina O'Casey."

"Me? I'm fine," she said, waving her hand to emphasize her point. "After I drove Daisy to the Jackson Police Department, I just wanted to make sure she was safe and taken care of, then I gave a statement to the cops. Oh, and I called the Ellingtons to tell them the good news. Skylar hired me to do a job and I wanted to report in about the successful results."

"You make it sound like it was no big deal," Jeremy commented. "But like I said, you put yourself in danger. You didn't have to do that. You could have called the police to report you'd found Nina and Daisy. They would have done the rest."

"But who knows what might have happened by the time they arrived? I didn't want to push it. Nina was clearly unravelling, and she couldn't be trusted with Daisy."

He grinned. "You have a habit of running headlong into danger, don't you?"

They both laughed.

"Where are my manners?" Reese stood. "Would you like something to drink? Water? Lemonade?"

"No, I'm fine, but thanks," he said.

"I need hydration after my run." She reached for her drink bottle on the table and took a swig, enjoying the coolness on her parched throat. She returned the drink bottle and continued talking. "I haven't checked in with the garage up in Jackson in a few days. I didn't realize they'd finished repairing my Bronco. You didn't pay for it, did you?"

"No, actually Leyla Ellington called them and took care of the bill. Then she asked if I'd drive it down to you."

Reese made a surprised sound. "That is so nice and definitely unexpected. I need to call and thank her. How is she doing, by the way?"

"Why don't you thank her in person and ask about her health? She's having a barbecue this afternoon and she wants us to come."

Reese considered the idea. "It's a long drive to the ranch. And I've got a ton of paperwork to do. But I love the idea of seeing the family again. Especially Daisy. You said she seems to be doing good?"

"Really good, in fact. She's the happiest kid I know, and she's smart as a whip. The Ellingtons are more than grateful to have her home. In fact, the city council in Sage held a huge celebration in the kid's honor, they were so happy to hear she'd been returned safely."

"That's wonderful," Reese said, thrilled to hear how well things were going for Daisy's family.

"It's all because of your persistence," Jeremy added. "You made this happen. You're good at what you do. As they say, you've got the right stuff."

"Well, again, like I said, it was my job to find the girl,"

Reese said, not wanting to crow about abilities. Silently, she admitted that finding Daisy didn't just solve a kidnapping, it's helped her regain much needed confidence. Going forward, she wouldn't doubt her abilities again.

"It's Saturday and you should take the day off," Jeremy persisted. "Let's go to the barbecue. What's a couple of hours?"

"Yes, well, I suppose I could." She sighed. "The paperwork will wait and honestly, taking a road trip sounds like a good plan to me."

REESE TOOK A shower and put on fresh clothes; a summer blouse, walking shorts and sandals, then drove Betty up to Wild Creek Ranch, with Jeremy riding shotgun. They talked the entire way, and time passed quickly.

Soon, she was turning down the familiar dirt road that passed through the low, rolling hills surrounding Wild Creek Ranch. She admired the split rail fencing that marked the property boundaries as she approached the log entry gate and stone pillars. It stood wide open, so she drove Betty toward the large, old-fashioned ranch house surrounded by shrubs and flowers.

"Nice place," Jeremy commented.

"I know, right? It's idyllic, like an oil painting." Reese rolled down her window and inhaled the fresh scents. Only in her dreams could she ever live in a place like this.

She parked in the gravel driveway and waved at Skylar and Leyla who stood on the porch, watching her approach. Daisy began jumping up and down, her dark pig tails bouncing.

"She's here, she's here," the little girl shouted.

When Daisy ran off the porch into the yard, her mother—her injured foot encased in a walking boot—

and grandmother followed. Rocky flew around the corner of the house, barking.

Reese and Jeremy got out of the Bronco and walked onto the lawn. Her nose twitched with the distinct scent of barbecue wafting through the air. It smelled delicious, and her stomach growled in anticipation.

Daisy hugged Reese first, then she skipped over to Rocky, and the two ran in circles around the adults.

Skylar and Leyla hugged Reese, both talking excitedly at the same time. For a second, Reese couldn't breathe because they squeezed her so hard. At last, they stood back and allowed each other separate time to voice their thoughts.

"When Officer Savage came to confirm the good news about Daisy, I could hardly believe it," Leyla said. "You saved our girl."

"I'm sorry all I could muster was a phone call to let you guys know I'd found her," Reese said. "I realized there would be a lot of procedures involved getting Daisy all settled in, and I didn't want to be in the way."

"We appreciate that," Skylar said. "It was amazing how you managed to handle Nina. Daisy's told us all about how unstable she was behaving."

"Daisy did her best to take care of me," Reese said, smiling at the little girl. "She saved my life. She's a hero."

"Heroine," Daisy called out, correcting her.

"Right," Reese agreed with a chuckle. "Heroine."

"I'm so shocked by Nina," Skylar said, shaking her head. "I thought she'd gone off to college and had become some rich corporate executive. I was even jealous of her! Come to find out, she moved to Jackson Hole, tricked Jack O'Casey into marrying her, then paid Vinny to kidnap my daughter. All because she was jealous of me."

"She felt robbed," Reese said. "You got your father's

attention and she didn't. You could have children, and she couldn't."

"I always thought Nina was, well, a B-I-T-C-H, but it's crazy to think of what she did," Skylar said. "To think she jumped off that cliff—it's disturbing."

"She realized she'd backed herself into a corner," Reese said. "She knew she'd be put away for life. She couldn't handle it."

"Vinny surprised me too. I would never have suspected him of Daisy's kidnapping," Skylar said. "It creeps me out that he was so obsessed with me he'd take away my daughter to try and get my attention."

"It surprised me, too," Reese said, remembering back to when she'd entered Vinny's trailer and viewed the walls plastered with enlarged photos of Skylar and other memorabilia. "But Nina paid him big bucks to do her dirty work, so that also encouraged him."

"Jack O'Casey didn't deserve to die, either," Skylar said. "Now that I know how Nina manipulated him from the beginning, and that she spiked my drink that night at the club, I'd consider him one of her victims."

"I agree with you," Reese said. "How does that change things—knowing he's Daisy's father?"

"For one, my daughter will soon be a trust fund kid," Skylar said. "O'Casey made millions with his computer app. His mother and father are named in his will, of course. But he'd recently added Dawna Shae O'Casey to it, thinking she was his adoptive daughter. We're working through some legal hoops right now, since her name is Daisy Ellington, but we've proven via DNA she's his biological daughter. My lawyer said it should be cleared up soon."

"Speaking of Jack's mother and father, have you talked to them?" Reese asked.

Skylar nodded. "Clara and Stuart have called a couple of times. They had no idea what Nina was capable of, and they are very upset that she murdered their only son. All that aside, they've asked to remain a part of their granddaughter's life."

"What have you decided about that?" Jeremy leaned against a tree and folded his arms over his chest. "That's got to be difficult for you."

"Not so much, really," Skylar said. "They've loved Daisy from the moment Nina brought her into their lives. They've called and talked to her frequently, and they're coming to visit next weekend. Daisy loves them, too. It's like she sensed from the beginning they were good people."

"I'm glad to hear that, Skylar," Jeremy said. "Kids need to stay in touch with all the loving adults in their lives. It's healthy for them."

"Yes, that's wonderful news," Reese agreed.

"I'm a little jealous, though," Leyla admitted in a good-natured tone. "I hate sharing my granddaughter with her new grandparents, but I suppose I'll have to now."

Everyone laughed, and Reese met Leyla's gaze. "How have you been feeling? And how have you been handling, well, all the recent revelations?"

Leyla lifted a brow. "You mean the fact that my husband didn't tell me about his affair with Nina's mother? And the fact that he'd had a daughter with her?"

"Yes, that's what I'm referring to," Reese said. "It must be difficult knowing now."

"I feel fine, and as far as everything else goes, it appears Matthew managed to keep a very large secret from me," Leyla commented in a sad tone. "I had no clue, of course. For all those years, I only thought Nina was Skylar's friend."

Skylar patted her mother's shoulder. "Dad kept it well hidden. I know he loved you."

"Yes, I know he did," Leyla said. "I wish he'd have told me the truth because it wouldn't have changed how much I love him. If we'd discussed openly what had happened, we could have seen to it that Nina and her mother were taken care of. It's my hope that Nina wouldn't have become so bitter."

"You'd have forgiven Dad for the affair?" Skylar said, her expression lined with shock.

"I wouldn't have been thrilled," Leyla said. "But we are a family and we would have remained strong to make certain the right thing was done."

"I love you, Mom," Skylar said.

"I love you, too, Skylar. And I love that we have our Daisy home." Leyla grasped Reese's hand and squeezed. "We certainly appreciate all you've done for us, Reese."

"When Daisy disappeared, I felt the worst fear ever," Skylar said with tears shining in her eyes. "It was devastating. But you listened to me and you worked your butt off to find my little girl. I owe you so much, Reese."

"Like my mom used to say, all's well that ends well." Reese considered the multitude of other heartbreaking outcomes that she'd seen over the years as a police detective and felt relieved this story had a good ending.

"Thanks to your perseverance," Leyla said, then clasped her hands and looked heavenward, "and lots of prayers."

"My turn, my turn," Daisy chanted.

The little girl had been playing with Rocky, who had finally collapsed into the grass, panting. Now, she wanted to be heard. Dressed in a pink sundress and sandals, she looked excited, just like a four-year-old kid should. The dark, haunted edge had disappeared from her eyes and she bubbled with enthusiasm.

Reese was pleased to see Daisy so happy. If she hadn't pushed the envelope on her investigation, the child may never have been reunited with her family. When the dust settled and the courts sorted everything out, Daisy would be a very wealthy young lady.

Leyla and Skylar turned to shake Jeremy's hand and thank him for his help as well.

While they were talking, Daisy ran up to Reese and hugged her knees. "Your name isn't really Miss Shaw, is it?" she asked.

"You can call me by my first name." She smiled at Daisy. "Reese."

"Reese, I like that! Like Reese's Peanut Butter Cups. I love peanut butter. It's my favorite."

"I thought M&M's were your favorite."

"Nah, not anymore."

"You've developed new tastes," Reese said.

"That's 'cause I'm all grown up now," Daisy declared.

Chance sauntered toward them; a barbecue spatula clutched in one of his hands. "Hey, everybody, dinner's ready."

When he saw Reese, he grinned. "Thank you so much for finding my niece. You put our family back together and we can never thank you enough."

"You helped a lot, you know," she told him.

"Anything for my niece."

"Reese, Reese, go on the slide with me," Daisy insisted. Rocky loped behind the little girl as she beelined toward to a swing set. She patted the wooden structure that featured swings and a playhouse covered with a red and yellow awning.

"I don't know, I don't want to break it," Reese said. "These things aren't built for adults."

She hadn't noticed the playset before, so she decided it must be new. Possibly something acquired to celebrate Daisy's homecoming.

"Puh-leese," Daisy cajoled.

"You'll be fine," Chance told her. "It's designed to withstand a tornado according to the instructions I used to build it."

"Oh, why not?" Reese jogged over beside Daisy. As the little girl began climbing the ladder, she followed. At the top, she could see for miles around. The majestic mountain scenery took her breath away. No wonder kids loved these things.

They were magical.

"Hold me in your lap," Daisy insisted. "We'll ride down that way."

Reese sat on the slide and arranged Daisy in front of her. In a flash of remembrance, she considered how hard she'd worked during recent weeks as she searched for the missing child. Despite the major roadblocks, she'd triumphed, and she'd seen to it that Daisy could come home to her family.

She honestly looked forward to the future and what it held in store. No matter the difficulties she encountered, she must continue climbing that mountain of life, one step at a time.

Pushing off from the top, Reese held onto Daisy as they sailed down the slide, squealing with laughter.

* * * * *

ABOUT THE AUTHOR

BORN IN PORTLAND, OREGON, Cindy has lived all over the United States and spent five years in Misawa, Japan. She has visited Canada, the Philippines, Samoa, Hawaii, both the western and eastern Caribbean and New Zealand.

Currently, she lives in Cheyenne, Wyoming, where Cheyenne Frontier Days is held each year. CFD's well-known rodeo is often referred to as the "Daddy of 'em all."

Over the years, she has won or placed in various writing contests. She has also written for and edited numerous newsletters. Her non-fiction magazine articles have been featured in "True West" and "Wild West." She was a book critic for Storyteller Alley and is a freelance editor.

For the last 18 years, she has been a contributing editor and writer for Laramie County School District 1's Public Schools' Chronicle, which has a circulation of approximately 46,000 readers.

From baby alligators to glow worms, Cindy has seen a variety of life's wonders.